FOUL DEEDS

A Rosalind Mystery

Linda Moore

Vagrant PRESS

Nimbus Publishing Limited
PO Box 9166, Halifax, NS B3K 5M8
(902) 455-4286 www.nimbus.ns.ca

Printed and bound in Canada

Cover design: Heather Bryan
Interior Design: Margaret Issenman
Author photo: Cylla Von Tiedemann

This novel is a work of fiction. Names, characters, places, and incidents are either the product of the author's imagination or are used fictitiously. Any resemblance to actual persons, living or dead, events or locales is entirely coincidental.

Library and Archives Canada Cataloguing in Publication

Moore, Linda, 1950-
Foul deeds / Linda Moore.

(A Rosalind mystery)
ISBN 978-1-55109-628-5

I. Title. II. Series: Moore, Linda, 1950- Rosalind mystery.

PS8626.O67F68 2007 C813'.6 C2007-904583-9

We acknowledge the financial support of the Government of Canada through the Book Publishing Industry Development Program (BPIDP) and the Canada Council, and of the Province of Nova Scotia through the Department of Tourism, Culture and Heritage for our publishing activities.

Advance Praise for *Foul Deeds*

"In *Foul Deeds* Linda Moore weaves together two great tales of murder and betrayal. One is a theatre production of *Hamlet* and the other is the cold-blooded murder of a civic activist. Moore's story is both fast-paced and complex, the characters enjoyable and the setting a perfectly realized Halifax."

– Louise Penny, author of *Still Life* and *Dead Cold*

"In *Foul Deeds*, Linda Moore honours the first rule of strong writing: write what you know. Ms. Moore knows the city of Halifax intimately, and she has a scholar's passionate knowledge of the works of Shakespeare. Like Shakespeare, Linda Moore understands the human heart and the foul deeds to which our hearts can sometimes drive us. From beginning to end, this novel is riveting."

– Gail Bowen, author of the Joanne Kilbourn mysteries

"A delightfully old-fashioned mystery that somehow manages to combine Halifax, *Hamlet* and horticulture in a lively, page-turning package..."

– Stephen Kimber, author of *Reparations*

Acknowledgements

Sandra McIntyre, for being a patient, insightful and inspiring reader, editor and teacher

Sandy Moore, for always being there and for his genuine encouragement

Cliff White of the Council of Canadians, for speaking at length with me about various aspects of The Water Wars, and his New Year's Day Tea with Reading, where this all began

Howard Epstein, for legal expertise

Niki Lipman, for the winter writing retreat, and her unwavering belief

All the listeners: Mary Ellen MacLean, Mary-Colin Chisholm, Patricia Reis, Christina Wheelwright, Alex Pierce and Paula Danckert

Molly; may she bound with joy in doggy heaven

William Shakespeare and Sam Shepard

Foul deeds will rise,
Though all the earth o'erwhelm them, to men's eyes.

HAMLET, ACT I, SC. 2

Chapter One

My heart was beating rapidly. I could feel it knocking against the *I Ching*, which lay open on my chest at the twenty-fifth hexagram—The Unexpected. I must have dozed off while the first winter storm lashed against the windows from over the harbour. The cat was sleeping too, one leg stretched out along my leg—a disgruntled afternoon sleep taken in resentment for suddenly losing the green garden under lumps of slush and ice. Something was scratching and banging against the outside wall—just the branches of the now-stripped maple, or was it a piece of loose eavestrough? It sounded metallic. I hadn't taken my blood pressure pill that morning—perhaps that was why my heart was beating so rapidly.

I climbed off the bed, poured a drink of water from the pitcher on the dresser and took the pill. The house felt cold and empty, and the light was going—dark by 4:30. November dark. Better move the car now on the unlikely chance that the snowplow should come by, then eat something and get ready for rehearsal.

Glancing at my desk, I noticed the flashing red lights on the telephone and realized the power must have gone off for a moment while I was snoozing. Pushing aside the piles of books and dictionaries, I pulled the phone towards me to re-record the voice message. I was now deep into the Shakespeare work, analyzing an old favourite—*Hamlet*—and it was proving a perfect way to avoid working on the case. Besides, after the last gruesome investigation, I was trying to change my life—find a more noble pursuit. Shakespeare was a long-held passion of mine, but this recent theatre jag I was on was not one that my boss, McBride, could understand. I was his researcher, his sounding board, his errand girl and general dogsbody. It was too much. As I lifted the phone back to its place, it rang and I jumped, knocking Northrop Frye's *Myth of Deliverance* onto the floor.

It had to be McBride. Hot on the trail, he would be anxious for my list—the names of obscure poisons that might have been used in the crime. It was a long shot, but that was his forte. By the time they hired Private Investigator McBride, people were usually desperate. He was the last resort. In this instance, the Office of the Chief Medical Examiner had pronounced our client's father dead by natural causes, and the police saw no reason to make a case out of it.

I decided not to answer the phone. Let him leave me a message, and I'd call back after I moved the car. I started to pull my boots on, listening to my new recording: "Hi, you've reached Rosalind at 423-9762. You know what to do." The response was an ungodly yelp from the phone, followed by a muffled sound, scuffling, some grunts, and then silence. The loud cry had startled the sleeping cat into a hiss. Suddenly the wind rose and slammed the piece of metal eaves-troughing against the window. The lamp by the bed flashed and the power went out as the metal clattered to the ground below.

I was trembling. Was that McBride, or a prank, maybe? The room was dark. I fumbled for some matches in my cosmetics bag and lit the small votive candle on the mantelpiece. The cat leaped to the floor, and I crouched down and put my hand on her. She started as I touched her, then wrapped her tail around her feet. Her fur was electric, her eyes huge—she looked like an owl. Best to try and reach McBride. I rose and looked at my desk in the gloom. The phone was dead, so the strange recorded cry would be lost. Cellphones weren't my thing, but I had an old rotary dial phone in the cupboard in the laundry room. Really they were so much more practical—no fancy features but they worked when the power was out. Only two flights down. I pulled on the black cardigan that was lying on the back of the chair, picked up the little candle and descended into the dark.

The crypt beneath the gothic-styled cathedral was constructed with ancient ironstone, quarried at Purcell's Cove, and the walls were several feet thick. The room, once an underground chamber where the dead were laid out, was now used as an intimate performance space with a few stage lights and some wooden risers for seating. The ad hoc company of young out-of-work actors was preparing a bare-bones production of *Hamlet*. At this particular moment, they were trying to solve the problem of making the ghost credible. How should the spirit of Old Hamlet appear? It was a question that could stymie even well-heeled theatre companies with real budgets and a bag of technical tricks up their sleeves, so arriving at an effective, inexpensive solution was frustrating everyone.

"The old king should look like he's floating, like he's walking but his feet aren't actually touching the ground."

"He could be miked so that his voice has an echo. '*Swear! Swear!*'"

"Maybe we could put him behind a scrim and then with just a tiny bit of light on him he would materialize out of darkness, the way an apparition actually would."

"But isn't it more scary if he's just there in the flesh—like totally real. Like you or me? Wouldn't that freak you out even more if you knew the person was dead?"

This group directing could get rather tedious, which is why Rosalind had been proving useful. Though not a theatre director—in fact, a criminologist by profession—she seemed to be a text genius with real insight into the scenes and a deep passion for words. She had won them over immediately when she celebrated their choice of location for the production. "Crypt," she had told them, "is from the Greek *krupta*, meaning vault, and *kruptos*, meaning hidden. In *Hamlet*, the idea of the hidden, of hiding, of secrets and conspiracy, is key. We're in the perfect place for this old story to be revealed."

But where *was* Rosalind? Had she forgotten rehearsal started at six o'clock? As the actors began to ask one another whether they should just get started without her, Sophie, who was playing Ophelia, borrowed George's phone. There was no signal in the bowels of the cathedral so she ran up the little stone stairwell and stepped outside through the arched wooden door to make the call. No answer and no recorded message. Strange. Well, there was a lot of heavy weather going on. Maybe Roz was held up by the storm, or having trouble with her car—could be anything. Sophie, already half drenched and shivering, ducked back through the low archway into the building. Hamlet's words swirled up from below as she descended the stone stairway.

The time is out of joint: O cursed spite,
That ever I was born to set it right.

McBride had left the driver's window turned down a crack so Molly would have some fresh air to breathe, and had made his way carefully across the icy parking lot in the pelting sleet towards the other car. But now the other car was long gone and Molly could see McBride's legs on the ground. He wasn't moving and no one was coming. The wind whistled around the car as Molly began to whine and bark.

"God, this crazy weather calls for a drink!" It was ten o'clock and everyone was wired from the rehearsal. They had gotten through

Laertes' departure for France, and the admonishing of Ophelia by both brother and father for risking her chastity with Prince Hamlet. Rosalind hadn't shown up at all; they had plunged on without her.

Bundled up and hurrying through the stormy night to their favourite drinking hole, The Shoe Shop, the gaggle of actors passed the parking lot at Grafton Street and Spring Garden Road. Sophie, who had a special place in her heart for all animals, stopped when she heard frantic barking coming from an old Subaru station wagon parked with its back bumper against the wire fence.

"Hey, wait. Do you think that dog's okay? Doesn't that look like Rosalind's friend's car—you know, what's his name?" She moved through the gate and, brushing away the snow, peered in the driver's window. "Yes. I think that's his dog Molly…"

"What are you doing, Sophie?" George called out. "Come on. I'm soaked!" The rest of the troupe had hurried on, anxious to get out of the wind.

"I'm just making sure she's okay," Sophie said, trying the car door. It stuck a bit with the ice, but was clearly not locked. "I'm going to open the door and just see what's going on."

"—Sophie!" George protested, but she gave the door a good pull and it came open. She was almost knocked off her feet as Molly bounded past her and scrabbled across the lot to where McBride was lying—his legs protruding from behind a large garbage bin. Sophie, who regained her balance and raced after the dog, stopped cold as Molly reached her target.

"George!" Sophie cried out. "Someone's lying there in the snow!" She moved slowly towards the body. "Oh my god, it's Roz's friend. Is he dead? He's not dead is he?" He wasn't dead, but he wasn't conscious either. George called 911.

After the ambulance left the scene, Sophie had no interest in continuing on to the bar. She said good night to George and took

Molly home with her. As soon as she got into warm, dry clothes, she broke up some bread and soaked it in milk to feed Molly—just the way she remembered her father doing for their old collie, Lochie. She could see the dog was distressed and needed a little comfort. Molly gulped down the repast in true Lab fashion, drank some water, and curled up on a mat beside the cast-iron radiator, but didn't close her eyes. Sophie had been trying every few minutes to reach Roz to tell her about McBride, and to find out why she hadn't come to rehearsal. But there was still no answer, still no message. Suddenly there was a loud, frantic knock at the door. Molly started to bark.

Chapter Two

I COULD HEAR A DOG BARKING and wondered if I had the wrong apartment, but after what seemed like forever, Sophie unlatched the chain and opened the door. I practically fell into her flat.

"What on earth? My god, Roz—what's happened to you? I've been trying to reach you. Do you know about McBride?"

That caught my attention as I was stamping the snow and ice off my boots and putting my dripping hat and scarf on the hall radiator. "What do you mean 'about McBride'?"

"He's in the hospital. We found him—George and I—after rehearsal, out cold in that lot at Grafton and Spring Garden. We called 911."

"Well, is he going to be okay? What did they say?"

"His vital signs were good. I gave them my number in case the hospital needs to call. They thought it was a concussion from a blow to the head. The police showed up as well—they think he was assaulted."

"Oh my god, Sophie," I said. "That's got to be what that bizarre phone call was."

"What bizarre phone call?"

I was suddenly shivering like mad. Something sinister really was afoot. Sophie started talking about Scotch and urging me towards her couch. Molly had picked up a small cushion and was trying to get me to take it. I sat and pulled Sophie's mohair throw around me to stop my teeth from chattering. She was right—a good belt of Glenlivet would sort me out. She put the glass in my hand.

"Now when you've downed that, you can tell me all about it," she said. Molly dropped the cushion and climbed up beside me on the couch. Several minutes later I concluded my story: "So the phone was dead, and there I was in the dark, going down the stairs with a candle. I felt like Lady M. after the murder."

Sophie was sitting opposite me in an old wingback chair she had inherited from a production of *Hay Fever*, with her legs stretched out and her feet on the couch. I was wrapped in the mohair, and Molly was curled up between Sophie's feet and me.

"There was something wrong with me when I first woke up from my little nap," I continued. "I could feel my heart pounding. Then, with that wild phone call, the crash against the window, and the power going out, I must have gotten really tense. Anyway, I don't remember passing out, but I came to about an hour ago on the cement floor in the laundry room. The candle had fallen and gone out. I was completely freaked out and it was bitter cold. I didn't even bother to try and find my keys—the car was half buried anyway. I just set out for your place on foot and thank god you're here. I can't believe I'm finally getting warm." I pulled the mohair more tightly around me.

"Wow, what a weird night," was about all Sophie could manage. "What do you make of the McBride thing?"

"I don't know what to make of it. I mean, there have been a lot of random attacks recently, but in this weather—in that parking lot—it doesn't make sense."

"And it doesn't seem like it was a robbery either," Sophie added "because the police found McBride's wallet in his pocket. As a matter of fact, the police seemed to know exactly who McBride was."

"Oh yeah, I'm sure they did," I said. "McBride hasn't exactly ingratiated himself with the local constabulary. He's been one step ahead of them too many times. Possibly this beating has something to do with the new case he's on. This man's son has hired McBride because he suspects his father was murdered. It could be that McBride is getting close to the truth."

"Murder most foul?"

"That's right, Ophelia." I smiled at Sophie. "So, how was rehearsal anyway?"

"Oh it was…you know…hard, but there were some interesting moments. I mean, we totally missed you. We've gotten spoiled by having you there to explain all the tricky bits. I've just got to be careful not to let Ophelia get trounced too early, don't I—I mean she has to keep her spirits up, right? She can't let Polonius utterly destroy her in her first scene. Besides, she has to be attached enough to him to be totally distraught by his murder. That's the final straw for old Ophelia, isn't it—her father's murder? That's when she goes around the bend. *He is dead and gone, lady. He is dead and gone. At his head a grass green turf—at his heel a stone….*"

Sophie was half-singing Ophelia's sad lament, and I started to drift. The Scotch had warmed me and I sank deeper into the couch. Molly closed her eyes and put her chin on her paws. Clearly anxious about McBride, she heaved a little sigh.

The carts of medication were rattling down the corridor, and McBride was dreaming there were clowns on roller skates coming after him like a gang of paparazzi. He knew he couldn't outrun them, so he was trying to call for help. But he couldn't make a sound—it was that old paralysis dream of his. If he could just open his eyes, he could save himself. He had to open his eyes. With enormous effort he managed it—just a little. Just enough to see the fluorescent lights of the hospital's hallway through the fuzzy blur. There was a dark form leaning in. A cop, maybe. He had schooled himself for so many years to play his cards close to his chest that he knew he mustn't say anything. He must stay silent to protect himself. The dark figure straightened and stalked away.

He closed his eyes again. Slowly, he began to recall what had happened to him—the voice calling out to him in the sleeting night.

"Who's there? McBride?"

"That's right."

"You're right on time."

"It's bitter out here. What have you got for me?"

"Back here—it's in the trunk."

Then it must have been someone hidden behind the next car suddenly hitting him across the back of the head. He staggered away from the car and pulled out his phone, hitting the speed dial for Rosalind. He could hear the recording before he was hit again, hard. He yelped and tried to fight back but was fading fast, his knees buckling. As he went under, his face in the snow, he felt the phone being pulled from his hand.

And now, finally, he was surfacing and he found his voice, his words blurting out into the hospital corridor. "Molly. Where's Molly?" His mouth was dry. From a chair near the foot of his bed someone in a uniform stood up, moved towards him, and began to speak.

"The girl who found you. She took the dog. She said she'd come round to the hospital tomorrow to see how you're faring. You took quite a crack on the head there, buddy. Do you know who it was that did this to you? Can you answer some questions? Mr. McBride?"

The Girl Who Found You. That was a nice phrase; he liked it. It made him feel warm. He began to drift down again into the dark. The Girl Who Found You. Maybe there was something redeeming about life after all. You could get beat up and lie bleeding in an icy parking lot, and a girl would find you.

Chapter Three

When Sophie and I picked our way through the storm-stayed city to the hospital the next morning we found McBride sitting up in a bed in the corridor of the over-crowded emergency ward. His head was bandaged and he looked very cranky. Though I was concerned and anxious, his appearance had me suppressing a grin.

"So why didn't you answer your damn phone?" he griped over the general din as we walked towards him.

"I was...the power went out. It was crazy. Are you alright?"

"Dandy."

Oh boy, if looks could kill.

"McBride, this is Sophie. You met her and some other friends of mine at that cast party shindig last spring. Anyway, she's the one who found you last night."

"So you're the one who's got Molly. Where is she?"

"McBride!" I exclaimed.

"What?"

"Rude, my god! Try 'Thank you for saving my life Sophie.'"

"Oh no," Sophie jumped in. "The credit goes entirely to Molly. She was making quite the ruckus—I mean, you would have frozen to death in that storm if not for her. And she's just fine, by the way, so don't worry. They wouldn't have let us bring her in here I don't think. Anyway, um—here...." Sophie reached in her bag and took out a tartan thermos. "I brought you some cowslip tea. It'll help you sleep. Really, it's so amazing."

"I'm not much for the herbal tea," he muttered. I cleared my throat and glared at him. "But yeah, thanks—that's...thoughtful."

He took the thermos and looked back at me.

"So how on earth did this happen to you?" I asked.

"I got tricked, sad to say. I got lured."

"Seems like someone's trying to send you a message loud and clear."

"No mistake." His reply was terse. It was obvious he wasn't interested in elaborating there in the hospital corridor. A hall speaker just above his bed was busy with pages for doctors, annoying electronic bell sounds, and various indecipherable announcements. Several teams had wheeled stretchers by in either direction, squeezing past us as we attempted to talk.

"I bet you just love hanging out here in the middle of all the action," I said. "Were there a lot of accidents last night or is it always a zoo, I wonder."

"All I can tell you is it's been non-stop crazy. Anyway, I'm out of here tomorrow morning."

"Are you sure? They told you that, did they?"

"No, I told them that. Now you get Ruby if she's not already towed. You've got a set of keys don't you?"

"I do," I said. "So, why don't I pick Molly up at Sophie's and come and get you—say around ten? You can catch me up on everything then."

"I'll be ready."

"Can we get you some water or anything?" I asked.

"Nope."

There wasn't much left to talk about. I was anxious to get out of there and McBride was clearly not feeling particularly affable.

"Okay. Well. We'll go, I guess...Take it easy, eh."

"You bet."

"Bye McBride."

"Bye Sophie."

As we walked out of the hospital, I found myself apologizing yet again for McBride's annoying lack of social grace. But McBride had always been at his worst around my friends, and under the circumstances anybody would be in a lousy mood.

"You guys are pretty connected though, aren't you?" Sophie asked.

"Oh yeah—we've been through some wild cases together," I said.

"How did you meet, anyway?"

"Well, he was a guest at one of my criminology classes that year I was doing the sabbatical replacement gig at Saint Mary's—I brought him in a couple of times to speak to the students. He was really great with the class, and we kind of got to be friends. So then he started hiring me to do little research projects for him. Eventually, I started doing a lot of the legwork—you know, the boring but necessary stuff. So there you go—we've been working together for almost five years now. I've learned plenty from him. He's a smarty-pants when it comes to the criminal mind. It's strange that he got suckered into that trap last night. I think he was behaving badly just now partly out of embarrassment."

"Don't you think it's weird, Roz, that the whole time McBride was unconscious, you were too? I mean you passed out in the laundry room only a few minutes after he tried to call you—and you were probably coming to on that cold cement floor at the same time we found him in that parking lot. It's like some kind of parallel experience or something."

"It's just a flukey coincidence, Sophie, that's all." I was attempting to dismiss it but her observation was unsettling and gave me a little chill. I had often had the sense, when we were in the scary depths of some sordid investigation, that working for McBride might be the death of me.

Before going our separate ways, I told Sophie I'd be by to get Molly in the morning and she reminded me that there was a *Hamlet* rehearsal the next evening. "I'll be there this time. Promise," I said. "What scenes are you working—do you know?"

She immediately began speaking Ophelia's lines to Polonius, "*My lord, as I was sewing in my closet, Lord Hamlet/With his doublet all unbraced—*"

I chimed in, "*—No hat upon his head; his stockings foul'd/Ungartered and down gyved to his ankles.*"

"That's the one," she said. "What's 'gyved' anyway, Roz?"

"Gyve is a fetter or a shackle, so 'down-gyved' means undone—unfettered down to his ankles. Bare and exposed."

"Well no wonder she's distraught," Sophie twinkled. "His doublet's unbraced too; he's practically naked. I could handle it, but apparently Ophelia can't, or she would never make the mistake of telling her father."

"Yep," I said. "And it's a big mistake because after that, things get a whole lot worse."

I decided to head home before going to get Ruby out of the parking lot. I needed a little time to get my bearings. As I pushed my way through the snow on the porch and entered the house, I could see the cat sitting on the hall table just inside the door. If she'd had a watch on, she would have been looking at it.

"Yes, yes," I said. "You had a cold and lonely night, but here I am at last—you'll be eating before you know it."

She jumped down and headed straight for the kitchen, her ears flattened to make sure I was in step behind her.

The house was chilly. I reluctantly turned up the thermostat in the kitchen, imagining the old furnace voraciously gobbling litre after litre of expensive oil. There's got to be a better way to heat this behemoth of a house, I thought, cursing my father for the increasingly cumbersome inheritance.

"You know, Dad," I said aloud, in case his spirit happened to be hanging around, "I could take a tropical vacation on what I spend on fuel. A long tropical vacation!"

Living alone was for the birds anyway. I should have tried to find a housemate. But past experiences of neurotic, messy, noisy students had made me gun-shy. The cat was enough to contend with. I loaded her dish with her favourite soft food, and she practically knocked me over purring and rubbing up against my legs. "There," I said, holding her back so I could actually set the dish down, "life's not so bad after all, is it?"

She gave the food a brief inspection and then casually strolled away, sitting under the kitchen table long enough to let me know it had all been a set-up—she didn't really need me. But she went back and attacked it as I put the kettle on for a blessed cup of tea. While the tea steeped in the little blue pot, I could hear the heating pipes banging as the hot water moved through them and warmed the kitchen.

Okay Roz, I said to myself, make a list: shovel out the car, clean the snow off the porch and the front sidewalk, go downtown and get McBride's car, carry on with the Shakespeare work, and, oh yeah, The Case. McBride would really want that research done by the time I picked him up in the morning. Besides, I needed the money.

Chapter Four

"Okay, I'm worried," McBride said as he lowered himself painfully into the passenger seat of my Peugeot sedan, Old Solid. You're the only person I know, he once said to me, who names your car but not your cat. His car, Ruby Sube (which I also named) had in fact been towed away, and now we had to go and pay a lot of money to get her out of hock. Molly had finally stopped leaping around him and we coaxed her into the back seat, but her nose was between us and she was panting eagerly, her eyes riveted to McBride.

"Molly, down!" I commanded. "Sit! Back!" All to no avail—selective hearing isn't confined to humans. McBride was no help. Oh well, I supposed she should be allowed this display of unabashed worship after the trauma. She probably thought she'd never see him again.

"Why?" I asked after we were finally settled.

"Why what?"

"Are you worried."

"Well, whoever it was who took my cellphone, they've got a good record of my contacts, not to mention your number."

"Okay. Start from the beginning," I said. "What were you doing in that parking lot in the first place?"

"I got an anonymous call regarding some confidential skinny on the Harbour Cleanup deal. You know—the $350 million that was contracted to go to the Europa Conglomerate. Apparently, our client's father, the deceased Peter King, may have been instrumental in helping to put the kibosh on that deal, and diverting the funds back to local interests. From what I could gather, King seemed to be making it a personal mission to hamper their activities not only here but around the world. So anyway, this telephone contact wouldn't give me his name but did say he was a part-time clerk in Planning, that over the past few months he had collected some very intriguing information, and that he was concerned there had been a vendetta against our victim. He sounded legit, Roz, and this call felt like the break I was waiting for."

"So you set up a meet to get the poop on the poop," I said, "and instead you got a whack across the back of the head. But why would anyone risk a pre-emptive strike unless you were a real threat? And why just rough you up if they've already done a murder? Why not just get it over with?"

"Good questions but don't forget: As far as the police are concerned no murder was committed, so if they've been lucky enough to get away with that one they wouldn't necessarily want to commit another. But I do believe these thugs were out to scare me off, hoping to just bully me out of the way."

"Well that's foolish! Obviously they don't know what makes you tick."

"That's right." McBride smiled for the first time. "Bring it on."

"At least it makes one thing clear," I said. "We do have a case here."

"Right. So, how are you doing on those poisons?"

"I've got a list for you. It's interesting in light of the Yushenko case in the Ukraine with dioxin. I mean, maybe poisoning's back in vogue. The problem is, in order to prove anything we'd have to get enough evidence together to insist on an exhumation and an autopsy. Not popular—especially at this time of year."

"Popularity's not my thing."

"Really? Could have fooled me, McBride."

We swung into the police compound and McBride handed me his driver's licence and registration and persuaded me to go in and do all the talking while he held a love-in with Molly.

"Do you want me to put it on my Visa too?" I said, leaning in through the window.

"Great, thanks Roz."

"I was joking McBride. Hand over your credit card. I'll bring the receipt out for you to sign so you don't have to move. And by the way, it's time for you to give me a paycheque, so you'd better get to it before you get knocked off."

"Are you good to go?" I asked as he slowly moved from my car into the rescued Subaru. Molly was already sitting at attention in the passenger seat. She looked as though she could drive if she had to.

"Never better," he replied. "Fax me your poison research and let's meet later." McBride inconveniently refused to get email—I was his link to the net, and was forever faxing information off to him.

"I have rehearsal at six," I said. "So we'll have to meet either before or after—or how about tomorrow morning, when you'll have had time to sleep on it?"

He looked hurt. The idea of being alone for that long never appealed to him.

"Six is a ridiculous time for a rehearsal. Why don't they have it in the day?"

"Most of them have jobs," I said, "to try and make ends meet."

"Does Sophie have a job?"

"No—not a straight job anyway. She does television and film stuff and charts for people—you know, astrological charts. But her heart is in the theatre, so she's happy to do this gig and split whatever they make at the gate."

"Crazy."

"Yeah. So tomorrow morning, then?"

"Come over."

As I was walking back towards the gate where Old Solid was parked, I heard him yell: "Bring breakfast!"

Back at my desk, I organized all the material I had gathered on the poisons, faxed it off to McBride, and started into *Hamlet.* I was pretty sure that the rehearsal would get beyond Ophelia's frightened description of Hamlet's visit to her sewing closet, and into the oily arrival of Rosencrantz and Guildenstern at the court. Polonius would by this time be convinced he had found the reason for Hamlet's unruly behaviour and would be zealously preening while presenting Ophelia's private correspondence with Hamlet to the King and Queen. It was a zesty bit of evidence that would justify their heartless set-up of Ophelia for her next humiliation—the nunnery scene. But as I opened the script, my eye caught the ghost's description of the poisoning:

> *Upon my secure hour thy uncle stole,*
> *With juice of cursed hebenon in a vial,*
> *and in the porches of mine ear did pour*
> *The leperous distilment, whose effect*
> *Holds such an enmity with blood of man*
> *That swift as quicksilver it courses through*
> *The natural gates and alleys of the body—*

Such treachery, I thought. It had been given out that the old King had been poisoned by a serpent during his afternoon nap in the orchard. Meanwhile, the real serpent—his brother Claudius—had slithered into the garden with the deadly vial and poured the poison into the King's ear. What exactly is "hebenon," I wondered. Looking it up in one dictionary, I found it defined as a nonce word, created for this occasion by Shakespeare. But the OED connects the word "hebenon" with "Eibenbaum," the German word for yew.

I sat up straight. That rang a bell. I grabbed the pile of paper I had faxed to McBride and started flipping through it. On the list of lethal plants was the popular landscaping shrub or tree the yew, "widely available in Nova Scotia. The pulp of the arils—the red berry-like fruit that is found only on the female plant—is harmless, but the seeds inside can be fatal, causing trembling and breathing difficulty with suppression of heart action, and in some cases, death can occur suddenly without any prior symptoms at all"!

I felt electrified. I had the eerie sensation of being guided towards the truth. I dialed McBride.

"Did you get the fax?" I asked as soon as he picked up.

"It's here," he said.

"Okay. I'm coming over now."

"But I thought you said…"

"It's okay—it's not even two o'clock."

"You've got something for me?"

"I think I've got a lead," I replied.

"I've got something for you too."

"I'll be there in a few minutes."

"Bring lunch," he said and hung up.

Lunch? Oh brother. I had nothing but some ancient sliced ham and half a loaf of bread. I didn't want to poison McBride—that would be just too ironic. Besides, all the evidence would point to me. I had a can of tuna I could take over. With any luck he'd have a bit of cheddar or something. I tripped over the cat while taking the bread out of the freezer. I hadn't seen her for hours, but suddenly there she was, looking distinctly offended by my hasty manner.

"Well," I said, "you can finish your favourite, but it'll be the dreaded crunchies tonight. I don't have time to go to the store." She swished her fluffy tail and sat down by her dish. "You've had fair warning," I said, scraping the last of the fancy "chicken in gravy" out of the tin for her.

"So, in your opinion what makes this form of poisoning more likely than any of the others?" McBride asked as he scarfed down the last of the tuna melt sandwich I had made for him.

"Well," I said, "it's widely available here, and all parts of the yew tree contain significant concentrations of taxine. While taxine is now being extracted to make a drug called Taxol, which is effective in fighting breast cancer, the actual substance is a complex mixture of alkaloids that are highly toxic and can bring about death in less than an hour—a death that looks like heart failure. And, even if the poisoner didn't have access to the deadly seeds from the female plants, the toxin in the actual foliage increases in the winter to a dangerous level. I have a strong feeling about it—intuition or something. And it's an age-old method."

I was reluctant to let him know I had been led to my conclusion by a somewhat dubious connection to an obscure poison mentioned in a play written over four hundred years ago. He was already cranky enough about my time-consuming obsession with *Hamlet*.

"I mean the least we could do, McBride, is check out the landscaping. Maybe the Kings have yews growing on their property. Peter King died on a Sunday, didn't he? So we should find out if there's a possibility he was poisoned right in his own home on the weekend. And since the yews are evergreen, it will be fairly easy to spot them in this weather. Besides—you're the one who wanted us to look into poisoning in the first place!"

"No stone unturned," he conceded. Enough of my hunches had yielded results that McBride knew better than to dismiss the yew tree idea out of hand, but he looked skeptical.

"So what do you have for me?" I asked him.

"Wait until you hear this, Roz." He got up and pushed the message button on his telephone. It was a male voice speaking in a hasty whisper:

"Hello, Mr. McBride—I hope you get this before you go to meet me as we'd arranged. I—I can't make it. I'm afraid I'm being watched. I'm sorry but I'm too nervous to go through with it. I'm really sorry."

"Wow. This changes the water on the beans. Do you have an actual record of the time the message came in?"

"The telephone gives the time of the message as just shortly before our appointed meeting time, but I'd gone out earlier that day and didn't make it home to pick it up."

"So it doesn't appear that you were tricked by the original caller as you thought, because if you'd gotten this message you never would have gone to meet him. That meeting was hijacked," I said. "And whoever took it was counting on you showing up."

"Yup," he said. "They got lucky."

He had nothing in the place to drink but tap water, but it was filtered and cold, and I took a long drink. Molly, thirsty from scouring the tuna tin, went to her big red bowl and followed suit.

"So now what?" I asked, putting down my glass.

"I've got more reason than ever to keep digging through all this water resource business," McBride said. "It's hugely fraught with power struggles and corruption and will only get worse as the fresh water supply dwindles in the world. Peter King believed that communities should have control of their water rights, and he had enough smarts, wealth and clout to really rock the boat."

"So you're saying he may have been gotten out of the way by someone who stood to gain from these privatization deals."

"You know Roz, there are millions, probably billions of dollars involved in this stuff. I'm learning that what the multinational conglomerates like Europa do is first move in on the bottom rung—say, as experts in sewage treatment. That garners them a bundle to begin with in construction and management contracts, and then they go for control of the water supply, maintaining that if they're responsible for what comes out in sewage it only makes sense they have control of the water supply to monitor toxins and all that. And you know what? That all makes good logical sense, and is a service a lot of places really need. The problem is greed. Given all that control, many of these corporations limit people's access to the resource, charging everyone an arm and a leg for their tap water. What should be reasonably available to everyone becomes an out-of-reach commodity."

"So our man King was a hero," I said. "I mean it sounds as though he was instrumental in stopping Europa from getting a foothold here in Canada."

"I think he was, and the irony is that most people simply have no idea what's going on."

"This is giving me the willies, McBride. We need to be really careful."

"Always," he replied.

"No comment." I looked pointedly at his bandaged head.

Suddenly I felt a creepy, clammy wave of fear. I picked up a pen and wrote on the paper towel he was using as a napkin, "Bugs? Maybe they got you into the hospital so they could do a number here."

He took the pen from me and wrote: "Or before, even. Maybe that's how they knew about the meeting in the first place."

We stared at each other. McBride got up and started to look around. I began searching carefully too. Listening devices had changed since I studied them years ago in a criminology course on surveillance. Now they were a lot smaller—tiny, in fact—and a lot more sensitive. Our chances of actually spotting them were slim. Besides, McBride's place was its usual knot of untidiness. We needed some sophisticated detection gear. Molly, who had been lying down under the kitchen table, moved to the back door and wagged her tail, signalling that, in her opinion, there were better ways to pass the afternoon.

Chapter Five

I GOT TO REHEARSAL ABOUT TWENTY MINUTES EARLY. Sophie was already there working on her lines. As I was taking off my coat, she interrupted herself in the midst of, "*O what a noble mind is here o'erthrown*" to ask, "How's McBride?" I decided to leave my scarf on—it was damp and chilly in the Crypt. "You got his car and all that?" she added.

"Oh yes—all done. I spent part of the afternoon at his place. We took Molly out for a run on the Commons."

"She's a great dog. Very special, I think." Sophie spoke as though she knew all dogs.

"I'm fond of her. And believe me, I don't take easily to dogs. But I kind of think of Molly as a person. I've known her since McBride rescued her—must be about four years ago now."

"Really? From what?"

"I'll let McBride tell you sometime," I said. "How's it all going?"

"I'm working ahead a bit, looking at that pesky nunnery scene. We probably won't get that far tonight but I'm so antsy about it. If I know it really well, it'll be easier to play. I mean, she really gets messed about by Hamlet in that scene, doesn't she?"

"Well, she's totally set up, Sophie. I mean she knows Polonius and Claudius are using her. She must feel like a complete jerk. What does Claudius say to Gertrude right in front of Ophelia?" I took the script from her and looked at the scene. "Here it is—'*Her Father and myself, lawful espials, will so bestow ourselves that seeing, unseen, we may of their encounter frankly judge.*' God, lawful espials! Sounds like the Bush admin. And then Polonius hands her a prayer book and says—'*Ophelia, walk you here. Read on this book that show of such an exercise may colour your loneliness.*' He's telling her how best to play her role in order to sucker Hamlet in. Ophelia's not by nature deceptive, but she's obedient to her father. That Shakespeare scholar Harold Bloom—you know him?—he writes that when Ophelia says, '*I shall obey my Lord*,' in that very first scene with Polonius, her tragedy is already in its place. So, okay, inwardly she's compelled to obey her father, but at the same time she cares deeply for Hamlet, who realizes the second he encounters her that something's up—he can smell it. The whole situation just releases this venom in him."

"I see what you mean," Sophie said. "He must be horrified she's become part of the dissembling he sees all around him at the court."

"That's right," I said. "So then at the beginning of the scene when she starts the conversation by trying to return the things he's given her—an obvious artifice—something in him just snaps, and he rages on, completely insensitive to her fragile state. He's partly railing against his own mother and partly lashing out hard for the benefit of the listeners—those "espials"—and he gets very carried away. It's ruthless, but he's in a world of treachery and he knows it. Part of what is truly tragic in this play is the bulldozing of the sweet love between Hamlet and Ophelia. They don't stand a chance."

I stopped ranting. The others were starting to arrive. Sophie nodded, taking the script back from me, "Okay, thanks Roz—that really helps."

As she walked away, I thought about how the suspicion of being spied on had made me feel just a couple of hours earlier. When McBride and I had taken Molly out to the Commons where we could talk freely, we decided he should call on his old buddy Andy—a specialist in the surveillance biz—to check out his place, his phone, and maybe even his car, just to make sure it was all clean. After our walk McBride was heading off to a meeting with our client, Peter King's son Daniel.

The actors were setting up for the scene between Ophelia and Polonius—her description of Hamlet's visit to her sewing closet, to be followed by the arrival of Rosencrantz and Guildenstern in the court. Sophie had pulled on her long rehearsal skirt and she came over to where I was sitting with my script, waiting for things to get rolling.

"By the way, Roz, in case we just do this one scene with me and I leave early, why don't you come over after rehearsal for a drink or some tea?"

"Sure," I said. "I will. That would be great."

"I have a surprise for you. "

"What do you mean?" I said, ever wary of surprises.

"Well it's…no it's just a little present, really."

A little present? What on earth could that be, I wondered as I drove along Gottingen Street to Sophie's apartment building in the North End. She lived at the edge of the Hydrostone, the part of the city that had been completely rebuilt following the devastating Halifax Explosion of 1917. The brainchild of renowned town planner Thomas Adams and architect George Ross, featuring design variations, gardens and wide boulevards, the Hydrostone was a remarkable success story. Over three hundred homes were completed in 1921, all constructed out of the compressed concrete blocks known as hydro-stones. The dwellings were modern for that era—all equipped with electricity and plumbing—practical—they wouldn't burn down easily—and beautiful. Still beautiful, I thought as I drove by the little row of shops that ran along Young Street.

Sophie had indeed left rehearsal early; I stayed on to work Hamlet's wonderful fishmonger scene with Polonius, followed by his first scene with Rosencrantz and Guildenstern. After a stressful day, I was feeling exhilarated, truly connected to something greater than greed and malice. While that was exactly what the play was about, the sheer joy of Shakespeare's language lifted my spirits. I was enjoying my work with the actors and they were all doing a superb job. Even though they had no money, no production support, no costumes, they were embarking on the *Hamlet* journey with full passion and commitment.

I parked in front of Julien's Bakery and walked across to Sophie's building and up to her apartment. She had the tea on—a new chai she was trying out—and the familiar bottle of single malt was sitting on the low table by the couch with a couple of small glasses.

"How did it go after I left?" she called from the kitchen.

"Really well," I said, spreading some of our favourite St. Agur cheese on a stoned-wheat thin. "Lots of comedy in those sections, watching Hamlet get the best of those characters as they stand on their heads trying to figure him out. It's about as light as the play gets. The company seems to be relaxing more too," I added as she came into the room with tea things. "I try not to interfere with what they're doing, and now they're readily coming to me to puzzle things out, so I think we've figured out our working dynamic. I'm really into it."

"You sort of spend your life puzzling things out, don't you? I mean that's what you do with McBride too."

"It is, although he takes the lead, directing me to do certain kinds of research and various other tasks. But occasionally I get very involved with the cases."

"He's not married is he?"

I looked at her. "Oh my god, Sophie. Are you interested in McBride?"

"But is he…or does he have someone in his life?"

"He's married to Molly," I said dryly.

"No, seriously—what's his story?"

"Well, he's divorced and his ex lives out in BC—Victoria, I think—with their teenage son, Alex. He used to lean pretty heavily on the bottle, and I guess she got as far away as she could. Honestly, in many ways he's your classic hard-boiled gumshoe, Sophie. It would be a tough slog trying to live with McBride."

"Oh for heaven's sake Roz—I don't want to live with him. I'm just curious about him."

"Well, just so you know," I said. "Anyway, moving right along… where's the present?"

"Well, it's not really a present, I mean, not an actual thing. I have this old friend in Montreal—he's an actor that I went to theatre school with there, and we used to do tarot readings and stuff like that all the time. So recently, out of the blue, he sent me this deck of cards he found in an antique store—it's probably a collector's item, like a really old set of the Tarot of the Marseilles. The strange happenings of the other night got me kind of worried, so I decided I should do a reading for you."

Sophie was a perfect combination of smart, independent woman, old world hippie-artist, and New Ager. There seemed to be nothing in the popular occult she hadn't familiarized herself with in some way.

"Do you know the tarot?" she asked.

"Not really. I think I had my cards read years ago. Remind me how it works."

"Well," she replied, "there are seventy-eight cards in the deck. Four suits—Cups, Wands, Swords, and Pentacles—make up the fifty-six cards of what is called the Minor Arcana, and then there are twenty-two cards in the Major Arcana—all of which have strong symbolic meanings which can be interpreted in many ways: images, numerology, astrology, archetypes. The cards are very potent if you're into interpretation."

The next thing I knew, she was opening a lacquered wooden box and taking out an oversize deck of cards.

"Okay," she said. "What you do is shuffle the cards for awhile and just think about your situation. You can actually fashion a question if you like, but really it's more about focusing in on your present circumstances."

She put the worn cards in my hand. I looked at them. They were about one and a half times as long as normal playing cards, and made of heavier cardboard with a blue and white-checkered pattern on the back. The illustrations were bold, medieval-styled line drawings in black filled in with vivid red, blue, and yellow ink. The twenty-two cards of the Major Arcana each had a tiny publisher's stamp on the illustrated side that said the cards were from B. P. Grimaud—Paris. The edges of the cards were grayed with use but not frayed.

I felt the weight of them.

"I don't know," I said. "You've kind of caught me off guard here. We might not like what we see."

"Look, don't worry. I'll just do a short reading—a ten-card one. Come on, it'll be fun and I know you'll get into it."

I started slowly shuffling the seventy-eight cards of the Major and Minor Arcana, thinking about the last few days, about McBride's incident in the parking lot, what I had learned about Peter King's work, *Hamlet* rehearsals. My mind drifted through the events.

Sophie had turned off the bright reading lamp at the end of the couch and we were in the candlelight. The air was scented with a mix of amber and patchouli aromatic oils, and she was sitting on the carpet on the opposite side of the low table, very still, watching me.

"Okay," she said, "first, you take one card out of the deck and that will be your Significator; it will be you. Go ahead."

I pulled out a single card and gave it to her. She placed it in the centre of the table face up. It was number seventeen from the Major Arcana, The Star.

"What does it represent?" I asked.

"Gifts of the spirit—the Water of Life," she responded.

"Get out of town!" I said. "Water…is definitely on my mind. It's what our case is all about."

"Well, water is at the heart of this card. The naked woman pours the water of life from two ewers—one onto the land and one into the stream. She is replenishing the stream so that those who are thirsty may drink, and watering the earth so that the seeds will grow. Behind her rises a hill with a shrub or a tree on it, and in the night sky are seven—"

The telephone rang, startling us both. She looked at me and I nodded for her to go ahead and answer it.

"Hello. Oh, hi! How are you feeling? Oh that's great—I'm glad to hear it. She is, yes. How's Molly, by the way? Good. Here she is. Guess who?" Sophie handed me the receiver.

I set the cards down on the table. "What's up? Lonely?" I smiled at Sophie. "What? Well, no kidding? See! What did I tell you!" Standing up, I put my hand over the phone and asked Sophie if I could invite McBride over.

"Why not?" she said.

"I'm sure Molly will show you which apartment it is," I said, giving him the address and then hanging up. I looked over at Sophie. "I'm right!" I said.

"Right about what?" she asked.

"They have yew trees. Daniel King confirmed it."

"Yew trees?"

"*The juice of curs-ed hebenon*," I answered. "Ring a bell?"

"The poison that Claudius used to kill his brother is from the yew tree?"

"This might bring us a step closer in our investigation. Let's take a rain check on the tarot for now Sophie," I said, feeling relieved. The water imagery in The Star card was already too unsettling, and the idea of a tarot reading was making me nervous. "I'm too wired about this yew tree thing."

"Hey, isn't the yew part of the runic alphabet?" she said.

"You got me," I replied.

"Yes, I'm sure it is. It represents death, doesn't it? I believe the yew tree was traditionally planted on graves. I have some runes here." With that, she pressed her finger on a decorative motif on the side of the low table and a drawer suddenly popped forward.

"That's pretty cool," I said.

"Yes, it's my secret drawer," she said, taking out her set of rune stones. "In fact, this will tickle your etymological fancy. The word 'rune' comes from *Runa*, the Germanic word meaning 'secret.'"

"Really?" I said, getting interested.

"We could read runes instead of cards," she said, teasing me with a wicked laugh.

"Another time I think, Sophie."

"You don't like anyone getting too close to what's going on with you, do you?"

"Can I see the yew stone?" I asked, changing the subject.

The letter carved into the stone looked like a tilted backward letter "Z"—a kind of zigzag that in itself represented a double-ended staff of life and death and would have been originally carved from a yew tree. Sophie was reading this information to me from the little paper that was in the box.

"It's number thirteen in the runic alphabet. It says here the oldest existing yew tree is possibly nine thousand years old. The yew is considered a very magical, sacred tree—the tree of life—but with its enormous, far-reaching roots it also represents death and the underworld." She looked at me and raised her eyebrows. "Oh, and the yew can also mean assertiveness, masculine aggression, or master of the estate."

"You know, this is all starting to make sense. The runes were

Scandinavian, weren't they? That might explain why clever Shakespeare would have Claudius use the yew to kill Old Hamlet the Dane, thereby becoming the new master of the estate, in this case the King of Denmark."

A sudden knock at the door took our attention. McBride and Molly hadn't wasted any time getting across town.

McBride settled himself in the wingback with a glass of orange juice and soda water—his current choice of non-alcoholic beverage—while Sophie whipped up a bread and milk special for Molly in the kitchen. Molly could make a variety of soft noises that McBride called whispers, and it sounded as though the two of them were actually having a conversation. I asked McBride how our client Daniel King was doing.

"He's a wreck. He looks like he hasn't slept since his father died and when I told him about the brutal little encounter I had in the parking lot, and my anonymous caller being too spooked to show up, he took it quite hard—since it likely proves his theory. I was sorry I had nothing solid for him except the certainty that we're on the right track. He'd like us to keep going."

"And at some point you asked him about the yew trees?"

"I just got him to describe all the plants and shrubbery around the property if he could. He also mentioned foxglove, which is on your list."

"That's right," I said. "Digitalis. Too much can stop the heart, but it's the wrong time of year to access it. If garden digitalis was used to poison Peter King, then this was planned several months ago."

"It seems King was an avid gardener. Daniel said he would often come home in early June to help out with the spring landscaping."

Sophie had entered the room with a new cup of hot chai. The aromatic scent of the sweet spice drifted over us.

"So I gather Daniel King doesn't live in Nova Scotia," she said.

"No. He's an architect with a firm in the Niagara district in Ontario, and he's got to head back to meet some deadlines for his current project. In fact," McBride paused, looking at Sophie as she sat down on the couch, "it's a theatre building he's designing."

"Really? I'd love to see it." Sophie made herself comfortable opposite McBride.

"What about Peter's wife—Mrs. King?" I asked. "What's her story? Is she also a gardener?"

"Daniel said she puts most of her landscaping talents into cultivating rose bushes. She's presently in London, England. Went over after the funeral. Apparently has an old friend there. He gave me a contact number for her in case we need to reach her."

"So Daniel's leaving when?"

"Early tomorrow morning," he said.

"And Gertrude's away in London. Well, tomorrow I'll go and see if I can get some foliage and berries off the yews on their property and have them tested."

"Good plan," he said. "And it's Greta."

"Right. Greta. Did I say Gertrude? What about you?" I asked him.

"I've finally got a response from the Mayor's Office. I've been trying to set up a meeting with him to find out exactly who the City was consorting with both overseas and locally before the Europa deal collapsed. And I'm curious about his take on Peter King's involvement in it all. So I'll be seeing him tomorrow."

Molly wandered into the room, her nails clacking on the hardwood floor, and came and stood in front of Sophie, giving her the look that meant could she climb up on the couch.

"Come on," Sophie said, patting the cushion. Molly climbed up, turned around twice and settled, putting her head on Sophie's lap. Sophie scratched her ears affectionately and looked intently through the candlelight at McBride.

"You know what? I gotta go," I said. "The cat. Let's have the regular coffee meet tomorrow at nine, McBride. And hey, if you're smart you'll stay and get Soph to do a tarot reading for you."

He looked dumbstruck as I got my coat. Making my exit, I could hear Sophie telling McBride to focus in on his situation and shuffle the cards slowly. I smiled all the way home.

Chapter Six

"So how was the tarot reading?" I asked McBride the next morning when we met up at Steve O Reno's Cappuccino on Brunswick Street.

"Oh I took a rain check."

"What? Oh no, poor Sophie...that makes two rain checks on the tarot readings. So what did you do, just leave? Honestly, McBride, you wouldn't know an opportunity if you fell over it."

"Reiki."

"What?"

"Yeah...she reikied me. Did you know she was certified?"

"Really."

"You wouldn't believe how hot her hands get."

"How hot her...What—were you naked?"

"Well Roz, you left me there."

"McBride! Then what did you do?"

"Afterwards? We played Scrabble."

"Oh—you're—you're just messing around with my head, aren't you?"

"No Roz. It's all true. Ask her."

"But you don't even like Scrabble."

"I know. We were like a summit meeting between two alien cultures."

"But you found common ground?"

"Common floor—we found common floor."

"You—you mean—are you saying you did it on the floor?" I sputtered.

"Well, the rug. She has a pretty nice one."

"Oh my god! When did you get home?"

"I haven't been home. I have to get there soon because Andy's coming in with his gear to check the place out, and then I'm off to that meeting with the Mayor." With that he swallowed the dregs of his coffee and stood up, suppressing a big grin. "See ya later!"

"Bye, McBride. Let me know what Andy..." I trailed off. Watching him go out the door practically dancing, I suddenly felt horribly lonely. Great—I'd watched two of my favourite people find each other, and now I felt left out. Time to grow up, Roz. Get real, and go to work on getting those yew berries tested.

I finished my coffee, got into Old Solid, and headed for the South End. The Kings had a grand old manor on Inglis just west of Robie. I pulled into the driveway, and got some large pruning shears out of the trunk. I hoped I would find yew branches with the arils still on them. I walked through the latched gate at the side of the house that led into the backyard. Over against the far fence opposite the house there was a variety of evergreen trees and shrubs, and that's where I headed. I walked past a mulched circular bed surrounded by a burlap windbreak stapled to wooden stakes. Within the circle were several kinds of rose bushes, all individually wrapped in burlap. Must be Greta's rose garden tucked in for the winter, I thought, and then I spotted the dark green yew tree on the corner of the property. I moved towards it, cross-referencing with the pictures and descriptive information I had brought with me.

This yew was in fact not a shrub at all but a large tree that reached up about twenty-five feet, and it had substantial girth. I started looking through the branches carefully. The yew foliage was so dense, I realized I should have brought a flashlight, but suddenly I spotted some of the dried scarlet arils near the trunk on two of the lower limbs. So this tree was a female. I took my pruners and leaned in through the thick growth as far as I could. "Thank you

Madame Yew," I said aloud, cutting the two small branches off and slowly backing out, untangling them as I went.

"Are you a gardener or something? What are you doing?"

I started and turned quickly. "Oh heavens! I'm sorry. I didn't see you. God, you caught me talking to a tree. You must be Daniel King."

Standing in the snow in a dressing gown and boots was a man in his early thirties. His eyes were red, as though he had been weeping or drinking.

"Yes, I am," he said.

"I apologize for trespassing, I thought you had gone back to Ontario this morning, or I would have rung the bell. I'm Rosalind, a researcher for McBride. I just um—well—I'm checking for poisons basically. Are you okay?"

"Not really," he said.

"Can I do anything for you? I mean, do you need a drive to the airport or anything?"

"I've decided to go tomorrow. I didn't sleep—nightmares—I just feel so..."

"—helpless," I said, finishing his sentence.

"More like haunted. But yes, helpless too. I mean he's gone. He's dead and gone, but I can't stop dreaming about him."

"Do you mind if I come in? Could we talk for a bit?"

"Please," he said. "I'll put the coffee on."

"I'll just put these branches in my trunk, if you don't mind my taking them."

"Be my guest. My father would always cut off most of the arils within reach in the fall—you can see places where it's been trimmed. This was one of my father's favourite trees—known for longevity. And located as it is on the edge of the property, it's supposed to be a symbol of protection too. All very ironic, eh?"

"Well, it's kind of a double-edged sword," I said.

"What do you mean?"

"Well, I understand the yew is also a symbol of death and transformation."

"Come 'round to the side door."

As I walked out to my car, I reminded myself I needed to take care. Speaking directly with clients was not my territory. Still, he looked so devastated. Surely a little commiseration would not be out of place. Besides I didn't set up the meeting. McBride told me Daniel would be gone. The truth was I had instantly felt an overwhelming empathy for the man. I knocked on the door.

"Just come on in," he yelled. "It's open." I stomped the snow off on the horse-hair mat, and bent down to take my boots off. I went up three steps and into a large beautiful kitchen. It had a green slate floor and the walls and cupboards were painted a lovely pale yellow. The harvest table sat in front of a large bay window looking out to the back garden.

The dressing gown was gone. He had put on a fleece pullover and a pair of sweat pants. "What do you take?" he asked.

"Just milk," I said, removing my jacket.

"Sit down. Here I'll take that," he said and walked out into a hall towards the front closet. Though he'd been staying in the house, it felt empty. I sat and looked out into the snowy garden.

"Must be gorgeous in the summer," I said.

"My father's pride and joy."

"Your father seems like he was a really spectacular person," I said. "I mean—close to nature."

"Yes, that's it—he was—he revered nature. In the last few years, preserving nature was becoming more and more central to his work and his life." He set a mug of hot coffee in front of me and sat down across the table. We both looked out into the garden.

"Daniel," I said, deciding to cut to the chase. "What do you think happened to him?"

"I just know," he replied, "that my father didn't suddenly die of heart failure. He was in great shape and he was gearing up to go into battle. We emailed each other fairly regularly because he travelled so much. He had sent me a message only a week before his death saying that the project he was involved in was really heating up—potentially another Cochabamba."

"Cochabamba?" I asked.

"It's a city in Bolivia where the people rose up against a conglomerate led by the US-based Bechtel Corporation. Under pressure from the World Bank in '98, Bolivia signed with Bechtel to take over the management of the entire Cochabamba water system. People's water rates rose immediately by 200 to 300 percent. Those who couldn't or wouldn't pay were cut off and they revolted. Ultimately there was bloodshed because the government used the military and the police to force people to bend to the corporation's demands. But eventually, the fight became a 'cause célèbre' and the entire country got involved. Commerce became paralyzed by strikes and protests. Finally the government caved in and threw the corporation out.

"It was a major triumph in the battle to keep the resource in public hands—part of 'the commons' as my father would say. He was a lawyer and over the last decade, he had become an expert on international trade law. He got deeply involved in the Bolivia situation. After that he began devoting himself full-time to what has been dubbed 'The Water Wars.' In the last several years, his testimony has frequently been instrumental in the rejection of corporate privatization schemes."

"Amazing," I said.

"Truly."

"Peter King. It's the karma of names," I said.

"I don't follow," he said.

"King," I said and proceeded to quote, 'Thus the Kings of old, rich in virtue and in harmony with the time, fostered and nurtured all beings.'"

"And that's from?" he asked.

"Do you know the *I Ching*?" I said.

"I know what you're referring to."

"Well, that quote is from the section called The Image in the *I Ching* hexagram—The Unexpected. I was just reading it the other day and it stuck with me. It really fits doesn't it? The gist is about the true value of Nature and the Spirit, and the danger of bringing about misfortune by manipulating nature for selfish motives. You know—the whole mess we're in on the planet basically."

"Well, if I'm right about my father, he may well have met with misfortune due to the greed of others."

"No kidding," I said. "Your father had demonstrated on numerous occasions that he was a serious opponent to this kind of profiteering. So if, as you say, he was readying for another battle and using his expertise to halt their activities around the world, it makes total sense they would want to get him out of the way. Does McBride know about that email your father sent you, and did your father indicate where this new battle would be taking place?"

"I believe it was a country in West Africa, but he often kept his travel plans confidential since it was a major part of his work. I gave McBride a copy of that email the first time we met, and now there's this awful assault that's happened to McBride and the fact that whoever called him with information is afraid to come forward. You don't have to be a brain surgeon to see that something very suspicious is going on. Oh god, it's so frustrating!"

"You can count on McBride," I said. "Really, Daniel—he'll come through for you."

"But I just feel totally isolated. It's like everyone's moved on. And it's only been a month—not even."

"What about your mother?" I asked. "Surely you're supporting each other through this?"

There, sitting at the table with me, he just fell apart. Uh oh, I thought. I've clearly hit a nerve. I reached over to the countertop behind me, grabbed the box of tissue that was sitting there, and set it on the table in front of him.

"Sorry to be so emotional," he said. "This is crazy, I just can't seem to pull myself together."

"Is it something specific about your mother?"

"I love my mother. She was devoted to my father, and he adored her. It's just—I found her behaviour so strange after the funeral."

"How do you mean?"

"She's always been very private but she was unusually distant. She was...in a rush. She just wanted to get out of here. He had named me the executor of his estate, so naturally I was staying on to take care of things, and as you say, I assumed that we'd be helping each other through it. But she...she decided to go to London. She has an old school chum there. Marjorie. They've always been very close, and most likely she's just dealing with her grief in the best way she knows how."

"But you did express your concerns to your mother about what you thought may have happened to your father."

"I didn't at first. She was so grief-stricken—crying all the time. I didn't think she could handle the idea that he may have been murdered, though I believed she'd have to face it when the Medical Examiner's report came out. But when it was declared a death by natural causes—heart failure—I certainly let her know how I felt. I mean, I was in shock. I'd been convinced they would find something amiss. And once the Medical Examiner's official report was in and the death certificate was signed it was a done deal—the police were not interested in pursuing it."

"So, am I correct in understanding that there was no actual autopsy?"

"The post-mortem examination on my father was external only—no examination of internal organs or toxicology testing. I was really bewildered by that and I wanted to go through whatever channels necessary to have them do a 'forensic' or 'medico-legal' autopsy, which is carried out in the case of unexplained or unnatural deaths. Well, my mother was dead set against it. She thought it was sordid and uncalled for, and she was angry with me. She wanted everything taken care of quickly and with a maximum of dignity and decorum—for my father's sake. So we had a tidy funeral and the next thing I knew, she was packing her bags, saying she needed some time to recover.

"Then, my insomnia set in. I couldn't shake the feeling that something wasn't right. I told her I might hire a private investigator and she just shook her head and said, 'It won't bring him back. We have to get over this. It takes time. Don't waste your money.' And then she was gone."

"Tell me, do you have a list of everyone who attended the funeral?" I asked.

"There's a guestbook that people signed, but I don't know if everyone did. There's a video too."

"I'd like to borrow them. Your father wasn't cremated, was he?" I asked.

"I think my mother would have had him cremated, but he'd requested a burial in his will."

"Tell me about your mother—does she have family here?"

"No, but my mother didn't get on that well with her family. My father met her in London, when he was attending the London School of Economics. After they married he brought her home to Canada. He studied law at Osgoode Hall and then they came here. But she went abroad to visit friends quite often over the years."

"And where in Europe is she from?"

"Zurich. In fact, I stayed with some cousins when I studied

there. I took a summer architecture course on exterior motifs a few years ago."

"Sounds wonderful," I said.

"It was. It was great. Those were the days." He rose from the table. "I'll get those things for you," he said.

For just a second, I caught a glimpse of the carefree Daniel, a young man on the road to success studying architecture, and coming from an interesting cosmopolitan family; a life full of promise. I realized that all that innocence had now been shattered. Everything had changed with the suspicious death of his father. It seemed to him that even his own mother had abandoned him.

"What's the next step?" he asked, bringing me the guest book and the video.

"Well, if we want to examine this question of a poisoning, we must get permission to exhume the body and do a thorough forensic autopsy. It's the only way to find out. I can prepare theories on what may have been used, and McBride will be working hard to dig for the who and the why. But in the end, we've got to go back to the body if we want to find evidence and prove murder. And if what we suspect is true, then there are those who will stand fiercely in our way. So we've all got to be brave and very careful, including you Daniel."

"Well, I'm getting on a plane to Toronto in the morning and going back to my life. It's going to be up to you and McBride."

"That's what you've hired us for," I said, "so give yourself a break. You're far too stressed. Sometimes work is just the thing we need to pull us through."

"That's what my father always said."

"Anyway, you've been here for several weeks. It's time for you to go home," I said. "Do you have kids?"

"No, but I am getting married," he said.

"Well good. Your fiancée will be glad to have you back. What's her name?"

"John." He smiled warmly for the first time.

"No kidding," I said. "Well there you are. You see, you are brave. And you're a groundbreaker. It bodes well for the case."

"I hope so," he said.

I had told Daniel King he was brave, but I knew he was confused and frightened. I felt close to understanding something—but what? I got into Old Solid and drove along Oxford, then up Quinpool to the rotary and out the Herring Cove Road to Crystal Crescent Beach. The sun was shining and it wasn't too cold. Sometimes the ocean and a brisk walk will clear my head. I had been affected by Daniel's story of his father's determined dedication to the greater good, and I felt the shadow of depression lurking—waiting in my periphery. Another courageous warrior gone from the battleground, I thought. We always have our child's eyes where everything seems simple—one does what is good for everyone, what is good for the planet. But our adult eyes have seen the face of greed and self-interest and they tell us that it's not simple—it's brutal.

I parked the car and walked along the beach. That brutality is what Hamlet was greeted with when he arrived in Denmark for his father's funeral and he was paralyzed by it. Though Shakespeare brings him face to face with opportunity and though he yearns to act, he cannot act, and he drives himself crazy trying to become an avenger. Sitting myself on a driftwood log, I looked out over the water to the horizon. In the far distance a container ship was plying its way towards the mouth of the harbour.

"Until," I said aloud, "until he returns with purpose after the perilous journey to England." His dark night of the soul. There, on the ship, his '*sea-gown scarfed around him*,' he had discovered the grand-writ that Rosencrantz and Guildenstern were carrying to the English King. The order for his own head to be struck off. Why? Because Claudius is now desperate; he knows that Hamlet is on to him. Claudius has already murdered once for power and now he is in possession of what his brother had—his kingdom and his bride, and he's not about to give them up.

So, I wondered, does someone have Peter King's bride now? Was there a reason, something more than grief that made Greta depart so suddenly for London? Had she been, as Hamlet says of Gertrude, '*like Niobe—all tears,*' only to post with dexterity to another life after the funeral?

My conversation with Daniel King had drawn me into the heart of the situation. I couldn't remember the last time I had actually cried, but suddenly my nose was running and my face was wet in the wind. Here I was longing for justice and grieving for a good man I'd never met.

Chapter Seven

Portly, ruddy-cheeked and rheumy-eyed, the Mayor had recently been re-elected with a sweeping majority, and he greeted McBride with his hail-fellow-well-met grin. Of course, at the mention of Peter King, the smile disappeared for a moment and his brow furrowed.

"A great loss, a very sad loss, terrific man!" His jowls shook.

"I understand he was involved in the harbour clean-up project," McBride said.

"He was involved in many things over the years—but absolutely, yes—he was commissioned by that bunch over at Ecology Counts to do a little synopsis for them on the treatment plants."

"I see," said McBride. "And what was Ecology Counts' interest in the project?"

"Well, between you and me, groups like this always presume we're going to make bad decisions so they start bombarding Council and Staff with horror stories. I mean, I'm not saying they don't perform a valuable service from time to time, but I wouldn't mind making it through one day without their holier-than-thou attitude coming at me. Of course, Peter King was a smart man with a terrific mind, but he was in cahoots with that woman—you know—the one who wrote that water book...I forget what it's called...blue something...Anyway, I've had it up to here with these trendy opinions that do nothing but prevent us from making real progress."

"So this little synopsis you refer to that Peter King wrote for Ecology Counts—was it general or very specific to our situation here?"

"Well, I'm sure they'd let you take a look at it if you asked them."

"But, you must have a copy here at City Hall. You read it, didn't you?"

"Absolutely. Of course I read it," he scowled. "I can tell you we had plenty of reports—not just King's. And what I read in all of those reports would just be the main points edited down by Staff." The Mayor was getting bored and irritated.

"Anyway, that business is all settled now and as far as I can tell, everybody's happy. We're set to run the plants ourselves, and that's mainly what they were after—and what King was lobbying for."

"Well, that must have produced some unhappy campers on the other side," McBride said. "My understanding is that the Europa Conglomerate stood to gain not only a long-term lucrative contract here, but basically a foothold in North America—and they lost both."

"Look, we were small potatoes for them. The truth is they were doing us a favour. Look how badly we've been managing our harbour for almost three hundred years. We don't have a leg to stand on. We could use a little expertise, don't you think? And expertise is what they were bringing to the exercise. They were not the criminals certain parties were trying to make them out to be."

"Who exactly were the individuals in Europa?" McBride asked. "Were they here on site?"

"From time to time. Listen, you know what? This is all water under the bridge now and I've got a busy day. I don't want to talk about this stuff. If you want to know who those people are, do your homework!"

"You're coming through loud and clear. Why don't I get out of your hair and drop in on City Staff...see if they have King's original report on hand."

"Fill your boots, McBride. Good to see you, again. Take it easy." The grin was back and he extended his hand—ever the salesman.

McBride's real goal was to drop in on the Planning Office. If his mysterious caller had indeed been a clerk there, it was possible that a visit to the office would prompt some clue. He was fairly sure they'd have models and drawings of the treatment plants and if he could get someone to show him these, he could hang around long enough to draw attention to himself. It was already well after eleven, and he wanted to get there before everyone disappeared for lunch. There was no receptionist per se, but a young woman going by with a roll of drawings under her arm asked him if she could be of help. He flashed her his best smile. "I've just had some business with the Mayor, and he suggested I come over and take a look at the plans for the Sewage Treatment facilities. Do you have any models or drawings?"

"I'm Denise," she said. "And you are?"

"Call me McBride," he said with spirited volume, prompting a number of people to look in his direction.

"Unfortunately Mr. Spiegle is not here. The treatment plants are under his supervision—but I'd be happy to get you some brochures." She disappeared down a hall, and McBride looked around. There were several library-style tables with maps and drawings on them. The room was open design with blue and grey padded baffles separating desks from one another. There was a large filing area with oversize blueprint drawers. The individuals in the office had quickly lost interest in him and gone back to whatever they were doing. Just behind him, the main office door opened and a young man who looked to be of Middle-Eastern descent entered with a large carton full of files. McBride stepped back to the door and held it open for him. At the same time, Denise reappeared with some brochures. He heard her say, "Here you are Mr. McBride." He purposely remained turned away from her and it had the desired effect. She raised her voice and called to him more loudly—"Mr. McBride!"

Once again everyone in the office turned and looked in his direction.

"Oh, thanks very much Denise. But can't I see some models of the treatment plants as well? I'm preparing a course for the community college and I want to get a good grasp of how it all works," he lied, rather well he thought.

"I believe all the models and plans would be with the engineering firm now—the project is well underway, you know."

"And I've forgotten which engineering firm the Mayor said the project was with."

"Look, Mr. McBride, these are all details that our Planning Head, Carl Spiegle, would be able to talk to you about. He's been working on this project for quite some time now. So I suggest you come back next month when he returns from vacation."

"Could I have Mr. Spiegle's business card?"

"I'll get you one." Now clearly impatient with him, Denise headed back down the corridor. The young man who had entered with the box was busy in the filing area. He looked directly at McBride, and nodded quite obviously.

McBride's pulse began to race. Could this be the contact?

Suddenly Denise was there, handing him the requested card. "You know the best thing to do is check out our website—there's tons of information there."

"Thanks. Great idea, Denise. I'll do that." He took a moment to stand reading the card while Denise walked away from him. McBride glanced at the young man, who hastily threw some empty folders into his carton, pushed past McBride and quickly exited out the door ahead of him. When McBride entered the hallway the man was waiting by the elevator.

McBride had been intending to make his next stop the City Staff office farther down the hall, where he would ask for a copy of King's report. Instead he went and stood by the young man at the elevator.

"Hi," he said. The young man nodded as before. "So, you must work here—for the City, do you?" He nodded again. God, thought McBride, maybe he isn't the contact after all. Maybe he's just a nodder. Or has a tic. Or doesn't understand me. Or maybe he is the contact and he's downright scared. McBride tried again, as the empty elevator arrived. "My name's McBride. I was just getting some information on the Sewage Treatment Plants. You don't know of any information other than what's in these pamphlets Denise gave me, do you?" Unbelievably, he nodded again the same way. "Well great—I'd like to get it," McBride said, as they stepped into the elevator.

Just as they arrived at the main level, the young man tapped McBride's shoulder and pointed down. "The archives," he said clearly.

Bingo! thought McBride as the doors opened. Three large men stepped forward. "This is going down," the young man said to them, pointing to the red arrow.

"Well, we're on now, Aziz. Might as well go along for the ride," the third one said crowding on, as the other two turned and looked at McBride. It wasn't sinister—it was just odd.

At that, McBride, following his gut instinct, said, "Oh, excuse me. This is the main floor!" and squeezed off just as the doors were closing. He could easily take the next elevator down and find the archives room. He stepped out the front doors for a second to get a breath of air. It was almost noon. The morning had been overcast but the sun was shining now, and the parade square was bustling with people passing between Barrington and Argyle. There was even a hot dog vendor braving the November chill. He wondered if the young man they had addressed as Aziz was indeed the same person who had initially contacted him. He stepped back in and headed for the elevator once again. As it opened before him, several people crowded off, including the Mayor, who frowned and said, "Still here McBride?"

Passing him to step into the elevator, McBride pointed up and said, "Just going to City Staff now to get that report." He smiled as the doors were closing.

McBride got out at the second floor and looked for the stairwell. With any luck it would go all the way down to the basement level and Aziz would still be in archives. He took the stairs two at a time, passing a door that said "Main Floor." He continued down. At the bottom of the stairs he found himself in a small basement corridor with one locked door and another that said "Supplies." He tried the handle of the supply room door. It opened into a small space lined with shelves where cleaning provisions and linens were stored.

He walked through the room and opened another door on the other side. Now he was in a dim but much larger corridor. He decided to go left. "Can I help you, Mister?" It was a voice from behind him. He turned to see a man in his sixties carrying an industrial vacuum cleaner.

"I'm uh...lost," McBride said. "I was taking the stairs to the main level and I must have gone too far."

"Yeah, you're right there, my friend—you did go too far."

Oh boy, this isn't my day, thought McBride.

"I guess I'll just give our security folks a little call. They're always happy to help out." He put the vacuum cleaner down on the floor and took a cellphone out of his pocket.

"Really, there's no need. I can just..." But it was too late. The phone conversation was already underway.

"How are ya now? Oh yeah? Yeah." This last "yeah" was spoken on the inhale. "Well, I've got a fella down here just outside the maintenance room, says he's lost. Says he must have gone too far. Good enough. We'll be right here. Waiting." He clicked the phone off. "Won't be a minute, fella." He stared at McBride.

"Thanks," McBride said. "Nice day."

"I wouldn't know," the man replied.

Approaching now from the direction toward which McBride had been heading came two blue-uniformed security guards, one large and one small. "We'll take it from here, Jake," the large one said.

"Fine by me," Jake said and disappeared into the supply room with the vacuum cleaner.

"So what's the story, buddy?" It was the large one.

"No story," McBride said casually. "I was taking the stairs down and missed the main level." He took the brochures out of his breast pocket. "I had a meeting with the Mayor this morning and then after that I was visiting the Planning Office to get some information on the Sewage Treatment Plants for a course I'm teaching at the community college."

"Oh yeah? What course would that be?"

"Uh. It's...Planning. You know, Environment and Planning."

"I see. I got a brother-in-law teaches at the community college in Truro. Which campus are you at?"

"Oh—uh—the main one," McBride wasn't feeling quite so clever about his lie anymore.

"I see. Got ID? Driver's licence?"

McBride took out his licence and showed it to the security guard, who took some notes.

"Well, come with us Mr. McBride, and we'll show you out." He put his hand on McBride's shoulder and they turned and led him towards a wide door at the end of the basement corridor. It opened into a finished area with several closed wooden and glass doors leading into offices, one of which was very likely the archives.

"This is more like it," McBride said.

"More like what?" the guard said. They were walking towards the elevator. He pushed the button.

"So Jeez, I can't be the only person that takes the stairs down," McBride said, attempting to lighten things up. "Haven't any other fitness freaks accidentally wound up in the supply room?"

"You took the wrong stairs." This was the small one, speaking for the first time.

"The wrong stairs?"

"That's right, the wrong stairs."

McBride was starting to feel like Alice in Wonderland after she fell down the rabbit hole. Aziz was the white rabbit and they were destined never to meet. They all stepped into the elevator and went up to the main level. The guards escorted McBride to the front door and watched him leave. He turned at the bottom of the outside stairs and they were still there watching him.

He'd be pushing it to go back in now. He'd have to get Rosalind to connect with Aziz.

Chapter Eight

After my jaunt to Crystal Crescent Beach, I took the yew branches and berries out to our regular lab for analysis of the taxine levels, then made my way home to prepare for rehearsal. I found McBride on my doorstep.

"I suppose you're looking for a cup of tea," I said.

"It can't hurt," he said.

"It's a comfort," I said, unlocking the door.

Over tea he caught me up on his failed mission at City Hall.

"I wouldn't call it a failure," I said. "It sounds as though you likely succeeded in finding your original contact. You just didn't get the information."

"Yeah, that little detail," he said cynically. "Otherwise it was a great success."

"Stop it," I said.

"I knew if I ventured back in to look for him in the archives, I'd risk putting focus on him, and there's no question he's skittish, and obviously with reason. Even my going around there today may have been a mistake. So now, it's up to you Roz to go down there, get King's report from Staff and then try to connect with Aziz."

"I can easily go over to Ecology Counts instead to get King's report. But as for the other," I said, "the problem is that because of the many, many errands I've done for you on past cases, a number of people at City Hall know me. They know me in person and they know me on the phone, and they know I work with you, so there would still be the risk of someone linking you with him even if it was me doing it."

"You think so?"

"How about this: Why don't we get Sophie to call using, say, a British accent? She's a wonderful actress, and she could call the Planning Office directly and say she's a friend or even a relative. It would keep the focus off you or me, and it shouldn't put him in any danger. We just need to figure out what she should say and what kind of arrangement she should make with him."

"Let me think about it," McBride said. It was against his principles to involve anyone unnecessarily in a case, but he was anxious to find a way to get at whatever information Aziz had.

"I have to go see her today anyway," he added.

"Oh really," I said, raising my eyebrows.

"I left Molly there this morning."

"Well, Sophie's got rehearsal at six and she usually goes in early, so you better get cracking."

"Right." He got to his feet and started to put his coat on.

"And hey, don't bother asking me how my day was," I said, picking up his teacup and carrying it to the sink.

"Okay I won't. Alright. How was your day?"

"Well, since you ask, I went to the King residence to get the yew tree samples this morning and I had a very interesting conversation with Daniel King, who surprised me by being there—it turns out he isn't leaving for Ontario until tomorrow."

"He must have changed his travel plans. And what was so interesting?"

"Well, he spoke quite eloquently about his father, but then he became extremely upset talking about his mother's strange behaviour after the funeral, how she more or less cut him off emotionally, packed her bags and left for Europe. Did you know about this?" I asked.

"No, I didn't—I mean—he told me she had gone, but not that she was behaving strangely."

"So," I continued, "I'm thinking that if we get the results I'm expecting on this yew sample—and I did get it out to the lab today—then we'll need to twist some arms and get official permission to exhume the body ASAP. And if we can prove poisoning, then I think we'd better be tracking down Greta King."

"You've got it all figured out, eh Roz? Maybe you should hang out your sign."

"McBride! For heaven's sake."

"I'll take all this under advisement kiddo—see you later." He was gone. I'd forgotten to ask him whether Andy had found anything untoward in his security sweep but I assumed since McBride hadn't mentioned it that everything was clean.

I had to get ready for rehearsal, so I decided not to stew about McBride's challenged ego, or about my own surprising feelings around his involvement with Sophie. I walked over to the cat and scratched her chin. She started purring immediately—warm from lying on the radiator. She stretched. "It looks like we're down to sharing a can of soup," I said. "But it's your favourite—beef with barley."

I put the new Cohen CD on and got a little repast together.

"Look at me Leonard. Look at me Leonard. Look at me one last time," I sang along.

"So," I said to Sophie during the break, "reiki eh?"

"What a character," she replied. "He's sweet, though. I like him."

"Sweet wouldn't be my descriptive choice," I said. "Don't forget I warned you."

"He mentioned this idea of yours to me this afternoon," she said, deftly changing the subject, "of calling this person and pretending I'm his friend or his cousin or something."

"Just make sure to keep it between us, Sophie, " I said, looking around to be certain we were out of earshot.

"Don't worry, I'm like the grave."

"Did McBride have a plan for what you'll say and all that?"

"He's working on it."

"Well, make sure to let me know what the plan is," I said to her, in case McBride decided to go ahead without filling me in.

"We're back, everybody." It was Michael, the stage manager.

For rehearsal that evening the space was set up for the play within the play, "The Mousetrap." There was a shadow drape that hung down from a high platform. Behind it was a red flickering light. Above on the platform, in full view, stood the player who would recite "The Prologue" and play a recorder to accompany the first part—the dumb-show. Player King, Player Queen and wicked Lucianus the Poisoner would be behind the sheet creating a shadow play. Claudius, Gertrude, Polonius and Ophelia were going to sit out among the real spectators, thus making the audience part of the court.

As Hamlet prepares for the arrival of Claudius and his entourage, he takes his old friend Horatio into his confidence:

> *There is a play tonight before the King:*
> *One scene of it comes near the circumstance*
> *Which I have told thee of my father's death:*

He then exhorts Horatio to keep his eye on Claudius. As the court arrives, Gertrude invites Hamlet to sit with her, but he declines, moving in on Ophelia saying, "*here's metal more attractive.*" The scene goes on:

> *Lady, shall I lie in your lap?*
> *No, my lord.*
> *I mean my head upon your lap?*

Ay, my lord.
Did you think I meant country matters?
I think nothing, my lord.

Tom was delivering Hamlet's dialogue quite flatly, as though removed from the action. Sophie stopped the scene for a moment to ask a question.

"Roz. Does 'country matters' mean what we think it does?"

"Oh yes," I said. "It's an Elizabethan double entendre. He's taunting her, purposely making her uncomfortable with lewd remarks and innuendoes."

"But why is he treating her like this on this occasion?" Sophie asked. Tom and the other actors in the scene were all looking at me, so I decided to go for it—tell them what I thought was going on in this key scene.

"Well, Hamlet has finally taken action—he's set a trap for Claudius—and he's so wired he's almost out of control. Look at the text. He starts the scene by answering Claudius's benign query about how he fares, with: '*I eat the air, promise crammed.*' In other words, he has an enormous visceral appetite for what is about to unfold. This spills over into crudity with Ophelia. Then, he can scarcely contain himself through the opening dumb-show. '*You are as good as a chorus, my lord,*' Ophelia says to try to quiet him down. And, '*You are keen my lord, You are keen,*' to which he replies, '*It would cost you a groaning to take off my edge.*'

"Next, hardly taking time for a breath, he goes after the players to stop their miming and get on with the play proper. '*Begin murderer! Pox, leave thy damnable faces and begin. Come—the croaking raven doth bellow for revenge!*' Next poor Lucianus hardly has his devilish speech out of his mouth before Hamlet fairly shouts to the whole court: '*He poisons him i th' garden for's estate. His name's Gonzago. You shall see anon how the murderer gets the love of Gonzago's wife!*'

"Then BOOM! All hell breaks loose. The story is a direct hit—Claudius leaps up and starts moving out of the room calling for lights, echoed by Polonius's '*lights! lights! lights*!' It's as though Hamlet has set a match to a fuse and has been impatiently watching the flame travel to the explosive point. You see, Claudius's reaction gives Hamlet indisputable proof of his guilt—he has just seen it with his own eyes! And he has corroboration from his trusted friend.

"'*Didst perceive?*' he asks Horatio. '*Very well, my lord,*' Horatio replies.

"'*Upon the talk of the poisoning?*' Hamlet asks. '*I did very well note him.*' '*Ah Ha!*' Shakespeare writes a shout of triumph for Hamlet here because now he knows the ghost was speaking the truth. The apparition of his father might after all have been a devil's trick or a hallucination. In the aftermath of The Mousetrap, he's absolutely beside himself with glee, tormenting Rosencrantz and Guildenstern as they attempt, at Gertrude's behest, to summon him."

Following my little dissection of the play within the play, the company tackled the scene again with new vigour. Hamlet found real appetite for the event, discovering that the hyperactive desire to expose Claudius overrode all social niceties. He was crude and rude to Ophelia, and to both the King and Queen. Following the rehearsal, they knew they had tapped into the relentless motion—the inevitability—of Shakespeare's tragedy. The Mousetrap is the turning point in the play. There's no going back once you catch the conscience of the King.

"What is it that makes this so powerful?" George wondered.

I thought for a few seconds before I replied. "I think it's Shakespeare's conviction that there is an undeniable morality. It's what makes his wicked characters like Claudius so fascinating; they act out of avarice or lust for power, blindly believing they can get away with it, but deep down inside they know they've transgressed.

Finally, they come face to face with their own wickedness and they recognize it. This raises them and makes them part of the moral tale that's being told. In the tragedies, the recognition comes too late—everyone dies—but it's recognition nonetheless, and it makes us better for witnessing it. Our humanity is what's at stake. As Hamlet says: *'Foul deeds will rise, Though all the earth oe'r whelm them, to men's eyes.'*"

Sophie added, "I believe the play is so popular today because... just look at this world! It's so in our face with greed and corruption that we find ourselves reaching for things that hold ancient truth and wisdom in them. *Hamlet* is one of those things."

Tom, who was playing Hamlet, said, "I think we find it meaningful because understanding the play helps us to believe we're capable of saving ourselves from ourselves."

The cast went on like this for some time, exploring and trying to articulate the rich feeling that the play gave them. As I drove home, I thought about my life. What was I doing? What was I striving for? Was I capable of doing any good—of raising myself up to something worthwhile?

While Shakespeare's poetry could lift you and make you feel grand, the sheer scope of his accomplishments could reduce you to utter insignificance.

When I got home, it was already after eleven. The message light was flashing on my phone. "Hello Rosalind. It's me, Daniel. I just wanted to thank you for our chat this morning. I'm sorry I had that little breakdown, but talking to you meant a lot to me. I'm flying back to Ontario tomorrow knowing that someone cares about my father and about finding out what happened to him. So thank you and good luck. Please keep in touch. Mr. McBride has all my numbers. Oh and if you need to reach my mother, he has a London number for her—but I tried to call her today and apparently she's gone on to Paris. I'm trying to get a number for her there. The contact name is Spiegle or something like that. Take care."

My mouth was open. This was too weird! Spiegle? Hadn't I already heard that name this afternoon when McBride told me about his City Hall fiasco? I immediately dialed McBride, but to no avail. He might be at Sophie's, but it was too late to call there. "Call me, McBride—it's urgent," I said in response to his message.

I opened the back door and whistled for the cat who had gone out when I came in. "Come on," I called, "bedtime!" Just as I was about to close the door and leave her out—she flew in—her long fur out to its fullest as she brushed past me on her way to her dish.

I locked the door with both bolts. Can't be too careful, I thought.

I was pleased that I had brought Daniel a little hope that the real story of his father's death would someday be told. But hearing his voice also made me feel anxious about whether we'd ever get anywhere. Go to bed, I thought, get a good sleep, and make something happen tomorrow.

I was in a dead sleep when McBride called at 2:00 A.M. "Sorry Roz. You said urgent."

God, I thought, nothing's that urgent. "Right," I said, trying to surface. "It's…um…oh yeah—it's Spiegle."

"What do you mean?"

"Wasn't that the name of the guy in Planning that you mentioned?"

"Yeah—Carl Spiegle. Seems to be the supervisor in charge of the treatment plants."

"But he's away, right?"

"On vacation, they said."

"Well, Daniel King left me a message saying his mother has apparently gone on from London to Paris. Guess what the contact name is?"

"That's pretty wild. Give me the number."

"He didn't have it—says he's tying to get it. What should we do?"

"I'll come over for breakfast and we'll discuss it. See you at nine for pancakes. I'll bring the bacon."

"Aren't you bushy-tailed," I said hanging up. He'd be lucky to get coffee.

Chapter Nine

BY THE TIME I'D BEEN ABLE TO FALL BACK TO SLEEP it was close to 4:00 A.M. and McBride was ringing my bell at 8:45. Molly bounded in as I opened the door. Only a Lab could be that happy to greet someone first thing in the morning.

"You're early," I said, standing there in my housecoat and bare feet. "You can start breakfast, while I get dressed." I headed back upstairs wondering what McBride would do to my kitchen.

"No, really, they're not bad, McBride. I mean eggs, baking powder and a little salt might improve them a bit, but it is possible to make them just with flour and milk as you've done." I reluctantly took a second gummy pancake from the heap. "Anyway, they're really just an excuse to eat syrup," I said, watching him empty the dregs from my maple syrup bottle onto his plate.

"And bacon," he said, taking the remaining crispy rashers. "Okay Roz, down to business," he said as I poured his coffee. "You're getting the lab results today? Don't you have any cream?"

"Sorry, just milk. I put a rush on the samples," I said, "but what are we going to do about looking into this Spiegle thing?"

"That's on today's agenda. I'll do a backgrounder and try to find out what his family connections are. I'll also call the London contact and try to get more information on Greta King's whereabouts. If that doesn't get us anywhere we may have to go back to the City and get Spiegle's vacation itinerary."

"Speaking of the City, Sophie mentioned at rehearsal that you wanted her to call the Planning Office and see if she could make contact with Aziz, so I guess that means we're going for that idea."

"Let's see how she feels about it later today."

"Doesn't it seem like we're just treading water on this case McBride? I mean, we have these avenues of pursuit, but we're just noodling around on the periphery. We're not really in the centre of it. It's driving me crazy."

"This is a tough one—one of those potentially perfect crimes. If Daniel wasn't questioning his father's death, the perpetrators would likely get away scot-free. You're not normally so anxious, Roz. What's going on?"

"Good question," I said. "Peter King has gotten under my skin. It's like he represents more than just himself to me. I want justice for him. I feel like the future of the world is on our shoulders."

"You know what I think. It's that crazy theatre stuff you're involved in. Whenever you work on a play, you get weird."

"I do?"

"Definitely."

"Definitely? Like this is some kind of pattern. Some kind of recognizable state I get myself into when I'm working on a play?"

"It takes you over, Roz. Anyway, you're going to Ecology Counts to track down that report, right, so you can learn even more about Peter King today."

Ecology Counts was housed in a mid-nineteenth-century house on Spring Garden Road, the office on the upper floor. The organization had been functioning for many years and had championed numerous environmental and greenspace battles as well as pushing hard for the Organic Waste system, which was a pioneer program in Canada.

Leading the charge was Eloise Radner, a transplant from Montreal who had been in Nova Scotia for twenty-five years but was still considered "from away." I had gotten to know her a little bit at the numerous protests prior to the Iraq War, when people from every walk of life and all the humanitarian organizations were out in full force. Eloise had been a spokesperson on the potential environmental damage the bombing of the Iraq oil wells would cause, as well as the risks of destroying the Iraqi people's water and electricity infrastructure.

"In fact," she said, as we reminisced about the pre-invasion marches, "it was Peter King who really got on the bandwagon about the threat to the Iraqi water system. And of course, everything he predicted has come to pass. The damage was so extensive that many Iraqis still have no access to water, in spite of the highly touted American engineering firms who've been paid millions to fix it. It's like that's the real new economy. Go in and bomb the shit out of a country— and then make billions rebuilding it."

"Feeling a little cynical these days Eloise?" I said.

"Goes with the territory, I guess," she replied. "I got depressed when Peter King died. I hadn't realized how much I was leaning on him to help me through some of the issues we deal with. He was an optimist in many ways."

"So you knew him quite well?"

"Uh, yeah. Quite well." Her tone made me curious about their relationship, but I was reluctant to pry.

"I understand you commissioned him to write an analysis of the sewage treatment development plans, " I said.

"We did. And he did a fantastic job investigating the Europa proposal that was before Council—looking at it for overall viability and for its ramifications in terms of international trade. He was dead set against it for many reasons. His report was excellent, very thoughtful and articulate, and even though City Staff tried to repress it—water it down, so to speak—it did ultimately have an impact. The councillors voted against the Europa contract on the final draft, even though they ran the risk of having to pay a penalty. I believe it's a valuable legacy from Peter—one of many."

"Why on earth would City Staff try to repress it?" I said. "How did they become so gung-ho about this notorious conglomerate that was already being taken to court in other countries for not fulfilling their obligations?"

"It's a mystery," she said. "We and other organizations presented them with so many reasons not to go forward, and yet it seemed as though they were intractable. Maybe they were all exhausted and just wanted to take the option that was right in front of them because it seemed easy. As I say, it really was a last-minute turnaround and I think that was through Peter personally meeting with each and every councillor. He was tireless."

"Did he ever say anything about anyone in particular at the City who was deliberately throwing up roadblocks?" I asked.

"He tended to be very circumspect about individuals," she replied, "although we used to share a bad laugh about how the Mayor and the Big Cheese from Planning must be sitting on Europa stock."

"The Big Cheese from Planning—who's that?"

"His name always escapes me…it's odd sounding. Um, Spiegle?…Carl, I think."

"I've heard the name before," I said. "How long has he been in the job?"

"He was hired four or five years ago. I don't recall him being on the scene before that. But you know who would know plenty about him is my good friend Harvie Greenblatt. He's a lawyer—used to be on Council. Very smart lawyer. Lefty. Good friend of Peter King's and very knowledgeable about the ins and outs at the City. He'd probably be happy to talk to you. I think I even have his card." She looked through her desktop cardholder. "Here we go."

"That's fantastic, Eloise, thanks," I said taking the card. "And could I also get a copy of the report that Peter King prepared for you?"

"Oh, for sure. We actually had them printed up for distribution." She walked over to a bookstand that held various flyers and publications and took a copy of the report from one of the shelves. "What are you researching exactly?" she asked handing it to me.

"I've gotten interested in all this water and sewage stuff and someone mentioned that Peter King had done a comprehensive study. I'm just educating myself about my own city, and about the work that Peter was doing. It sounds like you worked with him on all kinds of things."

"He was generous, gave us a lot of free legal advice. He ended up being a very good friend to me and just was—I don't know—the best. We should have lunch sometime."

"I'd love that—here's my card. Call me."

"Criminologist!" she said looking at it. "That's funny—I thought you worked in theatre."

"Theatre's a passion of mine," I replied, "but not really a job, though I am actually working on a production of *Hamlet* at the moment. Yeah, I guess I should change my business cards to read 'Criminologist and Dramaturge.'"

"Multi-tasking—it's all the rage," she said laughing.

"Keep up the good work Eloise…and your spirits," I said. "Oh, can I use a telephone for a moment?"

"Sure, on the desk at the front. Just pick any line that's free."

I called the lab to confirm that the toxicology report was ready. Picking it up was next on my list.

It was a beautiful day for the end of November. The snow from the recent storm was almost melted away and it was warm enough that the brine was in the air. I opened the car window on the way to the Burnside Industrial Park and took a deep breath. If only this was spring instead of the dark time of year, I thought, turning towards the old bridge.

The morning light was clear. From the bridge, I could see George's Island and out to the mouth of the harbour. Off to my left, I could see the new bridge and beyond into the Narrows. Approaching the Dartmouth side I moved into the left turning lane and it was as I was switching lanes that I first noticed the vehicle behind me as it switched lanes as well. It was an older-model, dark blue sedan. A Dodge? Something about the look of the driver rang a bell, and all at once I remembered seeing him sitting in his car when I left the Ecology Counts office. I'd been having a pretty good day, but now I was shaking. Was I being followed?

I tossed the bridge token into the toll machine and advanced, signalling to turn left. The Dodge was right behind me. I thought about the location of the lab—off the back end of a warehouse building in the more isolated part of the industrial park. Feeling vulnerable, I needed to think about this carefully before I got there. There was a Tim Horton's drive-through on my right. Without signalling, I impulsively turned in. He didn't follow me in. As I stopped to place my coffee order, he turned right at the intersection just past the doughnut shop. I breathed a sigh of relief.

When I pull out, I thought, I won't turn but will go through the intersection and take an alternate route to the park. I set my coffee into the holder and pulled out into the traffic. As I approached the intersection the light turned red. I was second in line. That's when I saw the Dodge in the parking lot of the Shell station across the road. So, he either turned around or he got into the lot from farther up the road. The driver was now out of the car, leaning on the trunk, smoking a cigarette. He was wearing a leather jacket and Matrix-style sunglasses—and he appeared to be looking my way.

Run or make a bold move?

I pulled into the Shell and drove up to the pumps. "Washroom?" I asked.

"Just around the side there. Key's inside," said the attendant. The side he indicated was exactly where my friend was waiting. After I paid for the gas, I pulled off on the other side of the lot, parked and walked into the station. I could see him through the narrow side window. The washroom key was on a peg behind the counter. There was a long-haired kid of about sixteen working the cash. "Can I get the key?" He handed it to me.

"Listen," I said. "Do you happen to recognize that man leaning on that blue car out there? Is he a regular?" He leaned forward and looked. He shrugged. "I don't remember seeing him before," he said.

"What kind of car is that, do you know?" I asked him.

"It's a Shadow," he said, knowledgeably, "a Dodge Shadow. They stopped making them in '93 or '94. My brother used to have one."

"A Shadow. Thanks." This karma of names thing was a bit uncanny. "Do you have a telephone I could use?"

"Payphone," he said, indicating a payphone on the wall just outside the door.

"Look," I said, "I need your help. I don't want that guy to see me making this call. I think he's following me."

His blue eyes widened. "Come down to this end," he said, suddenly engaging and pulling a telephone out from under the counter. The counter formed an L-shape going towards the back. "Thanks," I said and dialed McBride.

Miraculously, he answered.

"It's me. Do you remember what kind of car your thugs were driving that night?"

"It was too stormy to see details," he said, "but I'd say it was an older Dodge or Chrysler—nothing fancy. It was a dark colour."

"Well, I think he's on my tail. I'm at a Shell just across the bridge," I said. "Can you get out to the lab quickly, just in case? That's where I'm heading. I'll stall here for awhile."

"Where is he?" he asked.

"He's sitting out in the parking lot, bold as brass, just waiting."

"I'm out the door," he said and hung up.

"He still there?" I said to the kid, pushing the telephone back across the counter.

"Yeah." The kid leaned over the front side of the counter and peered out the side window.

"I'm going to the washroom. Just keep your eye on him for me, if you can. But don't do anything."

"Okay," the kid said, now completely intrigued by the idea of someone being followed.

Here it goes, I thought. I went out the front door and turned right, walking along the front of the garage. At the corner of the building I turned right again. He was dropping his cigarette to the ground and stepping on it as I turned. I didn't look at him directly, but glanced at the plate, which he concealed partially. I made out the letters "CSV." I walked straight to the washroom and went in.

Four or five minutes later, I opened the washroom door and retraced my steps. A quick glance told me he was now sitting in his car with the engine running.

I would take a longer route to the lab. If he didn't get behind me I would've brought McBride out for no reason—but it wouldn't be our first wild goose chase.

As I returned the key, the kid said, "I saw him get in his car."

"Thanks for watching." I decided it was almost time to leave the station.

To give McBride a few extra minutes, I sauntered over to Old Solid. I opened the trunk and took out the windshield wiper fluid. Then, I opened the hood and took my time emptying the fluid into the receptacle. After strolling over to the pumps to discard the bottle, I went back to the car, got in, and pulled round so I could drive past the Dodge and back out onto the main road. I had certainly delayed long enough for McBride to get across the bridge. I would drive the lower route slowly. I turned right out of the lot and proceeded, keeping my eye on the rear view mirror. There he was. He'd pulled out and was a couple of cars behind me.

A large district of warehouses and retail and wholesale businesses, the industrial park could be a mind-boggling maze if you weren't certain where you were going. Once you turned up one of the major arteries into the park, many of the side roads wound around in circles or became cul-de-sacs. My experience was that it was best to go directly to your location or risk getting hopelessly lost. Though the Shadow was quite far back, I could see he had made the turn and was still tailing me. Now there was a large transport truck separating us.

I turned onto a side road, went along towards the warehouse, drove past the courier depot through a narrow laneway and around to the back of the next building where the lab was located. I pulled in and parked the car near the lab office door.

I was hoping to see Ruby Sube waiting there, but there was no sign of McBride. And oddly, no sign of Matrix-man coming along behind me. I jumped out of the car and sprinted into the office.

"Hi Miriam," I said to the receptionist, who was standing at the water cooler swallowing some pills. "How are things?"

"Roz, I haven't seen you for awhile." Her voice was hoarse.

"No," I said, "I guess you were at lunch when I dropped the samples off yesterday."

"No, I just came back to work today—I was out sick for a week. Even though I got my flu-shot and everything."

"Don't believe in them myself, but lots of people swear by them. How are you now?" I turned to look outside through the glass door.

"I guess I'm a little better but it's still hanging on—you know, coughing at night and that—I'm taking these decongestants...Hey are you okay? You seem kind of jumpy."

"Right, I guess I am. I was expecting McBride. Can I use your phone?"

"Go ahead." She walked to her desk and pushed the phone towards me.

I dialed his number. No answer. So he was gone. But why was he taking so long to get here, and where was my pursuer? It was at times like this that McBride's cellphone would be just the thing. I made a mental note to push him to replace it.

"Thanks," I said to Miriam, hanging up. "So I'd better get those lab results."

"Right here," she said, taking a brown envelope from a box on her desk. She sneezed loudly as she handed it to me. "Oh god, sorry." She wiped the envelope with her sleeve.

"Bless you," I said, watching her blow her reddened nose.

"See what I mean? It's still hanging on. I don't know—maybe I should go home…"

She was still talking as I tore open the envelope and took out the contents. The report indicated that both the seeds and the foliage were highly poisonous. The analysis of the sample I submitted indicated that "the decoction from just 50–100 grams of needles or a mere 50 seeds could be fatal for an adult, depending on weight. The action of the poison is extremely rapid because taxine is quickly absorbed in the digestive system."

"Oh—here's your partner!" I looked up to see McBride exploding into the office.

"Dammit! There was a stalled bus clogging traffic on the Macdonald," he said. "I had to go around and take the MacKay. But you were right, Roz," he said. "I'd say same car, same guy. Oh, hi Miriam."

"You saw him?" I asked, before Miriam could respond to his greeting.

"I practically crashed into him two minutes ago. I was driving pretty fast to get here—and there he was at a standstill just around the side of this building. I almost rear-ended him. I managed to stop about two inches from his back bumper. He got a look at me as I was getting out of my car, put the thing in gear and peeled off in quite a hurry. You should have been able to hear the tires squealing from here."

"I didn't, but I'm all blocked up from this cold and I can't hear anything. I was just telling Roz—" Miriam started in on her saga, hoping for some sympathy from McBride.

"Did you get the plate?" I asked, interrupting her.

"Only part of it," he replied.

"Let me guess," I said. "CSV."

"CSV," he said. "Well, even with that, we should be able to get a lead through the Registry of Motor Vehicles. They should be able to narrow it down for us since we know the make. I'll give them a call first thing in the morning."

"Great. The sooner the better," I said. "That creeped me right out, being followed."

"Oh yeah, that would creep me out, too," Miriam added, and broke into a hacking cough.

"Now what do those test results say about the yews on the property?" McBride asked, indicating the report.

"The stuff's deadly," I replied, trying to keep my I-told-you-so vibes down to a dull roar. "So what's the next step, McBride?" I asked as we were leaving the lab. I turned back and said, "Thanks, Miriam—hope you're feeling better soon."

"Thanks, Roz. Bye." She waved a tissue at me.

"I guess we better approach the Chief Medical Examiner for a permit to exhume our victim."

"Hey! Great idea, boss," I said. "Why didn't I think of that?"

Chapter Ten

McBride had arranged to meet Sophie in the afternoon and he suggested I follow him to her place, where we could work out the details regarding Aziz. I was still edgy, but saw no further sign of the blue Shadow.

Sophie invited us in to have tea. She had just received a gift from a friend whose horoscope she had done, a personal blend of Indian and Chinese black tea; we all sat down at her kitchen table as the pungent brew was steeping.

"So what's the goal?" she asked, true to actor form, I thought.

"The main goal is simply to get Aziz on the phone and make a safe arrangement to meet him so he can drop the information to us."

"Okay. Do we know his last name?"

"I don't know it. I heard someone address him as Aziz—that's all I've got."

"Wait a minute—wouldn't I know his last name if I was his cousin?" Sophie said, cracking herself up. Her laugh was infectious. It felt good to laugh and relieve the tension of the day. Still giggling, she poured the tea for us and passed the honey in my direction.

"Okay, so I guess that makes me a friend or just some kind of acquaintance. What else don't we know, detective," she teased. "What's his position there?"

"Most likely some kind of file clerk," McBride said. "It's possible he floats between different departments. But when I saw him, he was in Planning, and if I remember correctly that's how he originally described himself."

"Okay, so I manage to get him on the phone. Then what?"

"You need to convey to him that you know me and that you'd like to set up a meeting. You don't have to say anything about delivering information. As soon as he hears my name he'll know that's what it's about, if he is indeed the contact."

"So what is it that you're after?" Sophie asked.

"He indicated that he may have information about what happened to Peter King," McBride offered. "He wanted me to get it that night in the parking lot, but then he got frightened off and seemingly for good reason—someone was keeping an eye on him. I might have been able to get it yesterday if I had followed him down to the archives, but three men he knew got on the elevator and I didn't want to put any focus on a connection to me."

"Okay. Leave it with me. I'll figure out a way to meet him. But, I have to be by myself to make the call," she said. "It's not just pretend, right. I have to get into it. I'll do it tomorrow morning. I'll let you know as soon as it's set up."

I could see McBride was a little nonplussed by Sophie's take-charge approach, but he didn't argue.

"Sorry to cut this short, but I have to get to work on Ophelia's mad scene now," she said. "I'll see you at rehearsal Roz."

That was it. We were out of there.

Once home, I got out the card that Eloise Radner had given me for the lawyer, Harvie Greenblatt. It wasn't five o'clock yet and with any luck I could set up a meeting with him for the following day. He was part of a firm that was notable for taking on high-profile civil rights cases and winning. No wonder he'd had a strong connection with Peter King. However, the secretary who answered said Harvie had recently left the firm and had gone to work for the Public Prosecution Service as a Crown Attorney. "We miss him," she said, giving me his new number. When I called I got his voicemail. I left a message, mentioning both Eloise Radner and Peter King, and asked him to call me back as soon as possible.

I went down to the kitchen to find something to munch on while working my way through the next section of *Hamlet*. The brutal Gertrude/Hamlet scene was coming up and I needed to look it over. "One egg and the heel of a loaf of sourdough. Looks like it's a fried egg sandwich," I said to the cat, who, in her customary style, materialized out of nowhere. She had clearly been down for her afternoon nap and was stretching, with her long fur every which way. I bent over and scratched her chin. She rubbed herself against my legs, and went and sat by her dish.

"You are endless," I said. "Well, there are crunchies here. I promise I'll go to the store on the way home from rehearsal." I filled her dish and changed her water. She looked long-suffering as she chewed.

I brought the egg sandwich to my desk and opened *Hamlet* to Act 3, Scene 4. I read through the rapid exchange between Gertrude and Polonius interrupted by Hamlet's offstage battle cry, *"Mother, Mother, Mother!"* Polonious then secretes himself behind the arras, and as I read Hamlet's entrance line, *"Now mother, what's the matter?"* the phone jangled. It was McBride.

"I'm just about to leave for the airport," he said. I could hear anxiety in his voice.

"What's going on?"

"It's my son," he said.

"Something's happened to Alex?"

"He was on a school ski trip at Whistler and he's had an accident. He's being airlifted to Vancouver."

"Oh my god," I said. "It must be serious."

"I think he's broken a bone in his leg—sounds like his femur."

"That's major," I said. "God, ski trips! Why? The only time I went on one, I got drunk and froze my hands."

"Yeah, I've got some stories too. Anyway, Carol is very worried, so I've gotta go."

"Of course. Do you want me to drive you out?"

"No thanks Roz. I'll take Ruby and leave her in the parking lot so whenever I get back, I can just drive myself in. But you could do me a favour and take Molly over to Sophie's later tonight—she's agreed to look after her for me."

"Not to worry. I'll pick Molly up at your place after rehearsal," I said.

"I'll be in touch," he said and was gone before I could ask him anything else.

When I got to rehearsal they had already begun to work. Hamlet was pressing Gertrude down on her chaise and forcing her to look at the two images: one of his father, which he carried with him, and the other of his wicked uncle, which was in a locket he tore from around Gertrude's neck.

"Hyperion's curls, the front of Jove himself…this was your husband. Look you now what follows. Here is your husband. Like a mildewed ear." What a strange image, I thought. "A mildewed ear," as though Claudius were covered with a thin coating of fungus—Shakespeare's theme of contamination emerging in a simple description.

I ducked quickly into the green room and sat down beside Sophie, who was going over her lines.

"So McBride called you about Molly?" I said.

"Yeah, that's fine. Terrible about his son, isn't it. He seemed really worried."

"It's one of those situations," I said. "You know—absentee dad. Whenever anything untoward happens, he's overwhelmed with guilt on top of everything else."

"What's Carol like?" she asked.

"I've never met her. She'd moved out west before I met McBride. I met Alex a couple of summers ago when he came out for visit. Really great kid. Smart and funny, and nice, you know? I think she's a good mom."

"Well, let's keep our fingers crossed that he's going to be okay."

"For sure," I said. "I'd better get back in there—see how they're doing."

"See you later. I don't know if we'll even get to this scene tonight."

"Well, in any case, why don't you take a ride with me after rehearsal, and we can pick up Molly together and take her back to your place."

"Thanks, Roz."

I went back into the Crypt proper. The Ghost of Old Hamlet had just passed through Gertrude's chamber—*"Look how it steals away. My father in his habit as he lived!"* Then Hamlet was instructing Gertrude to be chaste, *"Do not spread the compost on the weeds to make them ranker...Go not to my uncle's bed. Assume a virtue if you have it not."* Upstage of them, the old espial Polonius lay dead, one arm protruding through the arras. Gertrude was being forced to see the truth and she wasn't faring very well. *"Oh Hamlet, thou has cleft my heart in twain."*

Gertrude's plight got me ruminating once again on Daniel King's mother, Greta, and her strange behaviour after the funeral. McBride had departed for Vancouver without telling me whether he had learned anything about Spiegle. Should I now pursue this on my own, I wondered.

"I'll lug the guts into the neighbor room. Mother goodnight." The scene was over and the cast took a break.

Sophie was right. Ophelia's mad scene would not be staged until the following evening. After good nights all around, she and I climbed into Old Solid to go get Molly at McBride's.

"Everyone seems tired," I said, commenting on the evening's energy.

"Yes, it's difficult to keep up the intensity. Shakespeare doesn't really let down at all in this play. And of course most people are working at other jobs. Well, like yourself. How have things been going with the case, anyway?"

"It's been a bit scary. I didn't tell you when we were having tea this afternoon, but I was followed today when I drove out to the lab."

"Oh god, really?"

"Yes, and we think it was the same car and driver who got to McBride a few nights back. We got part of the plate and McBride was planning to track him through the registry tomorrow. Actually, there were a quite a number of things he was planning to do, which are now on hold." I knew I sounded discouraged.

"Well, I'm going to go ahead and make that call to Aziz tomorrow anyway. I'll let you know how it goes."

"I think it would be better to wait, Sophie," I said.

"Look, it can't hurt to make contact. I'm into it."

We pulled up in front of McBride's house on Harris Street. Molly started barking as I put the key in the lock.

"It's okay Molly," I said, pushing the door open. She could barely contain herself as she tried to jump up on both of us at once.

"Poor thing. She's been alone most of the day," Sophie said. "I bet she needs a walk. Why don't you go on home and we'll walk from here."

"I don't know. It's quite a long way and it's late."

"I walk home from downtown all the time. It feels good to get some air, and it's not even that cold. Really—go! Honestly, Roz. Go home, relax and get some sleep. You've had a stressful day. Come on Molly."

Sophie strode off towards Agricola Street with the Lab joyfully bounding along beside her.

I knew that Molly would put on a brave and noisy show if anyone tried to assault Sophie, so I let them go with no further protest. And she was right, Molly needed the walk.

As I was driving home, I remembered my pledge to the cat to pick up some soft food. It was almost eleven—too late to go the Superstore, so I stopped in at Joe's on the way down Cornwallis and splurged on several cans of her favourite. She would be over the moon. I also got some bananas and dug deep for enough cash to buy a container of Vanilla Swiss Almond Häagen-Dazs. Why not? The night felt bleak. McBride was gone and I was in the middle of a mess of loose ends. But maybe this was a good opportunity to catch up on my homework. I had to take a look at the guest book and view the video of the funeral, and I wanted to read Peter King's analysis of the Europa Conglomerate deal.

When I got in, the message light on the phone was flashing. The cat jumped up on my desk and straddled the phone as I hit the retrieve button.

"Hi Rosalind. Harvie Greenblatt here. I'll be at the office until midnight—I'm preparing a couple of cases for tomorrow—so if you get in before then, don't hesitate to give me a call, and we'll set something up."

"Great!" I said to the cat, whose agenda did not include me making phone calls. "Just a few more minutes. It'll be worth it." She didn't look convinced. Harvie answered before the second ring.

"Greenblatt."

"Hi, it's Rosalind."

"Oh…hi! Good, good, you got my message. Yeah, listen, I'd be happy to talk to you about Peter King. I'm in court tomorrow, but how about tomorrow evening?"

"Sorry I can't. I'll be in rehearsal," I said.

"You'll be in rehearsal?"

"Yeah, I'm working on a production of *Hamlet*," I said.

"Really? I love *Hamlet*! What, are you in it or something?"

"Hardly. No. I just help them with the text. Understanding it, what the scenes are about."

"So you're the director."

"No, I'm not. It's an unusual situation but they're doing all that themselves. What I do is just keep them clear on the meaning. Sort of like a translator, so everyone's on the same page."

"Okay, okay, I see—the language! That's so interesting. Great. Well, look, let's figure something else out. How about breakfast—8:00 A.M.?"

"Tomorrow? Are you sure?"

"Yeah, oh yeah. I never sleep. I'm always working or whatever."

"Okay, you're on. Where?"

"How about the Bluenose? It's right near the law courts."

"Perfect. I know it. See you at eight o'clock then. I'll wear a red hat."

"And I'll be the one with three briefcases."

"Okay," I laughed. "See you soon."

Following the call with Harvie, the cat and I indulged heartily in our store-bought treats. Then I crawled into bed and drifted off while reading Peter King's report. When it fell forward and hit me on the nose, I woke up, set the alarm for seven o'clock, and turned off the bedside lamp.

Chapter Eleven

SOMEONE WAS IN THE ROOM. It was pitch dark but I could hear them putting the video into the VCR and clicking on the television. There was ominous low organ music, and as the screen lit up, I could see a crowd gathered around a grave—but the grave was inside the church, by the altar. The two gravediggers were there too; they were busy digging. On the far side of the grave was Daniel King. He was wearing his dressing gown, weeping and pleading, "Please! Don't bury him yet. We haven't examined him."

But one of the gravediggers just grinned and handed him an empty flask saying, "Your water is a sore decayer of your whoreson dead body." Then he bent down and brought out a skull. He held it up and looked at it, and as he did, it became a floating apparition of Peter King. Suddenly, muddy water started bubbling up from the grave and gushing down the aisle between the pews. In the foreground on the lower right corner of the screen, there was a man kissing a woman while he slowly pushed her down onto the seat of the front pew. I couldn't see their faces.

She was dressed in a black suit with a hat and veil, and she looked like Jackie Kennedy—like the funereal image of her that is etched in our collective memory. Just as she was about to slip out of sight beneath the back of the wooden pew, she gripped it with her hand. I could see her long, red-painted nails. She turned her head away from the man so she was looking right at me through the dark veil. "Get out Rosalind! No one invited you to my husband's funeral. Just get out!"

Suddenly the man's cellphone started ringing. He fumbled for it in his jacket pocket and finally took it out and started pushing buttons, but it rang loudly on and on. "Turn it off. This is a funeral!" someone in the crowd hissed.

"It's not my phone. I've never seen it before," he protested, staring at the ringing phone in his hand.

"It's McBride's. It's McBride's cellphone!" I shouted out to the TV, starting myself awake, sitting bolt upright in bed and fumbling to shut off the beeping alarm clock—7:00 A.M.

"Oh god, must be the ice cream," I said to myself as the disturbing images from the dream flooded back to me. I climbed out of bed and checked to make sure the video was still in its box. "Weird." I dragged myself into the shower and got ready to meet Harvie Greenblatt for breakfast.

The Bluenose Restaurant was crowded with busy people starting their day with bacon and eggs. As I entered, Harvie spied my red hat and stood up and waved. He was seated in a booth along the windows—streetside. His regular booth, as it turned out.

"Good, good, you're here! Nice to meet you." He had a warm smile and shook my hand quite vigorously. "Sit down. I got you a coffee already."

"Excellent," I said pouring in some milk. "So, thanks for arranging this. I mean I know you must be extremely busy—new job and all that. I don't mean to pry but...what prompted the shift?"

"Flattery," he said. "They courted me." He grinned at my expression. "No, it's the money, actually."

"Now that really is a joke, right?"

"Yes, unfortunately, but money's never been that important to me. I just felt like it was time to cross the floor. When I was a young defence lawyer, I wouldn't have seen this coming, but the truth is, if you want to be really effective in getting the bad guys off the street—and go after corruption and all that nasty stuff—prosecution's the place to be. And it suits me. But it's so busy my head's spinning and it's the government, so there's way too much red tape."

"When Eloise told me about you," I said, "you seemed like the person to talk to about Peter King and his involvement with the City."

The waitress had arrived, and I put in my order for one egg, easy-over, bacon and toast. Harvie leaned towards me and said conspiratorially, "They have challah bread—get that instead, it's better."

"Oh sure—okay," I nodded at the waitress and she noted it down, giving Harvie a familiar little wink as she hurried away.

"It's not what you think," he chuckled. "It's just that I'm the one who got the restaurant to start offering challah. You know, like they have at The Senator in Toronto. It's a nice option and it's taking off."

"Well, I'm looking forward to it. But you didn't order. Are you eating?"

"Me? Of course I'm eating—I love to eat. I eat here so often I just nod and they bring me the usual. So tell me what you're doing exactly...you're looking into the sewage treatment deal?"

"You know, I'm wondering whether your new position as a prosecutor changes things. At this point in time I really need you to keep everything I say in confidence."

"It's my stock in trade," he replied. "No worries."

I spoke quietly. "I work for an investigator who's been hired by Peter King's son, Daniel, to look into his father's death. Daniel believes his father may have been murdered."

Harvie smacked the table and started nodding intently. "Oh boy," he pointed his finger at me emphatically. "Oh boy, this is good. I've been waiting for this."

"What do you mean?"

"I was amazed that the police didn't start the ball rolling. Peter was in his prime. His work invigorated him. I can't tell you what a horrible shock his death was. I was very troubled by it, and if I'd been working for the Crown then I might have been able to ask some questions."

"Okay, so what can you tell me? Peter was certainly against the Europa deal. Was there anything going on at City Hall that would make you wary, anyone who might try to stop him in his tracks?"

"The thing is," Harvie replied, "by the time Peter died, there was nothing left to stop. The conglomerate deal was toast and the City had smartly begun to make arrangements with the Water Commission to manage the plant. So what would anyone at the City have had to gain by getting rid of Peter?"

"That's the question," I said. "Last night I read the report that Peter prepared for Ecology Counts, and he was so articulate and so impassioned about the importance of keeping the plants in the public arena. Eloise Radner mentioned that City Staff did a major number on that report before Council saw it—really watered it down, apparently. Why would they do that?"

"That's not unusual," he said. "Council get so many reports, it's common practice for staff to just highlight the main points. Councillors are free to ask for the original."

"But do you think it's possible that someone at the City could have had some kind of inordinate interest in this company—a monetary stake perhaps?"

"Are you married Roz?" he asked suddenly.

"What?"

"Just wondered…suddenly I wondered whether you were married or not."

"No I'm not. Are you Harvie?"

"Divorced. I used to be married to a librarian. We've got a couple of kids."

"Really. How old are they?"

"Teenagers. High school. Good—they're good kids."

"Do they live with you?"

"Occasionally. Mostly with their mom. I mean, I'm never home."

Our breakfasts were suddenly in front of us. Harvie dived in.

"What time do you have to be in court?" I asked.

"Nine," he said chewing on the challah toast. "How we doing?"

"Eight-thirty by my watch. Do you know Carl Spiegle?" I decided to get direct, since time was running out.

"Oh yeah—Planning. He's a hard ticket, that one."

"What do you mean?"

"Well, he's very tough, very assertive. Has all his ducks in order. Usually gets his way."

"And in this case, what did he want?"

"Definitely wanted to go with the conglomerate—wined and dined them according to Peter."

"God." I started to get chills.

"Something wrong?"

"I just had the creepiest dream, and I think he was in it—though I don't think I've ever actually seen him. There may be reason to associate him with Greta King."

Harvie looked perturbed. "Really? Peter certainly never mentioned any such connection to me."

"Do you have any idea how long Spiegle's been in Canada?"

"I was on Council when he was hired. He came here from Germany. He has all kinds of impressive credentials in urban affairs—both admin and planning."

"Credentials from where?"

"Well, from Hamburg where he worked before this and prior to that…I think it was Zurich. He's Swiss you know."

I put down my fork and leaned in closer. "Greta's family is from Zurich. Look, would you do me a huge favour Harvie? Daniel gave me a video of the funeral. Would you come over to my house and view it with me to see if you can identify him and other people?"

"Sure I can, but when—you have rehearsal, don't you...Speaking of which, Roz, when are we going to talk about *Hamlet*? You know, I've been reading *Hamlet* for as long as I can remember. *Hamlet's* one hell of a great play."

"It is Harvie," I said, caught off guard by his genuine interest. "I'd love to talk with you about it."

"Well, what time are you finished rehearsal?" he asked.

"Usually around ten o'clock," I said.

"I can be there by 10:30 tonight. It shouldn't take us too long to view the video, although there were a lot of people at the funeral. The Anglican Cathedral was packed."

"Is that where the funeral was? My god, that's really strange. That's where we're rehearsing, underneath the church in the Crypt. No wonder my dream had Peter King's funeral and the gravedigger scene from *Hamlet* all mixed in together."

"I'd like to hear about your dream," he said, "but I'd better go."

"I'll get this," I said, indicating our breakfasts.

"Already taken care of," he said. I handed him my card with my address on it. "See you tonight Roz." He picked up his three briefcases and negotiated his way out the door. I watched him through the window as he crossed Hollis Street and headed down towards the law courts. His eager gait showed a dauntless enthusiasm that lifted my spirits.

Maybe we're getting somewhere, I thought, spreading a little strawberry jam on the last of my challah toast. Finally.

I got back home from the breakfast meeting around 9:30 and settled down at my desk. I picked up the guest book from the funeral. There were indeed several hundred signatures—some completely illegible. Peter had been a well-known and highly respected member of the community with plenty of connections. There were signatures of judges and solicitors and several politicians. There was Eloise Radner's signature. That's interesting, I thought, recalling her intense emotion when she had spoken about Peter. I was flipping randomly through the pages looking for the name "Spiegle" when the phone rang.

"Hi Roz—it's me." Sophie's voice.

"What's up?" I asked.

"I just spoke with Aziz."

"You did? That was fast work. Any problems getting him on the phone?"

"Remarkably easy. I called the Planning office and asked for him as we discussed. I said I was calling to confirm an appointment for him. And then the woman who answered the phone said he had just come in. Next thing I knew, he was on the line. So it was good timing or good luck, I guess."

"Wow!"

"Yes, and we made a plan. He's going to come to my place for a tarot reading."

"Oh, Sophie—not your place!"

"It's okay, Roz. Heavens, he sounds perfectly sane."

"When?"

"Tomorrow morning at eleven o'clock. Saturday right? He doesn't have work. I guess if he has anything to pass along, he'll bring it with him."

"Sophie, what if he's followed or something? I think you should postpone this until McBride gets back."

"Too late Roz—it's all set up and I'm looking forward to seeing McBride's face when I deliver the goods!"

"Well then, I should be there," I said.

"No, absolutely not. Besides, Molly will be here to protect me, won't you Molly? Listen I've gotta go—I've got some errands to run. I'll see you tonight. Get ready for that mad scene; I've got lots of questions. Bye." She hung up quickly so that I couldn't protest any further. I determined to talk to her again after the rehearsal.

I closed the funeral guest book and decided to have Harvie look through it if he had time. In the meantime, Sophie was right, I should do some preparation for the rehearsal. My brain was always better in the morning. I decided to spend a couple of hours going through the next section of the play. I'd always wanted to prepare an analysis of the symbolic meanings of Ophelia's wildflowers and this would be a chance to do so.

That night at rehearsal, as we got to Ophelia's entrance, the company stopped their work and sat around me while I gave them a little dissertation on the ditties and the flowers.

"What we refer to as Ophelia's mad scene is actually two scenes," I began. "In the first scene, where we stopped just now, Gertrude refuses to see Ophelia. In fact, her first line is—" I looked at Liz, who was playing Gertrude.

"I will not speak with her," Liz said on cue.

"That's right," I said. "She's emphatic about that and only when it's pointed out that seeing Ophelia may prevent dangerous conjecture in ill-breeding minds does Gertrude decide to allow her in. Ophelia enters the scene singing, '*How should I your true love know,*' a song about the grave, with the well-known, *He is dead and gone, lady* refrain. We can see this song having resonance for both Gertrude and Ophelia. Is she singing about Old King Hamlet, about her own father, Polonius, or about the death of her love with Hamlet? She insists not once but twice that Gertrude listen carefully—'*Pray you mark.*'

"When Claudius enters the scene, Ophelia greets him with, '*God dild you,*' and we cannot help but hear an uncharacteristic vulgarity in this greeting. She then says, '*They say the owl was a baker's daughter,*' based on the folktale that the baker's daughter was not generous to Christ when he asked for bread, so he changed her into an owl—'*Lord we know what we are, but know not what we may be.*' In other words, unexpected awful things can befall us. One day you're just a girl, the next you've said the wrong thing to the wrong person, and you've been completely cut off from the world you once knew. Everything is changed. She then sings, '*Tomorrow is St. Valentine's day,*' about a maid who gives her virginity to her lover and is then betrayed. '*Quoth she before you tumbled me, you promised me to wed.*' He answers, '*So would I 'a done by yonder sun, and thou hadst not come to my bed.*' The maid in the song has been cruelly tricked, much as Ophelia is betrayed by Hamlet in the nunnery scene. '*I did love you once,*' he says to her. '*Indeed my Lord, you made me believe so,*' she replies. '*Believe none of us. I loved you not,*' he says vehemently. Ophelia's songs and words in this first scene are filled with innuendoes, ironies and obscenities. They are a grotesque commentary on her bereft circumstances, and her extreme isolation.

"Barely a beat later, her brother Laertes bursts into the castle bent on revenge for the death of Polonius. Ophelia re-enters with her wildflowers, and Laertes is horror-stricken to see his sister so undone. The flower imagery in the scene begins with Laertes referring to her as the Rose of May, the symbol for purity, eternal spring and harmony. Ophelia's first gifts, apparently to Laertes, are rosemary and pansies—'*that's for remembrance, Pray you love remember.*' Rosemary is often used on graves as a pledge of remembrance. The name literally means Rose of the Sea and is also a symbol of constancy. '*There is Pansies*'—she says—'*that's for thoughts.*' Indeed the name pansy comes from the French feminine noun *pensée,* meaning "thought." Pansies can also be symbolic of shyness in young maidens and of the trinity: father, son and holy ghost—a possible echo of the *Hamlet* story. But more importantly, it is almost as though Ophelia is conducting her own memorial. And it reminds us of the ghost's command to Hamlet, '*Remember Me.*'

"Shakespeare leaves it up to the producer to decide who gets which flowers in the next section, so Sophie, you may want to try various possibilities to see what really rings true here.

"'*There's fennel for you and columbines.*' Fennel can be a symbol of paganism and witchcraft, but also of renewal and rejuvenation; it causes snakes to molt their skin. Columbine symbolizes cuckoldry, disloyalty and marital infidelity. Perhaps she gives these to Gertrude.

"'*There's rue for you, and here's some for me,*' she says. Rue, or 'Herb o' Grace a' Sundays' is meant to be effective against evil spirits and is a symbol of repentance and regret. Ophelia says, '*You must wear your rue with a difference.*' Is she asking Claudius to repent his sins?

"'*There's a Daisy*'—a symbol of the sun, the 'day's eye,' eternal life and salvation, but inverted, a symbol of lies and dissembling. Finally, she says, '*I would give you some violets but they withered all when my father died.*' Violets symbolize virtue, beauty and humility—her own attributes now withered.

"So while there can be a variety of meanings and inverted symbols for the flowers, Ophelia is finding a language which is hauntingly resonant with the truth—that those around her are flatterers, traitors, faithless to the point of evil, short on memory and thoughtless. Indeed, they are all so caught up in their own tangle that they do not even attempt to stop her as she makes her final heartrending exit to the willow, from which she falls and drowns."

"I like what you said about her conducting her own memorial," Sophie jumped in. "I mean, her life is over at this point and on some level she knows it. It does have that spooky sense of prophecy in it, so often connected to madness."

"Yes, I guess you could say it's already too late. But of course you can't really play it that way. It's more dramatic to be seeking rescue. That's why she is so determined to get in to see Gertrude. And at the end of her first scene, she says, '*I hope all will be well. We must be patient.*' And more importantly, '*My brother shall know of it.*' In other words, she's still fighting for her life, holding out some hope. When she returns for the second scene only a short time later, she's draped in the wildflowers and much further gone into the madness. Laertes is devastated and angered by her state, but he offers Ophelia only pity, not help. He's already grieving for her. This second scene has much more the sense of a goodbye ritual to it."

"God—poor Ophelia." This was Tom.

"Yes I guess that's what Shakespeare was saying about the nature of these power machinations. They leave the innocent destroyed. And of course it really sets the audience up to want some kind of retribution. When Claudius and Gertrude both die later, we have a sense that they deserve what they get. The brutal reality is that no one comes out unscathed. Even Horatio," I looked at George, "though he lives, is burdened with forever re-telling the tragic story."

The cast worked through the two Ophelia scenes a couple of times. Sophie had unnerving insight into Ophelia's desolation, and I was struck, as I had been so often over the years, by her luminous quality and the sheer force of her talent. The company decided to call it a night and tackle the section again the following evening.

After rehearsal, I stopped Sophie on the way out to try to talk her out of the appointment with Aziz the following morning, but she was determined.

"Look Roz, I've taken this on and I'm seeing it through."

"Sophie, if he does bring you something, it's best not to look at it, and please put it somewhere safe."

"I'll put it in my secret drawer," she whispered conspiratorially. "Remember."

"And promise me you'll call as soon as you can to let me know how it has gone."

"Promise," she said as we left the cathedral and walked out towards the street.

"Listen, I'd drive you home, but I have a meeting in a few minutes."

"That's okay, Roz. George said something about people going out for a drink."

"You could probably use a drink—that was stunning work tonight, Sophie."

"You too. You know it makes such a difference when you help us penetrate what's being said. It's inspiring. Thanks for doing all that research."

"Don't worry, I love it. See you tomorrow."

I was home just before 10:30. I'd made a hasty trip to the Agricola Street liquor store on the way to rehearsal and picked up an Australian Cabernet and a six pack of Keith's—I had no idea what Harvie drank, if anything. I also grabbed a few snacks from Brother's Deli. I pulled the bags out of my trunk and was just putting my key in the lock when Harvie ran up the front steps.

"Wow, I got here just in time," I said. "I wouldn't have wanted you waiting on the doorstep. You don't have a car?"

"Well, I don't use it much in the city. I try to walk whenever I can."

"But the three briefcases?" I said.

"Oh yeah. Well, I don't always have three—two of them are back in the office tonight."

"How was court?"

"Great, I think we're winning."

"Come on in, Harvie. It's chilly out here."

"So, this is your house."

"I'm afraid so."

"It's big—all yours?"

"For my sins."

"Must cost a bit to heat."

"It's ridiculous. I have this fantasy that the oil company execs raise their glasses to me at the beginning of every quarter. You know—'Here's to that crazy woman on Brunswick Street who single-handedly sends our profits into the stratosphere.'"

"Ouch!"

"I've got some beer and red wine here. What would you like?" I said, taking his coat.

"I'll take a beer, but I should have a bite first. I haven't eaten since our breakfast."

"Well, right in this bag, I've got some nice rye bread, some good cheeses and some pastrami. If you don't like that, I'm afraid we're out of luck."

"Sounds great. Let's go."

In the kitchen, I poured him a Keith's and put the food out on a big wooden cutting board. He opened my fridge. "Look at this Roz. You don't have any food in your fridge."

"That's not true. There's that can of cat food in the door and some ice cream in the freezer."

"So you should come with me tomorrow morning to the market. I go every Saturday. One of our city's great features! Come with me—lay in a few supplies, some fresh veggies, some nice fish, a chicken. It's all organic, and it's reasonable. It's local. It's not right you should have such an empty fridge."

"Okay. I'd love to. I always mean to go, but I never do it."

"It's a date. I'll pick you up at eight o'clock."

"Another 8:00 A.M. date? This is getting to be a bad habit," I said.

"Mmm! Good. This is good pastrami," he said taking a bite out of the substantial sandwich he'd made. "Brothers did you say? Very nice. So look, we'd better get going with that video."

"I hope you won't think this is a set-up," I said, "but the TV's in my bedroom."

"You're a goer, Roz."

I laughed, picked up my beer and the bread board and gestured for him to follow.

We didn't find anything of interest on the tape except the possible exit of Carl Spiegle from the church. The image was obscured and Harvie couldn't be sure it was him. There were no surreptitious hand-holdings with Greta in evidence. Harvie pointed out the back of her head where she sat in the pew next to Daniel, and from what I could see, she was blond and didn't look at all like Jackie Kennedy. Although there were some moving tributes to Peter King, the audio was poor and funerals make for pretty dull television. Both of us were so exhausted we fell asleep on the bed with the cat curled up between us. At some point, Harvie got up, put the quilt over me, turned off the TV, wrote a note to say he'd pick me at eight o'clock the next morning, and left quietly. Not very romantic, but better than I'd been doing for a long time.

Chapter Twelve

THE NEXT MORNING FOUND US HAVING COFFEE at the Trident Café on Hollis Street, getting ready to visit Harvie's favourite market vendors. We were both managing to avoid mentioning that we had fallen asleep together on the bed. "Thanks for coming over last night. I'm sorry the tape was so bad—what a waste of your time."

"Listen, I've found valuable evidence on much poorer videos. It's always worth a try. So tell me what you think is going on in this case."

I reviewed the facts as succinctly as I could, filling him in on what had happened to McBride the night he was at the meet to get information indicating that King was a target, my being followed by the same nasty character, the lab results showing that the yew samples were highly toxic and Daniel's confusion over his mother's behaviour after the funeral. "How well do you know Greta King?" I asked.

"Well, I've met her socially several times at fundraisers and so on for organizations that Peter and I were involved with. She's never been very outgoing in my opinion. Kind of private and enigmatic. But Peter thought the world of her, and she's a very beautiful woman. Bit of a fish out of water, I think."

"What do you mean?"

"Well, I don't think she's ever really felt at home here. She's kept herself removed, and I imagine she was lonely. I believe she travels back to Europe quite a bit, to visit friends."

"Yes, that's what Daniel said. Do you know him?" I asked.

"You know I haven't actually seen the boy for a few years. I do remember having quite a good conversation with him when he was going to the School of Architecture at TUNS. Peter took me to an exhibit of student designs and Daniel had a very interesting piece in it. He did well at the school. I certainly don't know enough about him to analyze his character. But Peter was proud of him and I would say that if he believes that something's amiss, it's certainly worth investigating."

"Well, it's his nickel at this point. We're far enough along in the case that the next logical step is getting a permit to have Peter's body exhumed. Harvie, do you know anything about how all that works?"

"I've actually never exhumed a body, but I wouldn't be surprised if it's a complicated, utterly exasperating administrative nightmare. But hey—that's the story of my life these days. I'd be happy to look into it and provide you with the information."

"I don't want to take advantage of you," I said.

"Feel free," he replied.

I could feel myself blushing. "God, Harvie," I said laughing. "We better go shopping."

"Yeah," he said. "What are we going to have for dinner?"

After thoroughly exploring a number of superb stalls at the market, we put our various purchases into the trunk of Harvie's funky 1990 pale green Mercedes and decided to amble along the harbour boardwalk. The market had been hectic and it was a relief to get away from the crowds. It was a brisk but bright morning and the sunlight glinted off the water.

"*La mer porte ses bijoux,*" Harvie said.

"The sea…wears her jewels?" I said, feeling rusty with my French.

He nodded, smiling.

"Nice," I said.

As we walked along I was interested to see that all traces of Hurricane Juan's devastation from the previous year had disappeared. The boardwalk had been restored and the five tugs and several familiar old ships were all in their berths. We made our way as far as the Wave sculpture at the Maritime Museum of the Atlantic and then turned and walked back to the parking lot. We drove along Water Street and then up to Brunswick. Harvie dropped me at home and as I got my parcels and bags out of his trunk, he invited me over to his place for an early meal.

"4:30," he said. "Just some salmon and a fresh salad. Set you up for your rehearsal."

God he is so great, I thought to myself as I watched him drive away. I can't believe he wants to cook for me. That's happened when? Never.

The message light was flashing. "Hi Roz, it's Sophie."

Harvie had distracted me so much I'd actually forgotten all about her eleven o'clock assignation with Aziz.

"I'm calling you so you won't worry. Aziz is in the kitchen finishing his tea, and I am just about to do his tarot reading." She was speaking softly, most likely from the bedroom extension. "I just wanted to assure you that all is well, and everything is in its place. See you later at rehearsal." She sounded quite pleased with herself.

It was already 12:30, so their meeting was probably over. Her message would indicate that she had safely stowed whatever information she had gotten from Aziz. I dialed her number and got the machine. "Hi Sophie—got your message. Hope to hear from you this afternoon. Otherwise see you later."

I put my groceries away—a rare experience for me—and settled down to work for a couple of hours on the Claudius/Laertes conspiracy, Hamlet's return to Denmark, and the gravedigger scene. Around three o'clock in the afternoon, I couldn't handle the knots in my shoulders any longer, so I decided to have a hot bath and disappear from the world for an hour before heading up to Harvie's. The cat joined me, revelling in the chance to pick her way along the curved rim of the old claw foot tub, repeatedly reaching her paw down to swat at the crackling bubbles. Though I did my best to discourage her from this daredevil sport, I always gave in. Otherwise, she would sit outside the bathroom door and find ways to make my life hell—like demonstrating her extended vocal technique or knocking over the hall lamp. Besides, I enjoyed her company. She would let me talk on, and had a slightly sardonic look that kept me honest. The water was nice and hot, and I took a couple of deep relaxing breaths.

As I lay back, I heard a thump from downstairs at the front door. I stretched my arm out and pulled the bathroom door open a bit. Nothing. Probably just some fliers coming through the mail slot. I closed the door and sank down further into the steamy bath. The cat had stationed herself in a crouch near the taps, her eyes half closed. I rested my neck on the curved rim of the old tub, placing the hot, lavender-soaked washcloth over my face and eyes. "Oh it just doesn't get better than this," I said through the cloth, letting out a sigh.

An unfamiliar shrill ringing made me sit up abruptly, the cloth sliding from my face. Startled, the cat fell right into the water. During the mad scramble to get her out of the tub without clawing me to pieces, the ringing stopped. So much for a blissful respite. Better get out and see what on earth had come through my front door. Barely dried, I threw on my old chenille dressing gown and ran barefoot down the stairs.

A manila envelope lay on the hall floor. On it was written in large scrawl, FOR ROSALIND. Okay, so this is from someone who knows my name and where I live. I picked it up and tore it open. It appeared to contain a cellphone—nothing else. As I was reaching in to take it out for a closer look, I stopped myself from touching it. It looked like McBride's phone. I laid the envelope carefully on the hall table so that the phone was lying on its back. I could see the little green message light flashing. Had the message been left just a few minutes earlier, while I was in the tub?

I took a pencil and, with the eraser end, depressed the message button. I then picked up the whole package and held the envelope to my ear. For a few seconds, I could hear the sound of dripping water, as though it were in an echo chamber. Then, a woman's voice, distressed, "*But long it could not be.*" Here she broke off to get her breath, and then again, "*But long it could not be, Till that her garments, heavy with their drink, Pull'd the poor wretch from her melodious lay, to muddy death.*" And then a sudden click off.

"Jesus Christ, it's from *Hamlet*," I said aloud, recognizing the final line in Gertrude's famous willow speech, in which she describes Ophelia's death by drowning. In a sudden panic I pushed the message button and listened again more carefully. There was no mistaking it—the voice on the recording was Sophie's.

My knees went and I dropped down onto the bottom step opposite the hall table and sat there, frozen. What could this mean? That the thug who had gotten the cellphone from McBride had possibly followed Aziz to Sophie's and was now threatening her? Or did we have this all wrong—was Aziz himself the threat?

I decided to call Sophie's place first. What if she were being held in her own apartment?

I was having trouble holding my hand steady enough to dial. No answer. Next? Go over there and take a look.

I called Harvie's number.

"Greenblatt." Again, he answered before the second ring.

"Harvie, it's me, Roz."

"Oh good. I'm just making this sauce base for the salmon. Do you eat onions?"

"Look I'm…I can't come for dinner. Something's happened."

"What's wrong?"

"It's Sophie, my friend. Someone dropped McBride's stolen cell-phone through my mail slot and—this is crazy but—it's her voice on the message. I have to go over there. I don't know where else to start."

"Start with the police. Listen, I have an old school friend there who's a detective."

"I need to see her place first. This could be just a weird scare tactic or something."

"Don't move."

"What?"

"Don't move. I'll be right there to get you. Two minutes."

He hung up. I stood still for a second. Dressed. Go get dressed.

I had brought the manila package with me and on the way over to Sophie's I pressed the message button. I held it up to Harvie's ear as he drove.

"Oh boy, that is creepy. That water dripping. She sounds scared."

"I know, and the weird thing is that in rehearsal we're exactly at the point where Ophelia makes her final exit to go to the willow."

"Then she drowns," he said.

"Oh god Harvie, I feel sick to my stomach. Can you...just pull over!"

Harvie stopped the car by the military gates on Gottingen and I got out and threw up on the curb. I felt dizzy but I took a deep breath and tried to pull myself together.

"I'm sorry," I said, getting back into the car.

Harvie got some tissue from the glove compartment.

"Thanks," I said wiping my mouth. I leaned my head back against the seat.

"You're white as a sheet. Are you okay?" he asked.

"Yeah—let's keep going. We're almost there."

We went into the building and up to the second floor. When I knocked on Sophie's door, I could hear Molly barking, but it sounded distant. I knocked again, and called out Sophie's name. More barking.

"I'll have to get someone to open up," I said to Harvie. I ran down the stairs and along the main floor hallway, praying for a little sign. At the end of the hall, there it was: "Superintendent."

"Please," I said to the woman who answered, "my friend lives in one of the second-floor apartments and I think something may have happened to her. Can you come up and open the door?"

"Against the rules," she said, cigarette in her mouth. "You have to have the police with you for me to open someone's apartment." I could hear the TV going. She was watching wrestling. Central casting.

"Yes," I said mustering authority. "I'm a criminologist and I have a lawyer with me." That seemed to confuse her enough to get some action.

"Okay—we'll take a look. But I have to be there."

"Of course," I said. "Thank you."

She closed the door in my face and reappeared a moment later without the cigarette and carrying a large ring of keys. "Which apartment?" she asked as we headed up.

"207."

"Oh yeah—the actress," she said.

"Yes," I said. "Sophie."

"No trouble. Pays her rent on time."

She was so slow on the stairs; I had to counsel myself to keep calm. Harvie had come to the top of the landing.

"This is the lawyer I was referring to." I was behind her looking directly up at Harvie. "So what we're doing is legal, right?" I said, nodding at him.

"Yes," he said on cue. "Perfectly legal."

In front of 207 she wheezed as she fumbled with the keys. Once again, there was the sound of Molly's distant barking. "She doesn't have a dog in there does she?"

"She's just looking after a friend's dog temporarily," I said quickly.

"No pets allowed here."

"It was an emergency," I said, trying to stay even.

"Well she should have asked me. Listen to that barking. I'll be getting complaints."

I was staring at the woman's nicotined fingers, waiting for the moment the door would open.

Finally, finally the right key! "Great, thanks," I said, and pushed past her.

As we entered it was obvious something horrendous had occurred. Drawers were turned out and papers were strewn everywhere. On the low table in the living room, a tarot reading was laid out. I followed the barking to the bathroom door, which was closed. Molly was making a serious racket now.

I looked over at Harvie as I reached out to open the bathroom door. He nodded, and stepped closer to me. "Molly," I called. "It's okay."

As the door opened the dog leaped out and was all over me, licking and whimpering.

"Come on girl," I said. "It's okay, Molly."

Harvie sped past us into the bathroom. I held my breath, expecting the worst. But there was no sign of Sophie. The Super was standing in the hall just outside the bathroom with her arms crossed, looking askance at the dog and the mess.

"What's been going on here?" she said following me into the kitchen.

The back door, which opened onto a series of fire escape porches, was ajar. I stepped out. There was crushed cigarette on the landing.

I got a baggie from Sophie's counter, put on her dish gloves and retrieved the butt. The kitchen drawers and cupboard doors were pulled open but not turned out.

Harvie called to me from the bedroom. Here was a much more chaotic prospect. Everything was upside down. The mattress was overturned and hanging over the foot of the bed. Lamps, books and cosmetics were all over the floor. Clothing and contents of the closet spilled out into the room.

I turned to the Super. "Obviously something has happened to Sophie. We're going to have to call the police. We'll stay here. Please go down and direct them up when they arrive."

"I better call them," she replied.

"No," I said. "I will. It's okay. As I said, I'm a criminologist. Please go down and wait."

As soon as she was out the door I turned to Harvie. "Okay, who was that detective friend of yours?"

"It's Saturday," he said as he reached into his wallet and took out a card. "Home number's on the back."

"Donald Arbuckle, Crime Division. I've heard McBride mention him. Would you mind calling him for me?"

"Not at all Roz."

"There's a phone in the kitchen."

The second Harvie went to the kitchen I was at the low tarot table. I felt carefully for the depression Sophie had showed me the night she had taken out the runes, and pressed it. The secret drawer released and sprang out a couple of inches. I pulled it open, and there inside was a green file folder. I opened the file quickly and spotted the City's letterhead.

"This is it," I said to myself. I closed the drawer and quickly slipped the folder into my shoulder bag.

Harvie came into the room from the kitchen. "Luck is with us—Donald was at work—and there's a team on their way."

"Good. Thanks for being here, Harvie," I said.

"Hey, whatever I can do," he replied, trying to keep things light. "How are you feeling, Roz? Are you alright?"

"Look, I need to be really careful here. I'm not going to fill the police in on the Peter King investigation yet. We're in the midst of gathering enough evidence to bring charges and we're not ready. If we blow it open now, we could lose everything we've got."

"Well, I would advise you to sit down privately with Arbuckle and come clean."

Within twenty minutes a crime unit was on the site, along with Detective Arbuckle. After introductions, I gave him the evidence I had found on the back steps, and told him about the back door being ajar. Somewhat reluctantly I also gave him the envelope with my name scrawled on it, explaining that it contained what I thought was the same phone that had been stolen from McBride a few nights before. I told him about my present work with Sophie on the *Hamlet* production and the alarming recorded message in her voice quoting from the play.

"Well, if this all comes back to McBride's cellphone, we can bet the situation is a lot more complicated than it appears at first glance."

"I know what you mean. Listen, I haven't touched the cellphone. With any luck you'll find prints on it."

I could see Arbuckle restraining himself from making a comment about me not needing to tell him his business.

"And where is McBride?" he asked.

"He's had to fly out west for a family emergency."

"What's his involvement here? Does he have a connection with this woman?"

"She's the one who found him the night he was assaulted, and she's been looking after his dog for him."

"Whoever turned this place upside down was obviously after

something. You say Sophie is an actress. Any lucrative sidelines, like drugs?"

"No, not her thing," I said.

"And you. Harvie says you work for McBride."

"I'm his researcher."

"So, do you have any idea what they were looking for? What else can you tell me about this situation?"

"I don't know what to make of it."

His eyes moved from me to Harvie and back to me. "I'm going to take a look around. Don't go anywhere." I looked at Harvie. I knew he wanted me to tell Arbuckle everything, but I was determined to get a close look at the file I had hidden in my bag before having to hand it over.

"Roz—" Harvie began.

"I know, but I have to talk to McBride first," I said under my breath.

"You have to think of Sophie's safety," he continued.

"Look, it's my fault she's in this mess. We're going to find her."

I went and sat down on the couch behind the little table where I knew Sophie would have been sitting during the tarot reading. I looked at the cards. The Significator—the card Aziz would have randomly chosen from the deck to represent himself—was the Knight of Swords, clearly an embattled figure. The Knight was covered crosswise by the card of Death. Even with as little as I knew about the cards, that was alarming. I decided to write the reading down for future reference. I took a notebook out of my bag and started to make a chart. Below the two central cards was The Hermit, an old man searching in the dark with a lantern, and above them was The Moon, with its baying dogs. To the left of the two central cards was The King of Wands and to the right was the Ace of Swords. Farther to the right were four cards not yet revealed.

I was about to turn them over when Arbuckle reappeared in the doorway holding a clear plastic bag containing a scrap of Indian print fabric. "Does this look familiar?"

I took it from him and looked at it. "Yes it does. It looks like a bit from a peasant skirt that Sophie wore frequently. Where was it?"

"It was snagged half a flight down on the side rail of the back stairs." Images of Sophie being dragged down the fire escape flashed through my mind.

"Have you asked the apartment dwellers on the lower level if they noticed anything?"

"You know, we thought of that," he said.

"And?" I asked.

"So far, no luck. Tell me what you're writing down there."

"This tarot reading," I said. "She must have been in the midst of reading someone's cards. She did do readings and horoscopes for people."

"Just for friends, or for strangers as well?" he asked.

"Well, if someone called and wanted a reading, she would make an appointment for them and they would come here. The thing is, most often it would be somebody who knew somebody who'd had a reading, so it was a kind of network of acquaintances."

For the first time, Arbuckle seemed genuinely interested in what I had to say. "Did she keep an appointment book I wonder?" He began to look around, picking some scripts and notebooks up off the floor.

"And," I continued, "it looks to me like this reading was interrupted, because four of the cards are still face down."

"So," he said, "we should be able to get prints of the person whose cards she was reading from those cards that have been turned over."

"Well," I said, "certainly from this one—the Knight of Swords—that would be the card he would have pulled from the deck himself to initiate the reading."

"He?" This question came sharply as he picked up the card and dropped it into a plastic envelope.

"Well, the person, I mean." I held his gaze.

By the time the crime unit was finished examining Sophie's apartment it was just after six. Harvie and I took Molly with us and he drove me over to the Crypt so I could check in with the cast. I had an irrational hope that Sophie would be at the rehearsal, going over her lines, oblivious to all that had gone on in her apartment. But she wasn't there. I was circumspect with everyone, saying that unfortunately neither she nor I could attend that evening. Since they were at the point of Ophelia's exit from the play, there would be only minor adjustments to their schedule. They would move on to the last scene of Act Four and into Act Five.

As I was on my way out, Liz, the actress playing Gertrude, asked me if I would mind taking five minutes with her while she went over the willow speech, which was coming up at the end of the scene. I knew Harvie was waiting for me but I agreed, and we sat down for a moment and began to go over it. By the time she got to '*our cold maids do dead men's fingers call them*,' I started to feel nauseous again. I was very fragile and concerned that hearing the end of the speech—an echo of Sophie's cellphone message—might well be more than I could handle.

"I'm sorry Liz, " I said to her. "I'll go through this with you in detail next week, but I think I might have the flu, and I certainly don't want to pass it on to you."

"Of course Roz," she said. "You really don't look well."

I made a rapid escape up the little stone stairwell and sat on an outside bench for a moment. I tried to breathe slowly as I looked out at University Avenue. It was Saturday and the streets were fairly free of traffic. Then, out of the quiet, I heard the shrill sirens of the fire trucks as they pulled out of the station just on the next corner at Robie. The noise brought the nausea back in full force. I put my head down on my knees. Harvie's gentle hand on my back was little comfort. "The sooner you can get me home, the better," I said to him. "I'm a wreck."

Chapter Thirteen

AT HOME THAT NIGHT, I was feeling pretty grim. I've got to track down McBride, I thought. This is ridiculous. I don't even have his ex-wife's last name. I decided to start with the Vancouver hospitals. I sat at my desk and took out a pad of paper and got ready to call directory assistance.

As I was reaching for the telephone, it rang. I looked at it. Isn't this where this whole thing started a week ago? I thought. Please god, be McBride. I answered it.

"Hi Roz. How's it going?"

"Thank heavens," I said. "I really need to talk to you McBride. How's your boy?"

"Well, it was a clean break and he's in good spirits. The team is conferring tonight to decide if he can go home to Victoria tomorrow."

"That must be a relief, " I said. "Listen, something not so good appears to have happened to Sophie."

I told him as much as I could and fought to stop myself from dissolving into tears.

"I don't know what to do. I brought the file home with me. No one knows I have it. I didn't tell Arbuckle anything about King or about Sophie's meeting with Aziz."

"So what he knows is that I was assaulted and whoever did it took my phone, and that when it landed back in your house it had Sophie's voice on it, and now she's missing and her apartment's been ransacked."

"Right. He has the phone—I gave him the package."

"Okay. I was planning to fly out tomorrow morning if all goes well. I need to be at the hospital for that meeting this evening, but let me see what I can do. Maybe I can catch a red-eye."

"Molly's here with me," I said.

"Sit tight Roz, and make sure to keep that evidence under wraps." He was gone.

How many times had McBride told me to sit tight? I felt as though every second was an emergency and I had to do something. I went to my bag, took out the file and sat back down at my desk. Okay, use your brain Roz, I said to myself. Find out what's so valuable. I flipped the file open.

Inside were three separate pages showing what appeared to be photocopied journal entries, some emails stapled to some official-looking correspondence and an envelope that felt like it contained a disc. The photocopied journal entries must belong to Aziz, I thought as I examined them. The first one was dated early August—more than two months before Peter King's death.

> Aug 3. Tonight I went to a special screening of Velcrow Ripper's excellent documentary Scared Sacred down at the Art Gallery. I saw the environment lawyer Peter King there and mustered up the courage to introduce myself to him. I knew he had personal experience in the Cochabamba story which is probably why he was so interested in seeing Velcrow's film. I told him I had seen him around City Hall, and asked him if he would let me interview him for my documentary film class. He said he was sure he could find some time for me, which is so awesome! I have a lot of respect for him and I want to ask him all about the Water Wars.

Based on this entry, I realized that there was much more to Aziz than we had presumed. He was not just a lowly file clerk working for the City, but a serious film student with activist leanings. The next entry was dated two weeks later:

> Aug 17. After work I took my new digital camera over to Peter King's law firm to interview him. He said he could spend the dinner hour with me. The secretary said he was on his way back from the law courts and let me in to his office to set up my camera. I couldn't help noticing a file sitting in a box on his desk with my boss's name on the label. Curiosity got the best of me and god forgive me for this but I opened the file and inside was a piece of paper with some disturbing notes on it. I took a picture of the page so I could study it more carefully later. This is what it said:
>
> Carl Spiegle:
> – silent partner in Europa Conglomerate/currently in planning stages for massive World Bank-funded water privatization scheme in West Africa
> – somehow connected to Aqua–Laben in Bonn, Germany, an aggressive bottled water company that is challenging for rights to Canadian bulk water—check Board of Directors again—pseudonym?
> – engineering planner with Thames Water '85–'92
> – raised in Switzerland, attended polytechnical university in Zurich

Aziz's third photocopied entry, dated September 15—less than a month before Peter's death—was even more intriguing:

> Sept 15. This afternoon all the councillors were at an in-camera session about the contract for the sewage treatment plants. I was staying late to finish up some work. Peter King arrived at the Planning office around closing time today.

> He and I exchanged greetings but he was clearly distracted. When the boss arrived a few minutes later I could tell he was fuming and they went straight into his office. They closed the door but their voices were raised. I could overhear the boss accusing King of undermining all his work on the Europa contract and manipulating the vote. I had my camera in my knapsack and I decided to surreptitiously record their conversation. I just checked the disc and the argument is fairly audible. I couldn't get the whole argument because some other people from the meeting came back to the Planning office, and I had to quickly put everything away. But I'm excited—I may be able to work some of this material into my documentary.

For the moment, I ignored the other paperwork in the folder and went straight to the envelope containing the disc. It was marked "Copy of King Interview Etc." I put it in my laptop disc drive and there was Aziz's office interview with Peter King. I advanced to the "Etc." section.

The camera shows a still shot of what must be the door of Spiegle's office. The audio is apparently the argument that Aziz refers to in his third journal entry. I turned up the sound on my computer.

King is mid-sentence saying to Spiegle: "...for god's sake, Europa was a disastrous choice and it's clear to me you were pushing so hard for reasons of personal gain. I simply made sure that every councillor got the information they deserved to have before the vote."

Spiegle replies in his Swiss–German accent: "The City has been working diligently to hammer out this agreement. This was a very good deal for us. I know precisely what I am doing and I resent your implication."

Peter King's response: "Let's put the cards on the table. I know about your connection with Europa and about your undisclosed business activities in Ghana and in Germany, all of which puts you, my friend, in a serious conflict-of-interest position."

Spiegle answers: "Let me warn you now: You will regret interfering in my affairs. You have no idea what you're playing at here."

To which Peter King replies: "I'm just getting started. I intend to blow you right out of the water, Spiegle. You and all your money-grabbing cronies."

That was the last of the information on the DVD. I was both horrified and exhilarated. This menacing exchange was more than posturing. The threats provided the justification to demand an exhumation of King's body. The fact that we could have had our hands on this information a full week earlier was exasperating.

I looked at the paperwork I had skipped over. It appeared to be promotional material for a program devised by City Staff to have the City provide certain enhanced services to councillors' districts in exchange for a smooth ride on the sewage treatment vote. Attached to this was an exchange of email correspondence between Spiegle and a female councillor in which she cited points that had been raised privately by—guess who?—Peter King. She felt his arguments were valid and she was having serious second thoughts about voting in favour of the deal. She had become disturbed enough to distribute the correspondence to the other councillors.

It was late. I poured myself a small glass of dry white port and moved over to the bed. I now had both cat and dog in the room. The cat was somewhat leery of the Lab, but had assertively claimed the bed. Molly was lying on the rug by my desk. She watched me as I reached out to scratch the cat's ears. I swallowed a little port, leaned back against the pillows, and tried to listen to the Saturday Night Blues program on the radio.

Around 2:00 A.M. the voice of the local newscaster slowly cut through my sleep. "In Halifax a young man of Middle East extraction was found badly beaten in the railway cut beneath the Young

Avenue bridge early this morning. He has been rushed to the hospital. Police are asking anyone with information about the incident to come forward."

I started awake. "Aziz!" I was still dressed and the bedside lamp was on. I wasn't even sure if I had really heard the news report or if I had been dreaming. The radio had gone back to Deutchavella on CBC Radio Overnight.

Molly stood and started to whine. She was agitated. "Oh my god, Molly. I guess you can tell I'm not a dog person. Do you want to go out?" She was immediately alert and anxiously moving towards the bedroom door. She hadn't been outside at all since Harvie and I had brought her out of Sophie's building. "You've got a champion bladder," I said. "Well, I have to find out more about this news report, so you and I are going to take a little hike up the hill to the police station."

I got up and put on my coat and boots. I looked at the file on my desk and McBride's warning about the evidence came back to me. I closed the file and took it over to my closet. I had a loose floorboard that had come in handy on a few occasions, and this would be one of them. I tucked the green folder under the board. Then I remembered the DVD in my computer. "Just one more second," I said to Molly, as I ejected the disc and put it in the file. I replaced the board and rearranged my shoes and boots.

"Okay, let's go." The hall was in darkness, lit only by the shaft of light coming from my bedroom. We began to make our way down to the front door. The cat stood at the top of the stairs watching.

Was it a trick of the wind in the trees? I distinctly saw a shadow moving away from the frosted glass of the front door. I stopped cold. Molly looked at me and gave an impatient little woof. I glanced up at the cat as she arched her back. "What?" I said to her. She turned and strolled back into the bedroom. I looked back down to the door and saw nothing. I decided it was all foolishness.

I pulled the door open and looked out. The street was empty.

We stepped into the chill night. Standing atop the porch steps, I bent over to attach Molly's leash to her collar. Suddenly she emitted a low growl. I started to turn but it was too late. My hands were grabbed, yanked behind me and lashed together at the wrists. I was pushed down onto my knees. Molly leaped into the air and snapped at my attacker but he gave her a hard push and she landed three steps down on the sidewalk.

She cringed, growling. I knew he wouldn't hesitate to hurt her, so I shouted, "Go home, Molly. Go! Go! Home." She knew her way to McBride's. She barked loudly. "Go!" I said again. She ran down the sidewalk a few paces, then turned back and started barking frantically. A Dartmouth taxi came along the road from downtown. I yelled out "Taxi! Help!" but my attacker, crouching behind me, put his arm around me in mock affection and used his hand to cover my mouth. He pulled my head towards him saying in my ear, "Shut up, bitch." The taxi slowed to a crawl but my attacker smiled and waved him on. As the cab turned down Cornwallis and disappeared, the thug hauled me up to my feet and backed me up against the door.

"Keys!" he yelled.

"My coat pocket," I said.

Keeping one hand around my throat, he pulled the keys out of my pocket, unlocked the door and pushed me into the house. He banged the keys down on the hall table and slammed me hard against the wall. We were nose to nose and I wasn't enjoying the close-up. He was a bug-ugly bruiser with a scar below one eye. He didn't look at all like the Matrix-eyed driver of the Dodge who had followed me to the lab. This must be the other one—the one who had whacked McBride across the back of the head.

"Today, you took a file from the girl's apartment. Where is it?" His breath was vile.

"Where is Sophie?" I said.

In a split second, he smacked me hard across the mouth. I'm not cut out for this, I thought. I'm not going to make it through this.

"Hand it over, or you'll take the kind of beating I gave to your nosey little Arab friend."

"You mean the body the police found tonight in the railway cut," I said, implying more than a beating.

I could see I'd caught him off guard. "What do you know about it?" he asked.

"I heard it on the radio. Just a few minutes ago. They found him," I said.

"So you know I mean business. So cough up the file."

My mind was racing. What were my options? Stall as long as possible while he beat the crap out of me? Agree to give him the file? Take him on a wild goose chase? I took a risk.

"Okay," I said. "You're right, I did find a file at Sophie's today, but I gave it to Detective Arbuckle. And I explained everything to him, so it's already too late. The beans have been spilled. So far you're not part of the story, but as soon as they figure out who Aziz is, they'll be after you for murder. And what's more they got some prints off the cellphone, and they're not McBride's so they must be yours." I was on a roll now. "So if I were you, I would stop trying to protect whoever is paying you and get the hell out of town."

I was leaning against the hall wall, my hands tied behind me, the cords cutting into my wrists.

Molly was still barking loudly, and sounded as though she was just outside the front door. I could also hear car doors closing and men's voices. Molly stopped barking and started whining. The doorbell rang.

He looked at me. I could feel the hall light switch jabbing into my back. If I forced my tied hands upwards, my fingers could feel the switch.

"Please," I said. "Where's Sophie?"

"That smart-mouthed little bitch is in deep shit," he said.

There was some loud rapping and we heard, "Police! Open up."

"Tell me where she is and I won't turn you in," I said hastily.

"Fuck you," he said, his spittle spraying in my face.

"HELP!" I screamed. "HELP ME!" He grabbed my throat and squeezed. I forced my hands higher and frantically switched the hall light on and off, on and off. There was a loud crack against the frosted glass.

My attacker turned and flew into the dark kitchen. I could hear him grunting and struggling with the back door. There was a sliding bolt lock a few inches up from the floor—you wouldn't notice it if you didn't know it was there.

The glass in the front door gave way and I called out again. "I'm here, help me."

From the kitchen I heard the bolt slide and the back door open as two police officers entered the front vestibule.

"Back door!" I said, gesturing with my head "He's escaping!"

One of them sprinted after him while the other worked at untying my hands.

"Why are you here?" I asked breathlessly, "How did you know to come here?"

"Two calls came in: one from a Blue Bell taxi driver to say something didn't look right and one from your neighbours next door who called about that barking dog."

"I think this guy is the one who hurt that young man the police found tonight," I blurted out as my hands were freed.

Wasting no more time, he turned and followed his partner out through the back.

Molly was scratching at the front door and whining. I pulled it open and stepped onto the porch.

"It's okay, Molly. It's okay," I said, trying to get my breath, and bending to give her a hug. I could feel myself trembling. She licked my face, which normally I would abhor, but it felt great. "Stay here now. Wait until I clean up all this broken glass."

Chapter Fourteen

It was three o'clock in the morning and I was at loose ends. The police hadn't returned though I expected them to come back or send someone else to question me. I could only think that they were so caught up in the chase they'd forgotten all about me. Their cruiser was still parked in front of my house. I had swept up the glass as best I could and had brought Molly into the kitchen and given her a bowl of cat crunchies and some water. Now I had the kettle on and was hoping to calm myself with a cup of tea. I picked up the cat and tried to settle her on my lap, but she was even more electrified by the night's events than I was. She scrambled down. I looked at the phone.

Though Harvie claimed he never slept, he was sound asleep when I called.

"I'm so sorry, Harvie," I apologized. "I know we had a wild and crazy day but tonight's been even crazier."

"What's up, Roz," he said. "What's happening?"

"You're going to think I'm nothing but trouble," I replied. "Can you possibly come over?"

"Five minutes," he replied, and hung up.

I felt so grateful I wanted to weep. The sudden shriek of the kettle's whistle had me almost jumping out of my skin. I took a deep breath, made the tea and left it to steep.

I didn't want Harvie or anyone to cut themselves on the jagged edges of the door's remaining frosted glass, so I dragged a piece of fibreboard up from the laundry room and was standing on the front steps attempting to tack it up over the upper half of the door.

"This is easier with two people, Roz." Harvie was suddenly behind me.

"Oh, god!" I exclaimed. "Sorry. I'm a little jumpy."

"It's okay, Roz, take it easy. Let's get this done and then you can tell me what happened." He reached out for the hammer and I handed it to him. "God, look at your wrist," he said, seeing the red marks that had been left by the cord.

"Wrists." I showed him both. I held the board in place while he tacked in several nails. Then we went into the kitchen for tea while I filled him in on the night's events.

"Oh boy," he said. "Oh boy, Roz. This is a very bad scene."

"I know, Harvie. I don't think there's any doubt that Peter King was killed. I mean these guys are brutal."

"Look, there are too many people getting hurt, including yourself. It's time to fill in the police and let the chips fall."

I knew he was right. Molly let out a low sharp woof as the doorbell rang. This time we both jumped.

"That must be the cops coming back," I said.

"Let's hope so," he said.

Though it hardly seemed likely my attacker would ring the front doorbell, Harvie and I went down the hall like two frightened kids. With the broken glass covered over, I now had no way of seeing though my front door, so I cautiously opened it to find none other than Arbuckle standing there.

"Haven't we met somewhere before?" he asked dryly.

"It's a relief to see you, Donald," said Harvie.

"Please come in." I pulled Molly back so he could enter. Then I realized this visit might not be about me. "Oh my heavens—have you found Sophie?"

"No luck there," he said. "Tonight I'm investigating a serious assault on a young man, and one of the officers who was here earlier contacted me to say you had indicated there might be a connection between your assailant and that case."

"That's right. He told me I would end up like 'my little Arab friend.' And I had just heard the report on the 2:00 A.M. news. How is he doing, do you know?"

"According to the most recent report from the hospital, he's still unconscious, possibly in a coma."

"Oh no, what a disaster," I said, my heart sinking.

We were standing in the hall. Harvie said pointedly, "I think we should all sit down so you can fill Donald in on the details, Roz."

"What's happening out there—have they caught the creep?" I asked as we walked into the kitchen.

"Not so far, but he lost a glove going over your fence. We're bringing in the dogs."

I poured him a cup of tea. "Milk?"

"Clear's fine," he replied. "Okay, I'm all ears. Fill me in."

"Right," I said, seating myself across from him. "There's a connection between Sophie and the young man who was beaten—'Aziz' I think is his name."

"It is," Arbuckle replied. "Aziz Mouwad."

"He was the one having his tarot cards read this morning. This all relates to a case that McBride and I are working on. Aziz carried some information to Sophie's that could help to bring a murder charge in the death of Peter King."

"The lawyer who died recently?"

"That's right," Harvie chimed in. "Environmental and Trade Law specialist. He was a long-time colleague of mine and also a good friend."

"And you're saying King was murdered?" Arbuckle looked at Harvie.

"I'm just learning about all this myself, Donald," Harvie said.

"We don't have conclusive evidence yet," I said, "but Peter King's son Daniel suspects that he was, and has hired McBride to investigate."

All at once, my eye was drawn past Arbuckle to flashing lights outside the kitchen window. I stood and walked over to look out. Figures with flashlights and a number of dogs were out in the dark treed area beyond my back fence. A kind of no man's land, once proverbially known as "The Jungle," it now surrounded a recently built men's shelter. Just below that and across the street was the huge dig for the new sewage treatment plant. Maybe that's where my attacker has escaped to, I thought. Maybe he's hiding down in the muddy depths of the enormous excavation.

"When is McBride due back?" Arbuckle demanded.

"Soon I hope," I answered, still looking out into the darkness.

"Had you told me all of this earlier today—and about your personal involvement—I would have been able to offer you some protection. You're a target, and you're playing a very dangerous game here."

"I know. It was stupid. I think I was in shock this afternoon." I turned abruptly and stared at them. "Oh my god!"

"What's happening, Roz?" Harvie stood up.

"I've just put two and two together. I....Yes, it makes sense. We have to go now—no time to lose!"

"Go where?" Harvie asked.

I turned to Arbuckle. "Can you find somebody who can get us into the treatment plant excavation? That's what my attacker meant when he said she was in deep shit, and that's what she meant by 'muddy death.' I think they've got Sophie down there!"

As Arbuckle stared back at me, there was an explosion of barking from out back. The police dogs had found something. We grabbed our coats and went out through the kitchen door and down into the yard. It was dark and very cold. There was a brisk north wind coming off the harbour and it was starting to snow. The gate was built to be indistinguishable from the fence; I showed Arbuckle where to unlatch it. We made our way towards the source of the noise and flashing lights, to where the dogs and several officers were focused.

What they had found was not the perpetrator but a long-time occupant of The Jungle who was too inebriated to be let into the homeless shelter for the night. He was doing his best to stay out of the elements by hunkering down under a tree in a haphazard structure made out of old, wind-whipped plastic, fallen branches and sheets of cardboard. He'd been unsuccessfully attempting to ignite a few twigs when he had been discovered by the dogs. His late-night cocktail appeared to be a can of Lysol, which would account for his completely docile stupor. Mercifully, the cops opted to move him to a cell for the night. They called in the paddy wagon and then huddled together in a brief meeting.

Arbuckle called a halt to the search out back, but instructed the dog wrangler to stand by at the station while he organized our visit to the excavation site. He assumed there would be a security guard there, but he wanted someone in authority to accompany us. His plan was to go to the station, track down a project manager from the engineering firm, then come back and get us. Harvie and I saw him to the front door. As he left I couldn't stop myself from blurting out, "Please be quick. Every second counts."

As soon as he was out the door, I ran upstairs to change into warmer layers and find a coat for Harvie to put on over the light jacket he had worn.

"No point in getting pneumonia," I said to Harvie, handing him a heavy wool coat.

"Good idea Roz, thanks. And do you have a hat? Like a toque or something for this bald head of mine."

"Sure. I can find you something...Won't be a minute."

I scurried back upstairs and into the spare room, where there was an old trunk in which I kept winter clothes. The overhead light was burnt out so I had to make my way across the room in the dark to turn on the bedside lamp. I thought I heard a noise coming from the closet and I stopped cold. Suddenly the cat leaped up onto the spare bed. "Oh aren't you everywhere," I said to her, turning on the lamp.

I went over to the trunk and lifted the lid. I was digging through old mitts and scarves when a shadow caught my peripheral attention. "I'm sure I remember seeing a wool toque in here, Harvie." There was no reply. I turned and there in front of me like a living nightmare was my scar-faced attacker. I opened my mouth to scream but he was too fast. He clapped his hand over my mouth.

"We've had enough noise from you tonight," he said as he ripped a cloth belt from a hook on the closet door and wrapped it around my mouth. He hissed into my ear, "All those pigs trying to track me down and where was I? Halfway up the iron ladder on the back of your house! The idiots never even looked up. By the time they got the dogs here, I was already inside. You should learn to lock your bathroom window." He was grinning as he forced me down onto a straight-backed chair. I winced when he tied my hands behind me with a leather cord from his pocket. He closed the spare room door and leaned on it, looking at me.

"Okay. We know the kid brought the file to the girl's apartment and we know you went there after we delivered the cellphone. You must have taken the file because it didn't just disappear into thin air, and I don't believe you gave it to the police. Now if you want to save your friend, you'll tell me where it is."

Just then I heard a voice in the hall. It was Harvie. "Roz? Are you ready? They'll be back to get us in a couple of minutes."

I started to grunt as loudly as I could. I tried to make my grunts sound like "NO." The attacker stepped aside so the door would mask him when it opened. More frantic no-grunts from me.

"Roz? Are you ok?" Harvie pushed the door open and looked at me. My eyes darted to behind the door to alert him—but of course it was too late.

The thug startled Harvie and let him have it with a good punch in the face. Harvie went down fast, but grabbed Scarface's leg on the way down and knocked him off balance. They wrestled and punched and made a lot of noise. The fight was fierce and I could hear Molly barking from downstairs. I was relieved when she finally stopped—I didn't want her to get into the fray. Harvie was valiant but he didn't stand a chance. As the thug hauled him to his feet and slammed him against the wall, I was horrified to see blood running down from a nasty cut under his eye. This had gone far enough. I started making sounds that were as close to "OKAY" as I could, attempted to stand then banged the chair back down on the floor. Scarface was winding up to hit Harvie again, but he stopped and looked at me. I nodded vigorously.

"You'll turn over the file?" he asked.

I nodded again.

He untied my hands and as I stood up I indicated the gag and grunted. He pulled that off too. He pushed Harvie into my chair and roughly tied his hands to the rungs, using the sash that had been wrapped around my mouth.

"Okay, let's go," he ordered.

Feeling shell-shocked, I stepped into the hall and moved towards my bedroom. He was following me at about three paces. I turned into my room and walked over to the closet where I had hidden the file earlier. I opened the closet door, bent down and started to move my shoes and boots around. He stood right behind me, towering above me and breathing hard, "I don't see it," he grunted. "Where is it?"

"It's under the floor here," I replied. I was shaking.

"No tricky business. Hurry up!"

In the next moment there was a commotion, a loud crack and

he crashed to the floor so close to me I covered my head with my hands. I heard a familiar voice saying, “Down you go, pal. Now we’re even.” I turned and looked up.

“McBride! Thank god!”

Chapter Fifteen

I STARTED TO LAUGH AND CRY AT THE SAME TIME. The cat, who had been attempting to get her beauty sleep during the fracas, jumped down off the bed, walked over and sat down beside me. She looked at the motionless Scarface lying halfway in the closet, face-down in my shoes and boots, and then up at me. It was oddly comforting.

The doorbell rang, startling me into action. I jumped up and ran into the spare room to untie Harvie, who had heard the commotion and was relieved to see me still alive and well.

"What happened in there, Roz?"

"Just a second. That's gotta be Arbuckle. I have to go let him in."

I sprinted down the stairs and opened the door, just as he was ringing the bell for the second time.

"Let's go!" he said.

"I've got a present for you first, courtesy of McBride. Come and take a look."

McBride had given Scarface such a good crack on the head that he was down for the count. Arbuckle didn't waste any time and called an ambulance, which arrived within three minutes. In the meantime, Harvie introduced himself to McBride and was filling him in on the night's events as the paramedics got the patient onto a stretcher. Scarface was taken to the hospital, followed by a couple of police officers who would keep careful watch over him. Harvie decided to go along in the cruiser to have the cut under his eye tended to.

McBride, Molly and I, accompanied by Arbuckle and his team, drove down the hill to the excavation, where we were to meet up with a project manager from the sewage treatment plant's engineering firm. Climbing out of his enormous SUV as we pulled up, Rich O'Toole was clearly not pleased to be gotten out of bed before dawn on a Sunday for what he considered an unfounded whim.

"First of all, you're twenty minutes late. Didn't you tell me this was urgent? And secondly, if there was a body or a prisoner down there, I would bloody well know about it."

"Not necessarily," I said. "If Sophie is down there, she would have been taken there just this afternoon or rather yesterday afternoon."

"That's ridiculous! The place is very well secured—" he fairly snapped at me. "No one gets in here on the weekends."

"Look," Arbuckle said, taking the engineer aside. "We know this is an uncommon situation, but better to be safe than sorry. We have some indications that the girl might be down there, and we're going to search the place and find out. We need your help. Now do your best to co-operate and try to think of any and all possibilities. It's a huge site and she's not going to be in plain view."

Arbuckle had the bit of material from Sophie's skirt, and the wrangler had brought their best tracker dog, a lanky German shepherd named Speed, who, like a true professional, was managing to ignore Molly. As for Molly, she was so delighted to be with McBride again that she wasn't allowing for any distractions.

The engineer typed a code into the electronic lock on the gate and as we walked through it, we were greeted by the night guard, who was dressed for the weather in a standard issue winter coat, heavy gloves and a hat with fur flaps that came down well over his ears. O'Toole grudgingly explained what the police were doing there in the middle of the night and asked him if he'd seen or heard anything. The guard said he'd just finished doing the rounds of the site and had seen nothing unusual. He added that he'd been on a double shift and that everything had been very quiet.

O'Toole shot a hostile look at Arbuckle. "You see? You're wasting your time."

"Look, we're going down there, O'Toole. Now let's go," Arbuckle said.

The guard led us over to a lift platform that would take us down about sixty feet. As the others got a little ahead of us, McBride said to me: "I feel like I've met the guard before—possibly he's one of the men who escorted me out of City Hall the other day."

We all descended into the depths. Because the elevator was just an open cage, it was possible to see all around and below, and to feel the frigid air surging past us as we descended.

When we disembarked, O'Toole walked over to a pole and pulled down a large lever, turning on a system of bright overhead work lights. The wind was swirling snow and sleet down into the site; it was a cavernous place and bitter cold. If Sophie has been down here all this time, I thought, she could well have succumbed to hypothermia. I pulled my wool scarf up and shoved my gloved hands into the pockets of my down jacket and tried to hope for the best.

"First of all," Arbuckle said, "let's have a look at any enclosed spaces."

The guard turned to O'Toole and suggested the access hatches along the tunnel.

"Good thinking," said O'Toole. "This way."

The team followed O'Toole through a maze of steel partitions and it seemed to me we were heading south, in the direction of downtown. The site narrowed into a three-metre-wide round tunnel located twenty-odd metres underground. I had heard about this tunnel on the radio—how it extended a full kilometre in length crossing the downtown area to Sackville Street, where it would eventually pick up the sewage that was carried down to that point from all over the city. While the sewage had always gone straight into the harbour, it would soon be diverted through the new tunnel to the treatment plant, where the "floatables" would be removed. There had been considerable controversy over the fact that the expensive and long overdue plant provided for "primary" treatment only. The several access areas the guard had referred to were located along the distance of the tunnel so it could be reached from external points if necessary. Each of these access points had a kind of hatch opening onto the tunnel; with O'Toole's help in releasing the sealed doors, we began to look inside these hatches. About halfway along the tunnel, I turned back to speak to McBride, only to discover that he and Molly had broken off from the group and were no longer following us. I looked back along the tunnel but couldn't see them. Typical McBride, I thought, but was relieved that our manpower was being spread out. Finally we inspected the last hatch near the end of the tunnel, which was blocked off at the point where it would be joining into the Sackville Street sewage pipe. We had found nothing. We began to retrace our steps, walking the kilometre back to the open site.

McBride, impatient with the hatch theory, decided to do a little investigating on his own. He quietly left the group. As he and Molly re-entered the open excavation site from the tunnel, he heard noise above. Looking up, he saw that the lift was rising—he could just see the top of the guard's hat as it moved higher. He quickly looked around. Across from where he stood was the small makeshift office that the security staff used. The door was open and the light was on. He was sure it hadn't been previously—he would have noticed the office if the light had been on. As the lift reached the top, about sixty feet over his head, there was a ruckus and at that instant something flew down from the lift platform into the site. Molly began to bark sharply and took off like a bullet, as though the object were a duck that had been shot out of the sky.

She had some retriever blood in her for sure. Within moments, she brought her prize to McBride.

He stared in disbelief as he took the object from her. He immediately sprung over to the elevator controls, but discovered that the guard had locked it off at the top. McBride would need either the code or a key to bring it down. Looking around he spotted a steel ladder attached to the concrete wall on the far side of the excavation. It appeared to go all the way to the top.

"Molly! Take this to Roz," he commanded, pointing in the direction of the tunnel. Molly barked sharply. "Go! Take it to Roz." She took the item in her mouth and ran towards the tunnel while McBride sprinted to the ladder and began climbing upward as fast as he could.

The distant sound of Molly's sharp bark echoed into the tunnel. Speed, the tracker dog, responded with a low woof and his hackles went up. He hauled on his leash and, as though we were suddenly one person, all of us began to run. We were just nearing the point where the tunnel widens into the excavation site when Molly appeared, clearly on a mission, racing towards me with something in her mouth. We stopped and I stepped forward.

"Drop it, Molly!" I commanded, reaching down. She let the object go into my hand.

It was a short, tan-coloured leather boot and I recognized it immediately. "Oh, my god, this is Sophie's boot." I looked with alarm at Arbuckle.

Everyone rushed past me into the excavation area while I just stood there staring at the boot in my hand. What did this mean? Suddenly I could hear their raised voices—"Up there! On the ladder. Somebody's escaping."

"This is a warning. Stop now!" I heard Arbuckle shout.

I turned and bolted into the open site. Looking far up on the opposite side, I could see what they were all focused on. The German shepherd was at the bottom of the metal ladder barking loudly.

"For god's sake!" I screamed at Arbuckle who had taken out his revolver. "It's McBride. He must be following someone." Arbuckle lowered his gun and the wrangler shouted a command at Speed, who immediately dropped away from the ladder. McBride disappeared over the top as the wind whistled down into the cold chasm where we all stood shivering and staring upwards.

O'Toole was at the elevator controls now. "It's bloody locked off up there. This makes no sense," he said. "I need the damn security guard. I need the code for this. Where the hell is the fucking guard?"

At that moment Speed began barking sharply. "He's got the scent!" the wrangler said to Arbuckle. Turning to the sound we saw that the tracker dog was in the little security office.

Led by O'Toole we hurried across and entered the office.

"Christ Almighty! What's this?" O'Toole exclaimed.

Screwed into the side of the desk were two lengths of chain. A padlock was lying on the floor by a small electric heater and the cement floor was splotched with what appeared to be vomit. Arbuckle knelt down and reached under the corner of the desk— another torn piece of Sophie's skirt. Possibly she had used it to wipe her mouth or perhaps she'd left it behind on purpose. Clearly this was where she had been confined and probably interrogated.

As I stared at the disturbing evidence in the security office, I suddenly realized who the night guard really was. He was the one who had followed me in the dark blue Dodge—the one I had named Matrix-man because of his fancy sunglasses and the one who was at the wheel the night McBride was knocked out. McBride had indeed recognized him, but hadn't been able to place him because his heavy winter coat and the security guard hat with fur flaps that covered much of his face had proved an excellent disguise. No wonder Sophie had been brought here. Spiegle, in his position as supervising planner on the sewage treatment projects, would have control over security on the site, and since no one was working here on the weekend it would make for a handy little torture chamber. This guy must be on Spiegle's payroll—his lackey, his bodyguard, his thug.

"The guard has taken her," I said to Arbuckle. "He was keeping her down here, and now he's on the run. I think he and the thug who attacked me tonight are working together." I felt the panic rising. I knew that things could now take a turn for the worse. Matrix-man was fleeing with Sophie and she would be a burden, not an advantage.

Arbuckle immediately tried his cellphone, but there was no signal at this depth. There was a land line on the desk and O'Toole—confused and angry, but now compliant—shoved it towards him. Arbuckle had the station put out an all-points bulletin.

"He's possibly driving a dark blue Dodge Shadow. The plate has 'CSV' in it," I said quickly to Arbuckle, who added this information to the bulletin.

When he hung up, he said, "O'Toole, get us out of here. Now!"

As O'Toole got on the phone to Elevator Emergency Services, Arbuckle looked at me with disconcerting intensity and pulled me aside. "You always seem to know more than you've let on. If you want to save your friend, you have to tell me absolutely everything!"

"I'm just putting it all together now," I said. "Believe me, I'm not holding back."

"You're not holding back but suddenly you know what he drives. Give me a break!"

"Look, I now realize that this guard is actually the same guy who was tailing me last Thursday. I didn't recognize him when we arrived here because the day he followed me he was wearing sunglasses and a leather jacket. He's also the same one who was driving the car the night McBride was roughed up, the night his cellphone was taken. McBride was on an assignation that night to meet up with an anonymous caller—whom we think was Aziz—to obtain some information on the murder that I referred to earlier. That meeting was hijacked—probably by this guy and the other one we sent to the hospital tonight. I'm convinced they're both working for someone else, and I believe I've got evidence pointing to who that is, but I'm not prepared to talk about that here." I glanced meaningfully towards O'Toole, who was still on the phone with his back to us. I was reluctant to discuss our suspicions of Carl Spiegle in front of O'Toole.

"Anyway," I concluded, "the important thing is I was right about Sophie, wasn't I? She was here. We are on the trail."

"But still one step behind. Don't you realize that if you'd let me in on your suspicions about the guard we might have found her before he pulled her out of that office?"

"You're right," I said. "I wish I'd recognized him earlier. He got away with sending us a kilometre down the tunnel so he could get her out of here. Thank god McBride left the group and came back here in time to see them escaping. With any luck, he's on to him now."

"Let's hope we're not too late—and that the boot came off a girl who was still alive and kicking."

O'Toole hung up the phone, having finally gotten the code. He went over to the controls, punched some keys and, to our great relief, the lift began to descend. We all got on the elevator—O'Toole, Arbuckle and the duty sergeant who had accompanied him, Speed and his wrangler, Molly and me. We ascended in dead silence.

There was a car waiting for Arbuckle and a van for Speed, the wrangler and the sergeant. I got into the car with Arbuckle, who was already on the phone to the station.

"Anything?" he asked. I looked at him as he nodded. "So our boy's coming 'round, is he? Good, I'm on my way to the hospital."

"I'll drop you off," he said to me as he snapped his cellphone shut.

"No you won't. I'm coming too. You're stuck with me."

Chapter Sixteen

WHEN MCBRIDE GOT TO THE TOP OF THE LADDER he was sorely winded from the rapid climb in the severe cold. Fortunately he'd had gloves, or it would have been an impossible feat.

He quickly got his bearings and realized he would have to take a different exit out of the site than Sophie and the security guard would, because the elevator platform was on the other side of the huge dig. Near him, a wide-gated entrance for trucks was barricaded with chains and a "Keep Out" sign. He had no problem scurrying under the metal gate. Finding himself just at the bottom of Cornwallis Street, he moved up the hill to the corner of Barrington and tried to assess the situation.

He had a good overview but there wasn't a soul anywhere. Just then, cross corner from where he stood, a car squealed onto Lower Water Street. It was a dark sedan, but it was not quite light enough to see anything more. The curious thing was that the car turned the wrong way on the one-way access road, convincing McBride that it must be the guard and Sophie. They were headed south into the city and apparently in a hurry.

Standing at Cornwallis and Barrington, McBride spotted a lone vehicle coming towards him. It was a Casino taxi heading south. He hailed the cab, jogged across Barrington and jumped in.

"Quiet morning," the driver said.

"Stay left," McBride ordered. "Go Hollis. And fast."

"Whatever you say, buddy. Where you off to in such a hurry?"

"I'm looking for someone in a car. We might be too late to spot them."

"Fellow steal your girl?"

"You must be psychic."

They were coming to the stoplight on Hollis at Duke. Ahead of them were very few vehicles, but the lone car that had turned right a couple of blocks ahead could be the one. In the increasing dawn light McBride could see that it was a familiar dark blue Dodge.

"I'm an idiot!" he blurted out as it struck him hard who the night guard really was.

"Got it bad, eh buddy."

"Just turn right at Prince."

The driver moved into the right lane and turned. McBride caught sight of the car. It was still climbing—going all the way up to Citadel Hill. It turned left at Brunswick.

Luck was with them and they just made the light at the top of Prince in time to see the Dodge taking the right turning lane onto Sackville.

"Take Sackville," McBride said.

The Dodge was stopped at a red light at South Park. As the light changed it took a left, heading along the Public Gardens towards Spring Garden Road.

"Left at—"

"I'm on him," the driver said.

They stayed behind the Dodge all the way down South Park, and followed when it took a right. McBride stopped the taxi when they reached the Robie Street intersection, paid the driver, then stood looking up the empty street to the house where the car had turned in.

"Well I'll be damned," he said aloud.

I wasn't eager to stare into Scarface's piggy eyes again, but more than anything I wanted him to spew out information about where Sophie might have been taken. On the drive to the hospital I filled

Arbuckle in on the evidence that implicated Carl Spiegle in the death of Peter King. I explained how there were direct references to him in the material that Aziz had gathered at King's office—all of which was in a file that Sophie had received from Aziz and which, I admitted, I now possessed; how McBride would be seeking a permit to exhume Peter's body to establish poisoning; and how I had a pretty good theory on the substance that was used. What we needed was proof that these two, Scarface and Matrix-man, were Spiegle's boys. And we needed real motive—proof that King's unrelenting interference with Spiegle's money-grabbing schemes had led to murder.

I knew I owed these details to Arbuckle now. I was serious and succinct, and he listened carefully. Everything that had happened during the last day—starting with the cellphone landing in my hall, the ransacking of Sophie's apartment, her disappearance, the violent attack on Aziz, the attack on me, and the startling occurrences at the sewage treatment site—all corroborated what I was saying. I respected him for not admonishing me any further about withholding facts or holding me responsible for Sophie's involvement. He could see I was already wracked with guilt and apprehension.

When we arrived at the hospital, we left Molly in Arbuckle's car and went directly to Outpatients to see if Harvie was still waiting for someone to look at him. He was nowhere in sight and I hoped he'd been attended to and was home in bed. We went up to the fifth floor where they were treating Scarface.

We stepped off the elevator and turned the corner, looking for B14. There, sitting on a bench outside Scarface's room, his right cheek bandaged, was Harvie. My heart gave a funny little leap when I saw him and I smiled. He stood as we appeared.

"Good, oh good," he said. "I was pretty certain you would show up here eventually. Is everything okay? What happened at the site?"

"Oh my god, Harvie, too much has happened." I spoke quietly.

"And we still don't have Sophie. She was there, but the site's security guard turned out to be Scarface's partner in crime, and he managed to get her out before we realized who he was. McBride's on the trail, I hope."

"How are you, Greenblatt?" Arbuckle was undoubtedly experiencing his own pangs of self-reproach about Scarface getting back into my house in the midst of the grand search his team conducted in my backyard, while he himself was sitting in my kitchen drinking tea.

"I'm good," Harvie replied, patting him on the back, "oh yeah, no worries—just fine. They stitched me up pronto. Okay, so now what's happening?"

"I'm going in to see if we can get some information from buddy-boy here," Arbuckle said, and with that he opened the door and entered the room. There was a constable in the room who rose when Arbuckle entered.

"Let's go in," I said to Harvie.

"How are you doing?" he asked.

"Your friend Arbuckle's a good guy, Harvie, and we're getting closer to solving the case, but I'm frantic about Sophie and Aziz. I'm very relieved that you're okay, though. As you said earlier, too many people are getting hurt."

"Keep the faith," he said, and pushed open the door for me.

Scarface was propped up, a bandage on his head, looking like a circus-mirror image of McBride the day Sophie and I had visited him in the hospital. He was staring straight ahead, mute. It seemed Arbuckle hadn't gotten anywhere. He gestured for me to go ahead and say something.

I looked at him and rallied my nerve. "So the tables have turned. You thought you had me, and you thought you had your hands on the information, but life is full of surprises."

"Shut up," he shot back.

"Charming as always," I said.

Arbuckle picked up the interview. "You can talk after all. Well, we have another surprise for you. We know that your partner was holding Sophie in the treatment plant site. Were you in on that part of the scheme?"

He stared out.

"I hope not for your sake," Arbuckle continued, "because now that the girl's dead and your buddy's on the run, things are going to get very serious for you."

He twitched. "She's not dead."

"I'm afraid she is. Your buddy got carried away, just as you did with the boy in the railway cut. How many murders will you be taking the rap for, while your partner skips town?"

"She's not dead. He was taking her to the house for a meeting. That was the deal."

"What house?" I interjected.

"If she was really dead, why would you care what house?" he shot back.

"And what deal? Who are you protecting?" Arbuckle asked.

"I want a lawyer. Now get out."

"Well, get one today because we'll be back."

Harvie, Arbuckle and I exited the hospital room.

"What house?" I repeated.

"I'll drive you home," Arbuckle said. "There's a possibility he's referring to your house, since that's where he went to find the file. They may have originally intended to drop Sophie there after scaring you into giving up the goods."

"Well, even if that was the plan, Matrix-man just saw me with you at the plant. He would never take Sophie there now."

"I'm going to take you to your house anyway, check it out."

Arbuckle waited inside the front door while Harvie and I took a quick look around. Molly seemed unperturbed. Nothing was out of place and there was no one there. Arbuckle left us and went to the police station to see if anything had come in from the APB.

Harvie went into the kitchen to make us a breakfast of coffee and fried eggs while I trudged upstairs to take a shower. In my room remained the chaos from when Scarface crashed to the floor a few hours earlier. He had knocked over the bedside table on the way down and the lamp was lying on its side. I stood the table up and replaced the lamp. In the closet, the boards were undisturbed and I neatly rearranged my shoes and boots. Pulling off my T-shirt, I walked over to the desk and saw my message light flashing. McBride?

"Hi Roz. It's Daniel King. I'm just calling to tell you that I'm back home in Ontario and have been proceeding with the work on my father's estate. I thought you'd like to know that my mother's been in touch. She should be flying into Halifax this weekend because she needs to sign some papers at the bank to complete the transfer of my father's funds. I know you wanted her permission to exhume his body and I thought you might get it if you talk to her in person. I hope you're making progress. Please let me know. Bye for now. Oh, I forgot to say, she'll be staying at the house..."

I stood under the hot water for almost a full minute before it hit me. I turned off the tap and jumped out, barely drying off as I scrambled into my clothes. "Harvie!" I yelled down the stairs.

"Breakfast is ready, Roz," he called back.

"No, I've got it. I've figured out where they are. We need to call Arbuckle. See if you can get him on the phone for me."

Chapter Seventeen

McBride was on his belly in the snow, camouflaged by evergreen shrubbery that was planted up against the back of the King residence. He was moving slowly towards a basement window, where he could see a glow through the frosty glass. He thought he could hear voices but the sound was indistinct. He needed to get inside. And it would seem that his best bet would be to enter through the basement somehow. A second window farther along at ground level showed no light, so was likely in a different section of the basement. The danger now was being seen from the kitchen window. If someone stood at the window and looked down, McBride would be visible.

He continued to wiggle along the wall of the house, partially hidden by the emerald cedars and juniper shrubs until he was in front of the second basement window. On close examination, it was well sealed and he wasn't convinced he'd fit through, even if he could get it open. He let his face drop onto the cold ground and sighed.

He was startled by the extremely clear and present sound of a woman's voice. Quickly, he looked around but could see no one. He shifted onto his back and looked up. He was staring at the underside of a small balcony that extended off the second floor, probably from the main bedroom. A hand holding a cigarette extended over the balcony rail. He pushed himself tighter against the wall.

"No, I will not speak with her. How dare you even suggest it. I can't believe he brought her here, to this house! He's a cretin—not a brain in his head. And why did he kidnap her in the first place?"

"I said calm down." It was a man's voice. McBride could detect a slight German accent.

"I asked you why he took her in the first place!"

"She was the recipient of some information that could be dangerous if it fell into the wrong hands. I sent him out to retrieve it and things got complicated. He couldn't get it from her."

"Well, what are we supposed to do with her now? Beat her up? Kill her? Is that your brilliant plan?"

"Look, she has no idea where she is. We've blindfolded her. He'll remove her to another location. But we want you to try to speak to her first. As soon as she tells us where the file is, we'll get her out of here."

"I don't understand any of this. You've turned my house into some kind of gang headquarters. I told you in Europe: It's all over. You have to accept that."

The cigarette dropped down from the balcony, landing a few inches from McBride's nose. He heard a door slam.

McBride continued to wriggle his way around the base of the house, moving through the shrubs. He got to the southwest corner and turned. There were no windows on this side until about halfway along, but as there were also no shrubs, the neighbours would have a good view of him if they were to look.

"This is foolish," McBride said aloud, got to his feet and brushed himself off. He moved towards the front corner of the house, having made a decision. There was an arched rose arbour that jutted out from the front corner of the house. He started to walk through it, but just then, the front door swung open. McBride tucked himself back into the webbing of the arbour, which was still thickly tangled with thorny canes, withered leaves and dead roses. The woman appeared with a suitcase and a smaller vanity case. She was wearing a fur coat. She put her luggage down on the brick steps, took her cigarettes out of her purse and lit one as a man appeared behind her.

"Greta, please."

"No, I'm not staying here. I won't be part of this. I'm going to a hotel today. I'm signing the probate papers at the bank tomorrow, and then I'm leaving. And by the time I leave, this house will be on the market, so you'd be wise to get your little band of thugs out of here, Carl."

Bingo! thought McBride. Carl and Greta.

A taxi pulled up in front of the house. Greta dropped her cigarette and stepped on it as Carl picked up her suitcases.

"No. Don't. I'm fine. I don't need any more help from you." She took the bags from him.

"You can't just walk away, Greta, you know that. You've tried it before."

But she did walk away. Down the front walk to the door of the cab. The driver opened the trunk of the taxi, got out briskly and came around to get her bags. She got into the back of the cab and pulled her fur coat close around her. The driver closed her door. She never once looked at the house. The car pulled away from the curb and drove towards Robie Street, where it turned left.

Carl stood on the front steps watching the cab vanish. Behind him appeared Matrix-man.

"Come downstairs. I think she's finally ready to talk." Carl turned and quickly followed. The front door closed.

When McBride had first stood up and moved towards the corner of the house, he had intended simply to go to the front door, ring the bell, and take his chances on what would happen, but now he decided to see if Spiegle had been distracted enough to leave the front door unlocked.

He tried the knob and the door yielded. He stood on the threshold and listened. It was silent. He pushed it farther open, entered the house, closed the door quietly and stepped lightly through the front vestibule into the main hallway. There should be stairs leading down to the basement, either off this hall or off the kitchen, he thought. There were stairs going up to the second level just to his left—sometimes the basement stairs were located directly underneath. There was a door there and he opened it, but it was a large storage closet set in under the stairs. Directly corner-wise to the closet was another door set into the east wall. It opened onto a small water closet, just toilet and vanity. No stairs going down.

He decided to inspect the kitchen. He moved cautiously into the yellow, slate-floored room and went towards the three steps that led down to the side door. He was right, there were steps continuing on down from the entranceway. But as he began to descend, he heard voices from the basement level getting close. He moved back up to the kitchen. Now he could hear them moving up the stairs. He quickly retreated into the main hallway and let himself into the storage closet under the stairs. The hinges squeaked a little as he pulled the door towards him. He left it slightly ajar. He could hear the sound of scraping chairs as the two men pushed Sophie down into a place at the kitchen table.

"Okay, I'll talk, but I want food first. I'm starving." The sound of her voice unsettled McBride.

"There was some leftover Chinese takeout from last night. It must be in the fridge." The voice was Carl's.

"That's fine," Sophie said. "Just rice would be fine. Heat it up in the microwave if there is one."

"Do it," Carl ordered, apparently of Matrix-man.

There was the sound of the fridge opening, a cupboard door, dishes being moved, and then the microwave beeping and turning on.

"And I need some tea," Sophie said. "Then I'll tell you what you want to know."

"Put on the kettle." Carl again. McBride could hear the water running into the kettle then cupboard doors slamming as they looked for tea.

"I don't see no tea." This was Matrix-man. McBride recognized his voice.

"*Any* tea." Sophie corrected him. "It's probably on the kitchen counter in a canister or something. If you untie me and take off this blindfold, I'll find it and make it myself."

"Don't be stupid," Carl said. "We're not going to untie you and we're not going to take off your blindfold. You'll have to put up with these discomforts until you lead us to the file. Then we'll take you home."

"First I want the rice and I want tea. Now, please…Did you find the tea?"

"For Christ's sake, find her some tea!" The kettle began to whistle at the same moment the timer on the microwave started beeping to signal that the rice was hot.

McBride took advantage of the racket in the kitchen to push the closet door open a little wider so he could hear them more clearly.

There was the sound of the plate being set on the table.

"Oh god," Sophie said, "it smells good."

"It's just rice."

"Will you untie my hands so I can eat. I'm not going anywhere."

"We can untie one hand. We'll keep your other hand tied to the chair."

"But first—please—I'm desperate to use the bathroom."

There was a silence while Carl considered what to do.

"Alright," he said, annoyed. "Take her. There's a toilet just off the front hall by the stairs. I'll go down to the bar in the basement and see if there's any tea there."

Matrix-man roughly hauled Sophie to her feet. Her hands were still tied behind her. He began pushing her towards the kitchen door that led into the hall.

McBride could hear the sound of a cellphone ringing and Carl's voice as he answered growing fainter as he disappeared down the basement stairs.

"Are you planning to untie my hands? I really don't think I can manage in the bathroom otherwise."

"Look, you want to go the bathroom, right?"

"That's right."

"So I'm taking you to the bathroom. So shut up."

McBride realized that Matrix-man had no idea where the bathroom actually was, so he was quickly tucking himself in behind the coats when the closet door opened wide. He stopped breathing.

"Nope. Closet." He returned the door to its almost closed position. "Okay...what's this? Jackpot! Toilet."

He had opened the powder room door, which was just around the corner from the closet. McBride could see Matrix-man's back through the narrow opening of the closet door as he faced into the bathroom. He was so close McBride could have reached his hand out through the closet door and touched him.

"Listen up princess," Matrix-man said to Sophie, "I'm going to untie your hands, see. And then I'm going to move you backwards to the toilet. Don't even think about removing the blindfold or you'll get a nice little reminder to be good like I had to give you last night." He turned Sophie around and untied her hands.

McBride could see part of Sophie's back. Then, Matrix-man turned her so she was facing him again. Her eyes were covered by a tightly wrapped black strip and her left cheek was badly bruised.

"Okay, now back up...Stop. Okay, now the toilet's just behind your legs. Can you feel it?"

"Yes."

"Yes, thank you!"

"Yes, thank you."

"Good girl. Nice and polite. No more smart mouth."

Matrix-man stepped back to the bathroom doorway and then

leaned on the frame so he could ogle Sophie while she peed.

"Oh, thank god," Sophie said in relief as she sat down on the toilet. "Eighteen hours is a long time to hold it."

"I kind of have to go myself," Matrix-man said. "Maybe you could help me out—you know—take my dick out for me."

"Really?"

"Yeah, baby."

"I doubt if I'd be able to find it."

"That was a pretty good punchline, Sophie." McBride's voice came from the closet. Matrix-man spun round like lightning, only to be met hard in the face by McBride's fist. He dropped to the floor. "And so was that," McBride added.

Sophie reached up and wrenched her blindfold off. She stood up from the toilet gaping at him in astonishment.

"Quick. He's out cold. Let's get him into the closet." McBride hauled him towards the back of the closet by the shoulders and Sophie jumped into action and pushed his legs in. "Grab a coat, Sophie. We're getting out of here."

She quickly pulled what must have been Greta's camel hair off a hanger and put it on. She was already wearing a pair of Greta's slippers, since she had arrived at the house with only one boot. McBride forced the closet door closed against Matrix-man's feet and turned the skeleton key in the lock. He stepped hastily into the bathroom and dropped the key into the tank of the toilet.

"Let's go," he said.

They crossed the hall to the front door and just as McBride opened it, a voice stopped them from the kitchen doorway.

"Not so fast." It was Spiegle—with a revolver.

"If you were smart, Spiegle, you'd let us go," McBride said. "You're only going to get yourself into a lot more trouble now."

"I'll be the judge of that," Spiegle responded.

"No, I'll be the judge of that. Now drop it." It was Arbuckle.

He had entered the house via the side door and was now standing in the middle of the kitchen with his gun trained on Spiegle. Flanking him were two sergeants. Spiegle glanced at them over his shoulder, but shifted his eyes back towards McBride and Sophie and raised his gun.

Chapter Eighteen

When I'd had my realization in the shower about the location of "the house," Harvie had contacted Arbuckle for me; he joined us as we devoured some breakfast. We quickly discussed the layout of the King residence. I was able to recall the side entrance I had used during my coffee meeting with Daniel. It seemed to me to be the entrance that offered the most options and the best protection. Arbuckle then made what I thought was the unusual and elegant decision to approach the scene not with blaring sirens and bullhorns, but in absolute silence, so the thugs wouldn't panic and possibly kill Sophie. In the interest of silence, I also decided to leave Molly home, under the watchful eye of the cat, knowing that if she got within scent or sight of McBride, she'd want to let everyone in town know about it.

Arbuckle swung the plan quickly into motion and within half an hour, Harvie and I found ourselves sitting in Old Solid a couple of doors down from the King house. We had just observed Arbuckle and two hand-picked sergeants enter the building by the side door, and we were anxiously waiting to see if they would find Sophie.

"What's going to happen?" I said to Harvie.

"You know what Hamlet says to Horatio, Roz, '*If it be now, tis not to come, if it be not to come, it will be now, if it be not now, yet it will come.*'"

"*The readiness is all,*" I said, finishing the line with him. "I'm just going to creep up to the house and see if I can find out what's going on."

"Best to wait," he cautioned. "The police just went in a couple of minutes ago."

He was right. We sat in silence for a few seconds, then the front door of the house opened slightly. I caught a glimpse of McBride, but then he stopped and turned back, leaving the door slightly ajar.

"That was McBride!" I said. "Did you see that? I can't stand it. I'm going to try and get close to the front door." I got out of the car and started sprinting towards the house.

Harvie was suddenly at my side. "Not without me."

We went quickly and carefully and got to the front steps without incident. I crawled up close to the door and leaned in towards the opening to listen. Harvie crouched close to me.

Then I heard McBride say, "You heard the man, Spiegle. Don't do anything foolish. Drop it now for your own good."

Clearly they were in the midst of some kind of standoff. Harvie and I looked at one another.

Suddenly a hand was gripping the slightly opened door, the fingers on the outside. It was Sophie's hand. Through the narrow opening I could see the long camel coat she was wearing—it went almost to the floor. I was trying to figure out how to let her know that I was right there, when all at once she flung the door open and threw herself out onto the steps, landing at my feet. This was followed closely by a loud gunshot, which must have been Spiegle attempting to stop her. Harvie and I quickly grabbed her and hauled her off the steps.

"Oh my god, Roz, what just happened?" she said. "McBride...He didn't shoot McBride did he?"

I looked back through the now wide-open doorway in time to see McBride take a flying tackle, land on Spiegle and pull him to the floor.

"Nope," I said. "He looks healthy to me."

"I shouldn't have moved. I didn't think...I just had to get out of there." She was trembling.

"It's okay Sophie, take it easy. God, you've been through so much. It's okay."

I helped her up and we all peered in through the open door. By this time, Arbuckle and the two sergeants had disarmed Spiegle and hauled him to his feet. They put cuffs on him.

As the three of us stepped into the house, Arbuckle began to read him his rights. "Get him out of here," he said to the officers when he was done. One of the officers immediately put in a call to the police van that was waiting around the corner on Robie.

Arbuckle looked at Spiegle and said, "Better get your lawyer on the phone. You've got a lot of explaining to do."

"What are you charging me with?" Spiegle asked.

"For starters try kidnapping, holding someone against her will, and attempted murder. You're just lucky I didn't shoot you when you discharged that weapon."

As he was being hauled out of the house, Spiegle looked back at McBride with pure venom.

McBride, who'd been leaning on the kitchen door frame getting his breath, looked at me. "That's two," he said as Spiegle disappeared. "Oh gosh, that reminds me, don't go anywhere, Arbuckle."

He walked over and opened the door to the water closet and lifted the lid off the toilet tank. Arbuckle looked bewildered as McBride was poking around in the tank.

"What's up?" I said to Sophie.

"Wait for it," she answered with a mischievous grin.

Finally, McBride pulled out the silver skeleton key, came into the hall and handed it, still dripping, to Arbuckle.

"Whenever you're ready for him, he's right in the closet there. He's having a nap."

"Matrix-man?" I asked.

"That's right."

"Now there's a nasty piece of work," I said.

"That's three," McBride said.

"We'll take care of this. Go home and get some rest," Arbuckle said.

We started out the door and I turned to Arbuckle. "When you were at the station was there any news about Aziz?"

"No change," Arbuckle said. "Still not conscious."

As we walked away from the house, we were silent. It felt good just to breathe and to know that we were all alive and well. The four of us got into Old Solid, and as I put the car in gear, Sophie let out a long audible sigh of relief.

"What time is it anyway?" she asked.

"I'm still on Vancouver time," McBride replied.

"But, do I have rehearsal?"

"Don't worry. I told them we have the flu," I reassured her.

"I'm starving," Sophie said.

As we drove along Robie Street towards the North End, Harvie suggested we all go our separate ways for a little rest and meet up at his place in a couple of hours for a good meal.

"Perfect idea," I said, turning right at the Commons and heading down towards Agricola.

There was a loud noise from the back seat. McBride was snoring.

Chapter Nineteen

LATER THAT AFTERNOON, Sophie and I got back into Old Solid and made our way up to Harvie's house on Black Street. I had brought her back to my place so she could have a shower and a decent nap and not have to face her ransacked apartment on an empty stomach. McBride had declined Harvie's dinner invitation, saying he was going to turn off his phone and sleep until he woke up.

"What a nice place," I said as we climbed the stairs into Harvie's flat. Harvie let the lower apartment and lived on the second floor.

"And—it smells delicious!" Sophie said. "What are you up to out there in that kitchen, Harvie?"

"Sit down and you'll find out," Harvie said, appearing at the top of the stairs in a dark brown "Guinness is good for you" apron and holding a bottle of Pinot grigio in his hand.

We sat down at the round table in his dining room as he opened the wine and poured us each a glass. We held our glasses out in a toast.

"Here's to McBride," Sophie said. "I think he saved my life today. I wish he was here."

We cheered him together and drank. The wine was superb.

"Yeah," I said. "From the moment he appeared out of nowhere last night, just as I was about to unearth the file for Scarface, and then climbing that insane ladder, right through to tackling Carl Spiegle today, he was definitely scoring hero points."

"So you did have the file?" Harvie said, scrutinizing me.

"I did, Harvie. I found it in Sophie's apartment, but I didn't want you to be compromised by knowing I had it."

"I definitely would have told Arbuckle."

"I know." I smiled at him.

"Well, in any case Roz, you were no slouch yourself. You handled a vicious assault. You sussed out where Sophie was being kept, and later you figured out where they took her. Amazing, I think."

"Stop it. I had lots of help," I said, pointing at Harvie.

"To Roz," Sophie said, holding up her glass.

"To all of us," I said in response. We drained our glasses.

"And now for my heroic act," Harvie said, giving us each a refill. "Getting the food to the people." He disappeared into the kitchen.

"What do you mean, climbing that insane ladder?" Sophie asked.

"Well, after you managed that clever manoeuvre of dropping your boot from the lift…"

"Oh yeah, that's when buddy walloped me." She carefully touched the multi-coloured bruise on her cheek. "Ow."

I described how McBride had climbed the sixty-foot ladder because the guard had locked off the elevator, how the tracker dog had led us to the frightening evidence in the security office, and how I then realized just who the guard was.

Harvie reappeared with a platter, then went back into the kitchen, returning immediately with a large china soup terrine.

He had prepared an astonishing Italian meal beginning with *Bruchetta con ruchetta*, or crusty Italian bread with arugula, accompanied by an excellent hearty soup, *Genoise minestrone*. Sophie and I wasted no time filling our bowls. We could feel the soup healing us with every spoonful. The dinner had the feel of a joyous festival.

"You're definitely living in a different economic bracket from me," Sophie teased Harvie as he produced another excellent wine to have with the main course. She was beginning to relax. I couldn't help tearing up when I looked at her.

"I'm sure it's just the guilt, Roz," Sophie said.

"It is the guilt. I can't tell you how stupid I feel for dragging you into this whole thing."

"Are you kidding? You tried hard to stop me from getting involved while McBride was away and you couldn't. I take full responsibility. Look, no guilt, okay?—just throw guilt right out the window and let's dig in to this fantastic main course."

Harvie was setting down a platter loaded with salmon-stuffed pasta triangles in cream sauce.

"This is unbelievable," Sophie said tasting it. "Maybe I did die."

"Well we have the incomparable Giuliano Bugiallis to thank for these recipes. Anyway Roz, I had to do something with that salmon I was about to cook for you when all this started yesterday," he said as we effused over the pasta dish.

"Yesterday?" I said. "Was that just yesterday?"

"It's still the weekend as far as I know. Otherwise, I'm in big trouble, I'd be missing court."

"So Harvie," I said, picking up the cue, "we need to discuss the trial. Don't you think that as the new, hot Crown Prosecutor, you can use this situation to put the spotlight on issues that were extremely important to Peter King?

"First of all, I would have to be assigned to the case by the Chief Crown Attorney. I'll look into that in the morning—let's take one step at a time."

"But you're perfect for this case," I said, pressing further. "I mean, you were once a councillor so you know the ins and outs at the City. You're familiar with the World Trade Organization and the privatization issues around water, right?"

"Right Roz. But given my involvement in the events of the last couple of days, I could potentially be called as a witness—which would mean I couldn't lead the charge. However, I'll certainly try to be an investigating attorney on the case for the present. And what about you? Do you want to be a researcher for us? We could work on it together."

"Are you serious, Harvie? I can't think of anything I'd rather do. This case runs deep for me."

"Let's keep talking," he said.

I smiled. "Excellent."

"And speaking of serious and deep," Harvie said, "I think it's time to bring out the *pièce de résistance*!"

"What! What is it?" Sophie asked.

"Time to unmask the Mascarpone Carnivale...my own invention...a triple cream extravaganza!"

Sophie and I shrieked and banged our feet and clinked our glasses in excitement, which made Harvie laugh.

In the midst of all this, the phone rang and Harvie went out in the hall to answer it as Sophie and I snuck gooey sweet spoonfuls of Mascarpone Carnivale.

Harvie appeared in the doorway saying into the phone, "I can't tell you how pleased we'd be to have you join us for dessert. We'll hold off until you get here. Hey! You two put those spoons down! Yeah that's right—just below Fuller Terrace."

"The man of the hour," Harvie said hanging up.

"Shit, you mean we have to share this?" Sophie said.

"Yeah, let's just eat it all now and give him a dry biscuit when he gets here." Sophie and I dissolved into hysterics.

When McBride arrived he was on his own, explaining that the events of the last couple of days had worn Molly right out.

"And how are you? Did you get some rest?" I asked.

"A little spinny—but getting there. I thought some sugar might help." He was eyeing the dessert.

"And can I pour you a glass?" Harvie asked.

"I'll pass, but a cup of tea would go down easy."

"You bet, anyone else for tea?"

"Yes please—I'll finally get my cup of tea." Sophie looked at McBride.

"That's right—those two weren't very accommodating, were they?" McBride said. "But actually, if Spiegle hadn't gone downstairs to look for tea for you…It's hard to know whether we would have had time to get that nuisance locked into the closet."

"I can't wait to see that creep in court," Sophie said.

"I heard Greta call him a cretin," McBride said.

"That makes sense," I said. "The word has a French-Swiss root."

"Now Roz, how do you know that?"

"I don't know. It must have come up in a play I worked on at some point." I proceeded to ask McBride about witnessing Greta at the house and what had transpired there. I explained that Daniel had left me a message saying his mother would be in town to sign papers at the bank. "He's going to be very upset about his mother's involvement in all this. It certainly sounds as though she's been having some kind of entanglement with Spiegle."

"He's so gross," Sophie shuddered.

"Like a mildewed ear?" I asked.

"That's it exactly," she said.

Harvie brought out the teapot and set it on the sideboard. McBride quickly moved to pour Sophie her tea. He brought it over and set it down on the table in front of her. Putting his hand on her shoulder, he leaned down, looking closely at her bruised face, "How are you doing anyway, Sophie?" he asked. "Are you okay?"

"Oh, you know…a little banged up, that's all. But I'm pretty tough, eh. And I'm safe now—thanks to you." She suddenly pulled him towards her and gave him a great big kiss that was ardently reciprocated.

Harvie, who had been watching this exchange with fascination, cleared his throat. "Well come on you guys. Serve yourselves. That mascarpone's not going to jump onto your plates by itself."

That was all we needed to hear. Ten minutes later we were fighting over the last of it and scraping the bowl out with our fingers.

The phone rang and Harvie answered it in the hall. "Yes they are, they're all here actually. How are you, Donald...No rest for the wicked? Okay. Let me write that down. Got it—yeah good, thanks. Good night."

Harvie reappeared in the dining room doorway and told us that Arbuckle had called to say that Aziz had come out of his coma and was apparently doing remarkably well. Arbuckle passed along the hospital room number since he'd probably be well enough to see visitors. "Oh boy, that's good news, eh?" Harvie said.

"Wow. That's fantastic news." I looked at Sophie, who immediately burst into tears.

"Oh thank heavens," she said. "I was so afraid he was going to die."

Chapter Twenty

As I MADE MY WAY HOME FROM HARVIE'S I wondered where Greta had gone after McBride watched her disappear in a taxi. I was almost numb from the day's roller-coaster ride of fear and exhilaration culminating in the arrest of Carl Spiegle. Harvie's wonderful repast and several glasses of wine had relaxed me to the point of wanting nothing more than to fall over into my bed, but I knew it was best to locate Greta sooner rather than later, so when I got in I called around to the local hotels. When this yielded no information I left a message for Daniel King in Ontario. He returned my call a short time later—but he had no idea where his mother was. He could only inform me she had an appointment to sign papers at the bank the following day. He said he would try to track her down for me.

I told him that a lot had happened and explained that his family residence had briefly become a kind of headquarters for the thugs who had assaulted McBride in the parking lot. I refrained from mentioning Spiegle's name or speculating on Greta's possible involvement with him. Nor did I let on that she had been observed at the house.

"My god. And you saying there are now three people in custody…This is unbelievable! What's the next step?"

"Well, we have several charges against them already, so they'll be detained until the arraignment. The investigation into your father's death has begun in earnest and will now finally include the police, Daniel. And I don't know if you remember an old friend of your father's, Harvie Greenblatt, the lawyer?"

"Yes, I do remember him very well."

"Well, he works for the Crown Prosecutor's Office now and of course he's very interested in helping with the case."

"This is all good news."

"But listen, it's vital that we find your mother, so if you hear from her, please find out where she's staying and what her plans are and let us know immediately."

We said good night and I sat for a moment staring at the telephone. I decided to get ready for bed. I was brushing my teeth when the phone rang.

"Hello."

There was a pause.

"Hello?" I said again.

"This is Greta King." I almost dropped the receiver.

"I'm, uh—we've been looking for you."

"Yes. I just spoke to my son."

"He managed to find you! Where are you staying?"

"I wondered if we could meet?"

"Now?"

"Yes, now."

"Where?"

"Your place? I'd like to have a private meeting. I know it's late, but..."

I didn't hesitate. "Come over then."

I gave her the address and hung up.

I wasn't sure what to do. How dangerous was she? Should I go it alone and speak to her one-on-one? Tell McBride? Or Harvie? I resolved to take the risk. I couldn't stand the thought of lawful espials hiding behind the arras. But I had broken into a sweat.

Deciding to treat her visit as I would any other, I put the kettle on. I was just pouring the water into the teapot when the doorbell rang. I opened the door and the cat rushed in—all fur. Greta was all fur too. Mink.

"Please come in," I said. "Sorry about the door, but I was attacked by someone last night and the police had to break the window."

She didn't bite. "Thank you for meeting with me. I understand you've had a busy day."

And so have you, I thought. "Can I take your coat?"

"No. I'm very cold. I've been walking."

"Let's go into the kitchen. It's warmer. We can have some hot tea."

"I could use something stronger."

"Scotch?"

"Thank you. Neat."

I reached up into the cupboard and pulled down the Johnny Walker Red, which had been up there for eons. There was just a heel left in the bottle. I poured her a substantial shot and set the glass down in front of her. I got myself a cup of tea and sat down.

"So," I said.

"So, you have been looking for me? It's Rosalind, isn't it?"

"Yes, it is. There's now an official investigation into your husband's death and you'll need to make yourself available, so I'm very glad you're here."

"Daniel said he liked you and trusted you."

"I like him too. You must be proud of your son. May I ask, why was it urgent that you see me tonight? Was there something in particular you wanted to tell me?"

"I've been away and I'm anxious to know what's going on. I'd like to hear it from someone who's been on the front line, so to speak."

"Well, for one thing, we're going to exhume your husband's body for an autopsy."

"I see."

"I understand this was something you hadn't wanted at the time of death."

"Well, the Medical Examiner determined that my husband died of natural causes. There was no need. I thought Peter deserved a dignified exit." She picked up her glass and took a drink.

I looked at her. She was keeping everything cool. I hadn't told Daniel that she'd been observed by McBride at the house, so she couldn't know we had seen her there. Maybe she had no intention of telling me anything but had come here to fish for how much we knew, and to find out if we were aware of her involvement with Spiegle.

She looked across the table at me. "Daniel said you told him there were arrests made at our house today. That is shocking news."

"Have you been there since you got back to town?"

"Not yet." An impressive, steady liar.

"Well, there were, in fact, two arrests at your house today."

"Good lord! What happened exactly—do you know?"

"My partner and the police pursued one of the men to your house. The other one was already there. That's where they were arrested."

"And what do you know about these two men? Who are they? What were they doing there?"

The questions were to the point. She wanted to know what we knew.

"I'm not sure yet who they are," I said.

"I'm wondering how these people got into my house in the first place. Was it broken into? At the very least you must have their names."

"I'm sure Detective Arbuckle has all that information by now. I strongly suggest you see him tomorrow; he'll answer your questions. And he'll have questions for you, things that you can shed light on."

The telephone rang. I looked at it.

"Please go ahead," she said. "Where is your washroom?"

"Go out in the hall and then just at the top of the stairs."

I picked up the phone.

"Hello."

"Roz, it's Harvie."

"My god, you're still awake?"

"I'm working. But listen, Daniel King just called me."

"I spoke to him a little while ago and I told him you might be involved with the prosecution. He said he remembered you very well."

"He had questions about the case, wanted to know who we were going after."

"And what did you say?" I was suddenly apprehensive that Harvie had told Daniel about Spiegle and Greta's apparent involvement with him, and that Daniel had passed it on to his mother.

"I told him I was tied up and couldn't answer his questions tonight but would be in touch soon. I wanted to speak with you and McBride before informing him of anything. I mean, he's your client."

"Good thinking, Harvie," I said quietly, "there are things we need to keep to ourselves for the moment. Listen, he did reach Greta and she is actually here right now paying me a visit, so I should go."

"Really? You're not in any difficulty are you? Do you want me to come over?"

"No, she seems harmless."

"Okay, we'll talk tomorrow."

We rang off. I could hear Greta coming down the stairs. I met her in the hall.

"You found it all right?"

"Yes, and thank you for the suggestion about seeing Detective… Arbuckle was it?"

"Yes. It's very important. Your son initiated our investigation, but now it's moving into the hands of the police and the Crown. So I'm sure you can understand that we need you here. Where are you staying in the meantime? Are you at a hotel?"

"I'm alright, thank you. It's very late and I've taken enough of your time. I'll go now."

You came to see me and you haven't gotten a scrap of information, I thought.

"Do you want a cab?"

"No, I'll walk. I can flag one."

"It's a bit dangerous to be walking around here, especially in that coat," I said. "There have been random swarmings and robberies. Please, let me call one. Or I could drive you somewhere. You didn't tell me where you are staying." Never give up, I thought.

"I'll be fine. It was nice to meet you, Rosalind." She opened the door.

I knew I'd kick myself if I let her go without at least finding out how to get hold of her.

"Greta, I know I haven't been very forthcoming. What we know at this point is just the tip of the iceberg, but I can give you some information about what the men were doing at your house and tell you the name of one of them—that is, if you'll tell me how I can reach you."

She paused, then said, "I can give you a cellphone number." She closed the door again.

"That would be excellent. I thought you didn't have one."

"That's how Daniel reached me tonight," she said. "He knew I didn't take it to Europe, but now that I'm back, I'm using it again."

"Would you mind writing the number down for me?" I indicated the notepaper on the hall table.

She wrote it down and handed the piece of notepaper to me.

"Thank you," I said.

"Now it's your turn. Tell me what you know about the men."

"Alright," I said, watching her face. "A woman was abducted from her apartment yesterday morning, treated brutally and eventually taken to your house. The men were interrogating her because they believed she was in possession of some incriminating information that could implicate one of them in your husband's murder."

"What do you mean—what kind of information?" Her demeanour was still cool, but I sensed a little increase in her heart rate.

"Business stuff, I think. Your husband often got in the way of powerful people getting what they wanted. The man who was calling the shots in this abduction incident is the focus of the incriminating information. He was one of the men arrested. His name is Carl Spiegle. Do you know him?"

She didn't flinch. "Where might I have met him?"

I was tempted to say Zurich but I didn't want to put her on the run.

"Through your husband possibly...This man works for the City, as a Planning Supervisor. You never heard Peter mention the name Carl Spiegle?"

I saw a moment of decision cross her face. "I don't know him," she said.

"That's all I can tell you at this point," I said. "We're still working on it. But back to your phone for a moment. You said you didn't take it with you to Europe."

"That's right." There was an edge of impatience to her voice. "What would be the point of dragging it around over there? It wouldn't work."

"Exactly. I get that. So I must have misunderstood you. I was sure you said you hadn't been to your house since you returned to Halifax, but you must have been back there to pick it up."

Caught. I could see it in her eyes.

"I—a friend had it."

"So you're staying with a friend?"

"You've got the number. Call me if you need me."

She was gone.

"Wow," I said aloud as I turned the deadbolt. I took a deep breath. She'd been wearing expensive perfume—Chanel—probably purchased in Paris during her recent assignation with Carl Spiegle. She had really dug herself in. Risky to lie and say she didn't know Spiegle when it would be easy to prove otherwise. McBride said that when she left the house, she had told Spiegle it was over. So why not take the opportunity to help put him behind bars? It didn't make any sense. I was missing a piece of the puzzle.

"Now can I go to bed?" I asked the cat, who had wandered into the hall from the kitchen, licking her chops. I put Greta's glass by the sink, switched off the kitchen light, and turned down the thermostat. "Come on," I said and trudged upstairs with the cat following.

Chapter Twenty-one

Six hours later, I opened my eyes and stared at the ceiling in the dawn light thinking about all the things that were going to be accomplished that day. Harvie was going to speak with the Chief Crown Attorney to find out how much involvement he could have in the investigation. In conjunction with the police he was also going to get the ball rolling on the exhumation of Peter King's body. Arbuckle was going to begin the interviews with Spiegle, zeroing in on the murder of Peter King. The two thugs would each have a string of charges brought against them for their various assaults against Sophie, Aziz, McBride and myself.

McBride would soon be on his way over to my place to review Aziz's file before we took it up to Arbuckle. After our visit to the police station, he and I were going to the hospital to see Aziz. Progress, I thought. At long last.

Fortunately, Sophie and I didn't have rehearsal until the following evening. Monday was almost always the day off—or, as the actors called it, the "dark" day.

And, oh yes…Greta! Her visit of the previous night felt so surreal. What's the best next step, I wondered. I had the feeling that calling her on her cellphone would prove fruitless. We could ambush her at the bank while she was signing papers, but could we force her to talk to the police? McBride would have to figure it out.

I closed my eyes. The cat stretched and stood up. She walked all the way up my body and stood on my chest, looking at my face. I opened my eyes again.

"Okay," I said. She purred in response, sensing that food was in the offing.

McBride and I were sitting in my kitchen over a cup of tea an hour later. I was filling him in on Greta's late-night visit, which he found perplexing.

"What an odd thing for her to do," he said. "It doesn't make sense."

"Well, that Greta's one crazy cat, I think. No offense," I said to the cat. "I had the impression that Daniel had encouraged her to talk to me. She told me she hadn't been to her house since she'd arrived in town, which as you and I know was a lie. She must have come to see me to find out what we know. Anyway she left just as mysteriously as she arrived."

"And what information did she actually get from you?" McBride asked.

I explained the story of our little exchange—her phone number for the information on the abduction and the name of one of the men arrested, Carl Spiegle, whom she denied knowing or ever having met.

"Curiouser and curiouser," McBride said. "Well listen, it's almost nine. Let me get a look at the Aziz file and then we'll take it up to Arbuckle and find out what his plan of attack is with those three."

"Great. I just have to get myself together. Why don't you wash these up and I'll be right back down with it." I smiled and pushed my teacup towards him.

I went up to my room and pulled out a warmer sweater to wear. It was looking a little nasty outside—that lovely rain-snow-ice combo it does so well. I put the sweater on and brushed my hair. Then I went over to the closet and pushed aside the shoes and boots with my foot. I bent down and pulled the old pine floorboard up.

At first I couldn't believe it. Then I reached in and felt around. My heart went into my mouth. "Oh my god," I said aloud.

"McBride—" I called from the top of the stairs.

"What?" I could hear the dishes clinking around.

"We've got trouble." I sat down on the top step.

He walked into the hall with the tea towel in his hand and looked up the stairs at me.

"What do you mean?"

"It's gone. The file's gone."

We just stared at one another. Then he took the stairs two at a time, sprinted past me and into my room. I followed, hoping, as he did, that I'd made a mistake.

"It's definitely not there," he said. "You're sure you didn't move it after they pulled Scarface out of here?"

"No. And I hadn't even gotten to the point of lifting the board when you knocked him down, so of course I just assumed it was still there. When I tidied up the lamp and the table, everything looked just as we'd left it. Sophie came back with me yesterday but other than that, no one's even been here, except…." I trailed off and looked at him.

"Greta." We said it together.

"That's it," he said. "Now her little visit makes sense. Did she come up here?"

I nodded reluctantly. "She went up to use the bathroom when I took a call from Harvie."

"Bingo," he said.

"But how would she know?"

"Scarface must have told Spiegle where he thought it was, and Spiegle must have told her. They've been in touch with each other somehow. Boy, they really don't want that evidence to surface."

"The thing is, Aziz would still have all those original journal entries and probably a copy of the DVD and everything else in the file. The evidence still exists right? And for that matter, when he gets well, he can be brought forward to testify."

"This could be bad for Aziz—"

"You mean, Aziz is now a target," I said.

"No time to waste." He jumped to his feet.

"Your car or mine?"

"Let's take Ruby. Come on Molly!"

At the hospital, we took the elevator to the sixth floor and followed the signs to the ICU, where Aziz had been recovering from his coma.

Even from a distance I knew something was wrong. At the end of the hall we could see a cluster of people around a bed; it looked like a scene straight out of *ER*. We picked up our pace.

"Oh Christ, it is him," McBride said.

Aziz appeared to be in extreme agony. He was clutching at his stomach and retching violently. A young nurse came rushing out of the room and quickly headed down the hall to her left.

"What's happened to him?" I said running along beside her.

"Sorry. No time."

"Look, I'm a criminologist, and he's a victim in a case we're working on."

"We're not sure what's going on. He was doing so well, but now—violent nausea and he may be going into heart failure."

"Arrhythmia?"

"Yes."

She had opened a locked door and was rapidly wheeling out a piece of equipment that I recognized as an electronic defibrillator.

"Did he have any visitors this morning?"

"A woman. Less than an hour ago. She was very nice, said she was his boss, I think." We were moving quickly back towards the room.

"Fur coat?"

"That's right."

"It's poison," I said bluntly.

"What?" The nurse looked straight at me for the first time.

"It could be taxine," I said. "From the yew."

She shook her head and picked up her pace. I pursued her.

"Look I know it sounds crazy, but it's not. It is possible that this woman had access to that substance. In a high concentration it works very fast, is easily absorbed. Was he eating breakfast at the time?"

"Yes he was. Okay, I'll tell the doctor," she said, wheeling the defibrillator into the room. Everyone leaped into action to get the machine ready.

McBride was across the hall on a pay phone to Arbuckle.

"He's on his way," he said, hanging up.

The door opened again and an older man—black, with piercing blue eyes—came out and looked at me.

"You said something about poison?"

"Yes, I did," I said, speaking fast. "Taxine from the yew. Can start with severe stomach pain, nausea, then there's an arrhythmia and the heart fails. No known antidote, except recently some vets swear by heptaminol. It's a chloride of some kind. It's animals who usually get in trouble—eating the yew leaves. Maybe call a vet! Oh, and I've also read about calcium channel blockers being helpful. Pump the stomach to reduce the amount of poison going through the system."

"We've done that."

"That's all I know," I said.

Quite understandably, he was looking at me with a combination of astonishment and suspicion. But he asked no questions, just turned and flew back into the room.

I looked at McBride. "She was here. She must be insane."

I could see the doctor giving specific instructions to several people. Someone immediately got on a telephone. A couple of minutes later, a technician came flying down the hall and entered the room.

Meanwhile, Aziz was still fighting for his life. More jolts from the defibrillator.

Arbuckle hadn't wasted any time. He appeared from around the corner and rushed towards us.

"How is he?"

"He might not make it," I said. "The stuff's deadly."

"What stuff?"

"It looks like taxine, from the yew. The same thing that I think killed Peter King. It sounds like Greta paid Aziz a visit this morning."

"You know, we have all three of those guys locked up and I didn't think we'd need someone here to watch over Aziz. But obviously I was wrong."

"Well, since you're beating yourself up, I have a confession of my own," I said. "Greta paid me a visit last night, and—are you ready?—she managed to steal the evidence file."

"She paid you a visit?" Arbuckle said. "Why didn't you call me?" He was clearly annoyed.

"I thought I could handle it," I said. "I didn't know until this morning that the file was missing."

"Look, the important question is: where is she now?" McBride said.

"The bank?" I offered lamely.

"My guess is the airport," Arbuckle said.

The door opened and the doctor reappeared. "I think he's stabilizing. We gave him an injection of heptaminol. It may have helped." The doctor was breathing hard, as though he'd just run a marathon. He went back in to the room. I looked through the narrow window on the door. Aziz appeared somewhat calmer now, and was breathing more regularly.

"Oh god, we might have gotten here just in time." I was shaking.

Arbuckle was on his phone. I heard him asking someone to check with every airline flying out of Halifax to find out if Greta King was booked on any flight.

"If you have to prioritize, check flights to Montreal, Toronto, New York and London first. Do this immediately and call me back on my cell."

He snapped his cellphone shut and looked at us. "I'm going to the airport now. She might not be there, but if she is, I'm going to head her off at the pass." He spun on his heels and walked away at a clip.

After the doctor confirmed that Aziz was out of the woods we left the hospital. McBride said he'd connect with the bank to find out if Greta had a specific appointment that day.

"What about you, Roz?" he asked as he dropped me off at home.

"I have to get my bearings," I said, getting out of the car. "This morning when I woke up, I knew how everything was going to unfold. Now I know nothing."

Chapter Twenty-two

The morning's events had left me badly out of sorts. I thought I might sit down with my old friend *Hamlet*, get my head back into something familiar. I made a pot of tea, and while I was waiting for it to steep I decided to give Sophie a call to see how she was feeling.

"I just heard from Michael," she said. "We'll be reviewing part one tomorrow—a stumble through."

"Oh that's good to know. I was just thinking I should take a look at it."

"Something's wrong. I can tell from your voice. What is it?"

"Everything," I said. "I feel like such an idiot." I proceeded to tell her about Greta's visit, the theft of the file and what had happened to Aziz.

"Oh my god, the poor kid. Like he needed that. But you think he'll make it?"

"I certainly hope so. The doctor thought he'd passed through the worst."

"And so now what are you doing, Roz?"

"I'm trying to figure out what Greta's up to. Honestly, when I picture her sitting at my table last night in that mink coat, it's like watching a scene out of a forties film noir. Like she was waiting for Humphrey Bogart or Cary Grant to come along and join her for a Scotch."

"Really? I didn't actually get to see her when they had me tied up and blindfolded in the house. But I heard her voice. She certainly had Carl Spiegle on edge. It seemed as though the whole situation was a complete shock to her—but obviously she's involved or she wouldn't have stolen the file, or tried to hurt Aziz. You're right. She does sound like one of those wild noir characters…like Ingrid Bergman in *Notorious*."

"What are you doing today Sophie?" I asked.

"Remember my apartment? I'm putting everything back together. Why…do you want to come over and forget about things and just watch a movie? Because speaking of Hitchcock, I happen to have *Strangers on a Train* sitting right here. We could watch that this afternoon, Roz. Let's have some fun."

"Okay. That actually sounds great. I'll get it together and come over soon." I hung up and went to pour my tea. Well, this will be just what the doctor ordered, I thought to myself. Just go and hang out with Sophie and watch—which one did she say?—*Strangers on a Train*. In the next instant, I was overwhelmed with that shivery sense of being "guided." I looked down and realized I was still pouring—my tea was running all over the counter. Oh my god, I've just figured it out, I think. I know what Greta would do! I mopped up the tea and hurried upstairs to my computer to look up schedules for VIA Rail.

The Halifax–Montreal train left at 12:30, but with a first-class ticket, passengers could board as early as eleven o'clock. It was almost eleven. I had over an hour to check out the train before it even left. I called Sophie and begged off. I thought about inviting her along but decided to learn from my mistakes. I'd gotten her into enough trouble already.

I went into my room and started searching on the top shelf of my closet for the gold plastic bag that contained a curly, red-haired wig I'd once used in a case. I found it and carefully pinned all my dark hair back, shook the wig out and put it on. I looked for my sunglasses with the light rose-coloured glass, the kind you could still see through even if the light was poor. I put them on and looked in the mirror. I found it a satisfactory disguise, and I liked it; it made me look kind of hip. I checked my watch. It was exactly eleven o'clock. I grabbed my leather coat and my car keys and headed downtown to the VIA Rail station.

I parked Old Solid at a two-hour meter on South Street and walked in to the station.

People were starting to congregate—seeing their friends or relatives off, waiting to board. I walked across the open area and stood in line for a ticket.

"When can you board?" I asked the ticket man.

"Not until twelve o'clock," he said.

"But if you have a first-class ticket I thought you could board early?"

"That's right. They let you stay in the lounge and then they take everyone on." He looked at his watch. "They've probably just gone up."

"What's the first stop?"

"Truro."

I paid him for a first-class ticked to Truro.

As I walked away from the booth with my ticket, I realized he hadn't asked for my name or for any ID. Just like the old days. This is perfect for Greta. She wouldn't even need to give her name, although she probably didn't pay cash if she was going all the way to Montreal. I was wondering how she might have paid for her ticket as I made my way to the exit that led out onto the platform.

"Sorry, they're not boarding yet. Take a seat in the waiting area."

"I have a first-class ticket."

"You'll have to wait. They've already gone up."

"Why do I have to wait? The reason I bought first-class is so I could board early!" Redheads are scrappy, I thought.

"Okay, okay, just a minute. Mick!" he called out to a porter. "Take this lady to her car please. First class."

"Come this way, ma'am. Ticket?"

I showed him my ticket.

"This ticket says Truro."

"That's right."

"Okay, but you'll barely be on the train long enough to even get a meal." He looked at me as if I had lost my marbles as he led me to the first-class coach.

We walked along the platform.

"Which are the bedroom cars? I'm thinking of taking the train to Montreal next month and I want to see what they're like."

"These cars that we're passing now are the bedroom cars," he said.

"And are they first class?"

"There are both economy and first class. First class is more private—much nicer, better service."

"Can I see those?"

"Other passengers aren't really supposed to be walking through those cars..."

"Most people probably aren't even on board yet, and I'm travelling first class myself. It would be worth something to me if I could get a look at them—just a quick look."

He gave in. "Sure—just a quick look. Follow me."

Ah, the language of tips.

We boarded the train, turned to our right and went through the heavy door at the end of the car. The bedroom unit doors were all closed to the corridor. He knocked on the first door we came to. There was no answer, so he opened the door and showed me the "bedroom." It was a double, with everything very compact and tidy. No surprises. A high recessed shelf for luggage and a little closet. A private sink and toilet. Wall sconces, a nice reading light and a heavy blind on the window.

"Very nice. I'll definitely book one," I said as we stepped back out into the corridor. I was almost knocked over by the unmistakable, intoxicating scent of Chanel. I looked down towards the other end of the car but there was no one in sight. "And where's the dining car for these passengers?"

"Just the next car up that way," he said. "Or you can have a meal brought to your bedroom."

"Could we see that car too?" I asked, starting to walk towards the far end, hoping my nose would help me pinpoint which bedroom the scent was coming from. My pulse was racing.

"Sure," he said. "Why not."

"You lead," I said, letting him pass me, so I could take my time. "Is there a smoking car?"

"There used to be, but not any more. You have to step off the train at certain designated stations."

The scent was definitely stronger about halfway down the car, but it remained strong as we walked along to the other end. We passed through the doors of the two adjoining cars and entered the dining room. He waited while I looked it over. The tables were set with silver, china and glassware on crisp linen.

"Very nice," I said. "Like something out of another era. Comfortable too." I sat down at one of the tables so that I was looking back towards him. I glanced out through the window.

That's when I saw her. She was standing on the platform with her back to the entrance of the car, smoking a cigarette. I would know that coat anywhere.

"We should probably go. This car isn't really open yet."

"Of course," I said "but this has been great. I think I've got all the information I need."

He opened the door again, and as we moved between the two cars another porter was on his way up the step from the platform, carrying a medium-sized leather suitcase and a matching vanity case.

"Hey, Mick buddy. How ya doin," he said, then turned and went into the bedroom car. We followed. "Here we go—G7," he said.

He opened the compartment with a key and went in with the luggage. I paused and looked in as I was passing. The waft of Chanel came straight out of the room to greet me. This room was bigger than the one I'd been shown, and there was a little armchair by the window.

"Gosh, this one's bigger," I said to Mick.

"Yes, that's called a suite."

"Lovely. I'll have to remember that—G7."

I made note of the car number as we left it.

We continued on, passing through two more cars until we got to the first-class coach. There were still many of the comfortable-looking plush seats available. I looked at my watch. It was 11:30. "I really appreciate your help," I said, handing him a twenty-dollar bill.

"Thanks! Just let me know if you need anything else," he said.

"I will. It's Mick, right? You don't have a cellphone I could use just for a minute, do you? A local call."

"No problem," he said, handing me his phone. "Just dial the number and then push send."

"I'll just step out on the platform."

He opened the door and we stepped down. I looked back along the platform, but Greta was no longer standing outside. I stood apart and dialed McBride.

"It's me."

"Where are you?"

"I'm the redhead with the first-class ticket to Truro."

"What?"

"I'm on the train. The Ocean. It leaves for Montreal at 12:30. Guess who else is on this train? I just saw her on the platform smoking. She's in Suite G7, Car 3204."

"She's on the train? Now how on earth did you figure that out?"

"It was just a hunch…"

"That must be what I pay you the big bucks for."

"That's why I can afford to give very large tips to porters who let me look in cars that are off limits and loan me their phone when I need it," I said rapidly in a half-whisper. "So quick, what should we do?"

"Well, our friend Arbuckle is still at the airport. I spoke to him about ten minutes ago. They discovered that Greta King was booked on a 1:20 flight to New York. So, he's out there with a couple of officers waiting to apprehend her."

"My god, she's so wily. Okay, how about this? Call him back and tell them to drive to the VIA Rail station at Truro. The train must get in there at 1:30 or so. Wait—I'll ask the porter—"

I asked Mick and he told me the train was scheduled to arrive at 1:38.

"Okay, did you hear that? 1:38. The airport is almost halfway to Truro, so they've got plenty of time to get there. In the meantime, how about you make your way down here pronto and join me."

"I was about to suggest that very thing," McBride said.

"You've got about a half an hour to get here. I'll be in car number..." I turned and looked for the number, "3207."

I clicked the phone shut and returned it to the porter.

He must think I'm really weird, I thought, watching him walk away. A woman with a first-class ticket to Truro who gives twenty-dollar tips but doesn't own her own cellphone. I guess they meet all kinds in this job.

I got back on the train and chose a seat. There were plenty. An attendant immediately brought me a *Globe and Mail* and asked if I'd like a beverage or something to eat. I ordered a ginger ale and sat back to wait.

As on many previous occasions, McBride arrived just in the nick of time. The train was huffing and puffing and getting ready to roll out when he finally appeared, entering from the far end of the car.

The car was only half-full of travellers, mostly businessmen busy ordering drinks.

"God, I forgot you were a redhead. I thought I had the wrong car." He dropped into the seat beside me. "It kind of suits you."

"I'm glad you think so. I want to look good for the task ahead, but most importantly, I don't want to show up in Truro with bad hair. So is Arbuckle meeting us there?"

"Yes, though he's feeling a little dubious about your so-called hunch. He left a lieutenant at the airport just in case Greta does show up for that flight to New York."

"I saw her. Unless she has a twin sister with the same coat, she's on this train. But it's wise for him to cover all the bases. Besides, after that magic trick she pulled last night, I'm not convinced she's human. She may very well appear in more than one place at a time."

"I told him that in the several years we'd worked together, you'd had many hunches that were right on the money."

"Wow, you admitted that? Have you been in therapy or something?"

"You know, that wig really affects your personality."

"I know it does. I feel much edgier, feisty in fact. I'm sure it'll wear off. It's just that I'm completely wound up about what's going to happen in an hour. Is there a plan?"

"Of course there's a plan! What do you take me for?"

"There's no plan, is there?"

"No, but we'll figure it out. I know this much—Arbuckle is going to be in contact with the conductor and the engineer and they're going to hold the train until we have her in custody. Presumably it will be up to us to know exactly where she is when we arrive in Truro, so that they can get her off the train without incident. We don't want any frantic, last-minute chase scenes."

"No, we don't. Alright. That sounds good. You gave Arbuckle the car number and the suite number, so they'll be very clear on where to get on the train."

"Yes, Roz."

"You know, she'll likely be stepping off the train for a cigarette, which would be ideal. They can just scoop her right off the platform. On the other hand, what if she's crashed out in her little bed, planning to sleep all the way to Campbellton or Rimouski. I mean, she's been pretty busy. She's probably exhausted."

"Well, then we have the conductor knock on her door, wake her up and ask to see her ticket."

"So when do we start to look for her?"

"We don't want to do anything that would alert her to the fact that she's being watched, so I'd say as late as possible."

"And what about all the people that are planning to get on in Truro? Do they hold them in the station until she's taken off the train?"

He gave me that long-suffering look to let me know I was taxing his patience. "I think we can safely leave that part to Arbuckle. He'll likely work things out with the station master."

"When are you getting your cellphone back? We really should be coordinating this with him."

"Roz. Chill. Read the paper."

"You're right." I tried to relax. I leaned back in my first-class easy chair and closed my eyes. I tried to concentrate on breathing deeply.

The conductor came along and said, "Tickets!" and I jumped.

He looked at my ticket. "Truro. That's the next stop," he said.

"I know." I said. "1:38. Are we going to be on time?"

"Should be pretty close."

The attendant then announced that the first sitting for lunch in the dining room would commence promptly at one o'clock.

I looked at McBride. "That's it," I said. "That's where she'll be. I'd put money on it."

Chapter Twenty-three

McBride and I decided to split up. We waited until 1:05. I entered the dining car first. The front section was quite full and Greta was not at any of the tables. I looked down towards the opposite end of the car and there she was, sitting at a table by herself, facing towards me in the direction in which the train was moving. She didn't even look up from her menu as I walked past her and took a seat at the last table in the car, just behind her, facing her back. My table was smaller and didn't have a window, so I was hoping no one would join me. An animated crowd of women travelling together spilled in, taking the three remaining empty tables in the middle of the dining car. They were a hearty bunch, laughing, eyeing the waiter, and calling to one another between tables. I gathered from their voluble chat they were writers heading off to a retreat at an abbey somewhere in New Brunswick.

When McBride entered next, the dining car was crowded. So far, so good. He appraised the situation and moved towards Greta. She shifted a little in her chair.

"Mind if I join you? The car seems to be full." He could be quite charming, and was managing to appear rugged and sophisticated at the same time. I stared down at my plate so as not to freak him out.

"Of course," she said, and gestured gracefully to the chair opposite her.

Good breeding. There's nothing like it.

"How's the menu?" he asked, flipping his open.

"Standard fare in disguise."

"In disguise?" he repeated. The word had sent my stomach into a spin. But it was just paranoia.

"Oh, all these exotic descriptions," she said. "I find it hard to know what to choose. What will you have?"

"Hmm. I see what you mean. Well, I'm looking for something light."

"Is it too early for a cocktail? Would you like a drink?"

Excellent, I thought. The longer this lunch takes, the better.

"I'm on the wagon, I'm afraid. But I'd be happy to buy you a drink. I'll have a soda or something. What would you like, a white wine?"

"No, I'll have a Scotch."

"Neat," I said to myself.

"Neat," she said.

The waiter came by and McBride said, "We'll be ordering in a moment, but we'd like to start with a cocktail. Scotch neat for the lady and I'll have a sparkling water—whatever you have."

"San Pellegrino, sir. Would you like the bottle?"

"Sure."

The waiter moved on to me, and I pointed to the clam chowder on the menu.

"Cup or bowl?" he asked

I pointed to the word "bowl." I didn't want Greta to hear me speaking in case she recognized my voice, but I needn't have worried. She was now laughing out loud at something McBride said and seemed not the least bit aware of me.

"That comes with a warm bread roll, " the waiter said.

I nodded and smiled, and he left me. He had plenty to keep him busy.

The clutch of writers in the middle of the car had ordered a bottle of wine for each table and were off to a rollicking start to their New Brunswick getaway.

"I hope they're not going all the way to Montreal," Greta said, as their laughter began to increase in volume.

"I heard them mention Moncton," McBride said.

"That's a relief. They'll be gone before dinner. Where do you disembark?"

I closed my eyes. What would he say?

"I'm just going as far as Sackville..."

"That's a pity," Greta said.

My god, I thought. She's flirting with him.

"I have some business at Mount Allison University," McBride added.

"Oh I see—you teach."

"No. I'm a consultant. It's environmental stuff. They have an asbestos problem in one of their buildings."

"Really? How unfortunate." The waiter set the Scotch down and filled McBride's glass from the bottle of San Pellegrino.

"But what about you?" he asked. "Your destination is Montreal?"

"Cheers," she said, holding up her glass.

There she goes—practicing the fine art of avoiding the question, I thought as the waiter set down my chowder. It looked good, but my stomach was in knots.

"Here's to Montreal," McBride said. They drank.

"It is a wonderful city," she said.

"Do you have family there? You seem—well—as though you might not be from here."

"I'm from here, there and everywhere. It's a long story and one I'd rather not discuss." We rumbled rhythmically along and everyone in the car seemed remarkably carefree. Greta sipped her Scotch and made charming comments to McBride. It was a clear day and there was snow on the fields.

"Would you like to order, sir? There is a second sitting at 2:00 and it's almost 1:30."

"Oh, I see," Greta said. "We're being shunted along. Well, I'll have the fettuccine."

"And I'll go for the chicken Caesar," McBride said.

Less than ten minutes to Truro. My nerves.

The train suddenly lurched slightly and we heard the squeal of the brakes and could feel the strain as the engineer tried to bring the train to a rapid halt. I just caught my chowder before it slid onto my lap.

"What on earth?" Greta said holding on to her glass.

The writers were all getting to their feet, carrying their wine glasses with them, and trying to see out the window.

"Something must be up ahead on the track," one of them said. "We don't seem to be anywhere in particular."

"I think there's a road up there," another added, her cheek pressed against the glass.

"Maybe someone was trying to race the train. God, I can't believe my brothers used to do that as teenagers," one of the others said. Every one of the writers suddenly had train stories to tell.

I made eye contact with McBride. What could it be?

"Calm down folks," the waiter said. "They'll be letting us know if there's a problem. In the meantime, we'll carry on as usual. Please enjoy your meals." The literary bunch began returning to their seats.

At that moment the door opened and the conductor entered.

"What's happening?" a man at a front table asked him.

"Just a momentary delay," he said, walking casually through the car, then turning and going back out. Everyone resumed eating.

Not a moment later Arbuckle, accompanied by two men in plain clothes, entered the car and without pausing walked straight down to the table where McBride was sitting with Greta. The conductor came back in and stood by the door. The entire car began to quiet down as one by one people started to zero in on the encounter.

Very quietly, Arbuckle said, "I'm detective Arbuckle with the Halifax police. We'd like you to come with us, ma'am. We have some questions for you." The writers were wide-eyed, all riveted to Arbuckle and Greta.

"What's this all about?" Greta was maintaining her cool.

"I assure you it would be best not to get into the details right here," Arbuckle said.

She looked at McBride intently, reached across and put her hand over his. "My husband and I are on our way to Montreal to see our family. My mother is gravely ill. You must be mistaking me for someone else." McBride was looking at her. He remained still and gave absolutely nothing away.

"I'm sorry to hear that," Arbuckle said. "Nonetheless, it will be in your best interests to co-operate and come with us."

Arbuckle was nothing if not patient.

Greta suddenly tossed back the rest of her Scotch and stood up. The eyes of everyone in the car were on her. She was wearing a close-fitting grey wool dress and I could see she was quaking, but she maintained her dignity and bearing. She picked up her bag from the chair beside her.

"We'll carry that for you," Arbuckle said reaching out. "Let's get your things from your compartment."

She handed him her bag. "I'll just go and sort this out," she said to McBride for the benefit of the watching passengers. McBride nodded. As they moved towards the front of the car, he looked at me and raised his eyebrows. The conductor opened the door for them, and they exited the car. The passengers all began talking at once.

"Amazing," I said over the cacophony of voices. "What now?"

McBride rose, moved to my table and sat down across from me.

"Let's stay out of it," he said. "We've done our bit and Arbuckle clearly has everything under control."

I could feel the relief move through my body. The waiter arrived with McBride's chicken Caesar. "Will you be paying for the lady's drink, sir?" he asked.

"I'd be happy to pay for it. And you can cancel the fettuccine."

The train started to move again. McBride ate his chicken Caesar and I watched him and thought back over the wild events of the day.

After a few minutes, the conductor entered the car and announced the station stop.

"How on earth will we get home from Truro?" I wondered aloud.

"We could…take the bus?"

This suggestion got me giggling. I looked at McBride and said, "Asbestos consultant?" We both cracked up at this, and were still laughing as the train pulled in to Truro.

Chapter Twenty-four

We really did take the bus. It left Truro at 4:00 p.m. McBride and I arrived in Halifax at 5:30, and immediately parted ways. I had gotten a parking ticket—he probably did too. Expensive afternoon.

When I got home, I dialed Harvie's number, but he wasn't in yet. I left him a message and went up to my bedroom, where I hauled off the wig and decided to take a quick shower, to wash the train off me.

I was toweling my hair dry when the phone rang. "Hi Roz. How are you doing? What's happening?"

"Things got a little complicated today, Harvie."

"Yes, I spoke with Arbuckle this morning. He told me about Greta's terrible antics. Did she show up at the airport?"

"What are you doing right now? Do you want to have dinner or something—I'll fill you in," I said.

"That would be great. Come on over."

"Harvie, you don't have to cook. We could go out."

"Are you kidding? I'd much rather be here. Seriously. Come over."

"Okay, I'll be there soon. Did you connect with the Chief Crown Attorney today?"

"I made my pitch. He has to have a meeting with the Director of Public Prosecutions. My situation is quite unique but he feels I can continue to work with the police on the investigation for the time being."

"Fantastic," I said. "Okay—see you soon. I'm hungry!"

Harvie was pounding filets of tender veal when I arrived. Some

Yukon gold potatoes were baking in the oven.

"It's a very simple dish," he said. "I cook the veal in a wild mushroom sauce with a little cognac added to it—very tasty. Wine?" He held up a bottle of red.

"Not just yet—I haven't really eaten today—I ordered clam chowder on the train but I couldn't eat it."

"The train?"

"Yeah. It was just a hunch. I went down and found Greta on the train."

"No! Tell me everything."

I reviewed the day's events, and Harvie was thoroughly absorbed by the story of Greta's capture. "So this whole case just got a lot more complex," I said.

"That's for sure. What was she thinking? Obviously trying to protect Spiegle, but why?"

"God Harvie. I can't even imagine where you'll start with all this."

"Well, I'll sit down with Donald Arbuckle and we'll look at everything and figure out how to proceed."

"Arbuckle was really something on that train today. Quiet authority, no big show, no bluster, nobody got hurt. He just got the job done. He's changed my entire opinion of the police."

"He's a mensch. I've known him for a long time."

"So what do you want me to get started on, research-wise?" I asked.

"Let's not put the cart before the horse. I have to get my own situation sorted out and if you're going to do research for us, I'm going to try to get you a proper contract—so you'll at least be earning a little money."

"That's very thoughtful of you, Harvie."

"Well, now that this case has moved along, Daniel won't be paying you and McBride for anything further, right?"

"That's right. His father's case is finally being brought into the justice system, just as he had hoped, but he's going to be a mess when he finds out what his mother's been up to. Deep down, he knew. We really need to get him out here to see her."

"And he should also be present for the results of the autopsy. Speaking of which, I was able to expedite the paperwork today. If everything goes smoothly we should have the coffin out of the ground by the end of the week."

"You're kidding. That's very impressive!"

"I know." Harvie smiled. "Shall we eat, Roz?"

Before sitting down I went to use the phone first, to find out how Aziz was doing. I called the ICU on the sixth floor and spoke to a nurse. She told me that he was still in recovery from his bout with the poison, still weak and very groggy.

"But is the doctor feeling confident he'll pull through?"

"Unless something unexpected happens. He seems stable."

Next, I dialed Sophie's and left a message to fill her in on his condition.

Then Harvie and I sat down at the round table. He held up the bottle of wine and beamed.

"Now?"

"Absolutely." I held out my glass and he poured some wine for both of us.

"Onward!" I said. "To the trial."

"May it bring justice to the memory of Peter King," he added, and we drank.

"Wow—that's extraordinary!"

"Nothing like a good Spanish Rioja," he said, clearly pleased with my response.

I took my first bite of Harvie's delicious meal. "Okay," I said, "yesterday's dinner wasn't just a fluke. You've obviously got a career as a primo chef if the new gig doesn't work out."

"You know the best thing about cooking good food?"
"Eating it?"
"Eating it *with* someone. Here's to us, Roz."

Chapter Twenty-five

HARVIE WAS RIGHT. The body came out of the ground early Thursday and the process was begun immediately. McBride had gotten in touch with Daniel and broke the news to him about his mother's arrest. He agreed to come in for the autopsy results. He flew in on Friday morning, just as the examination of the body was being completed.

I picked him up at the airport, and we went together to the Office of the Chief Medical Examiner on Spring Garden Road. The samples for toxicology testing had been taken from the corpse on Thursday and couriered to the RCMP Forensic Laboratory. They were prioritized so the results could be made available by noon the next day. McBride met us at the examiner's office; while we waited for the results, we went into the visitors' lounge to discuss developments with Daniel. We explained that the probable charges against Greta were theft and interfering with evidence—both relating to the stolen file—and attempted murder for the poisoning of Aziz, and that she was presently being held in custody until her arraignment.

We told him the police had recovered the evidence file from her luggage, and that the information in the file had allowed the police to move further along with the case against Carl Spiegle. Then we dropped the bomb: If the awaited results showed poisoning, it was very possible that Greta had conspired with Spiegle to kill Peter King.

Daniel was looking very pale and shaken by the news. If he hadn't started the investigation, his mother would still be a free woman.

"I don't know what to do now," he said to us. "I don't know if I can face her."

"Daniel, " I said. "You're here now. You have to remember why you started all this. If your father was murdered, it must be brought into the light. It's looking very much like you were right. You have to be strong enough to face whatever the consequences are—including finding out what your mother's involvement is. As hard as it is, go see her, talk to her. Ask her to tell you the truth."

He put his head down in his hands, clearly distraught. He's still a child, I thought. Well, he'll be a man when this is over—if he makes it through the fire.

The Medical Examiner sent one of her assistants up to let us know that the results were in. As we were going down the stairs, we were joined by Donald Arbuckle, who had also been called. We introduced him to Daniel King and we all went in together.

"Well, you were correct," the examiner said to me. "Peter King's stomach contents reveal traces of highly concentrated taxine. The poison appears to be from the seeds of the arils as opposed to yew foliage. As you suggested, we contacted the lab out in the industrial park and they forwarded us the results from the material you had brought to them. The tests that were done there on the seeds you gathered on the King property have matching characteristics. It's highly probable that the poison in the body is from the same source. At your request, Detective Arbuckle, we also tested the material that was pumped from the stomach of the fellow who was poisoned in the hospital. Again, matching characteristics. He's very lucky to be alive, by the way."

"It was a close call alright," McBride said, looking at me and remembering our frantic morning.

"The death certificate of Peter King will be amended and reissued," she continued. "Myocardial infarction due to taxine poisoning. I'll have it ready for you later today."

"This is not the sweet victory I had imagined," Daniel said, "but I want to thank you both for all your hard work on this case." He shook hands with McBride then with me. Then he offered his hand to Arbuckle. "And you as well, Detective Arbuckle."

"I can take you to visit your mother now, Daniel," Arbuckle said.

He looked over at me for a moment, then said, "Yes, alright. I'll go and see her."

"Are you staying at the house?" I asked.

"I am. I'll be here for the next few days."

"We'll talk again soon," I said.

He and Arbuckle went up the stairs to the main level.

"I'm going to leave a message for Harvie," I said to McBride. "He's in court today, but he'll be anxious for the news."

"Then what?" he said. "Should we have lunch?"

I looked at McBride and realized that for him the case was over. He would probably be called to testify but his investigation was done.

"Alright, let's have lunch. And then let's go visit Aziz in the hospital. He should know about all this too."

At rehearsal we'd been working on large sections of *Hamlet* all week, and that evening we were scheduled to have a complete run-through. Harvie asked if he could join us for the first half, and I had cleared it with the cast. I picked him up at the law courts at 5:30 and we made our way up to the cathedral.

"I got your message," he said. "Thanks for that. It must have been very gratifying to find out you were right about the taxine."

"Let's thank Shakespeare, Harvie. He's the one that pointed me towards the yew. The thing is—I knew I was right when Aziz was poisoned. His symptoms fit everything I'd read. He's doing fine now, thank goodness. McBride and I went to see him today. He's ready to leave the hospital, I think."

"Wonderful! That's wonderful news. He's a fighter."

"Yeah. He's actually talking about making some kind of documentary around the whole experience because he has that interview he did with Peter King that he could weave into it. And then there's the upcoming trial, right? Which could be part of it too."

"He wouldn't be allowed to film in the courtroom, unfortunately."

"No, but he could still interview various people and create a personal record of what's happening. It would be a way for him to turn all this horrendous pain he's been through into something positive. Also a way of showing the world what good work Peter was engaged in. Anyway, it lifted my spirits to see how he's bounced back from those brutal assaults and how he wants to be involved in spite of everything. Human beings are unbelievably resilient, aren't they?"

"And how will he get by?" We had arrived at the cathedral and were walking towards the door that led down to the Crypt. "Does he still have his part-time job with the City?"

"So far. They can hardly fire him for noticing what Spiegle was up to."

"Well, speaking of jobs…I have news for you, Roz."

"You do?"

"As of Monday, you are officially on contract as a researcher for the Crown in the cases against Carl Spiegle and Greta King."

"Seriously? Oh Harvie, I'm thrilled." I spontaneously threw my arms around him. "Thank you for going to bat for me."

Harvie looked very pleased with himself as we entered the Crypt. Several actors had already arrived and were getting themselves into partial costumes for the rehearsal—anything that would affect timing or be part of the action: outer garments, cloaks, swords, belts, hats, boots.

I introduced Harvie to the actors and then to Michael, the stage manager, whom I described as the best stage manager in the world because he seemed so to me—always good-natured, tireless, unbelievably well organized, detail oriented, and with a real love for the actors and the play. We were lucky to have him.

Sophie bounded in. "Oh god, I'm late," she said, meaning she wasn't early, which was her custom. "Harvie. Hi! Good to see you. We'll chat later—I have to get ready."

"Good, good, right. See you later. I'm looking forward to this. I love *Hamlet*."

"So you can just take a seat in any of those audience chairs that are set up. I probably won't sit with you because I'll be taking notes at the production table," I said.

Harvie went over and sat about three rows up on the risers. I took my place beside Michael's chair and opened my script.

"Five minutes to the top," Michael announced for all to hear.

A striking and very skinny blond girl sat down on the other side of me. She looked about twelve.

"Hi. I'm Rosalind—text stuff." I smiled at her.

"Margot," she said, "lighting stuff."

"Is this your first look at it, Margot?" I knew the actors had been having a difficult time finding someone to light the show.

"Yes. Thank goodness there was a run tonight. I'll figure out a lighting plot as soon as the rehearsal ends and start hanging whatever instruments I can scrounge up tomorrow. Preview's next Wednesday right?"

"That's right, there are two previews, then we open next Friday." It was Michael, suddenly appearing beside us. "Places, everyone!" he called out. "Did you guys meet?"

"Just now. I can't wait to see it with lights," I said to her. "But, my god, it's a tall order and there's probably not much available to you in terms of circuits either."

"Well, the good news is it's so intimate in here that one little lamp goes a long way. Basically, looks like I'll be using anything that takes a bulb."

"Roz, the actors want me to keep an eye on the blocking tonight, so would you mind being on book?"

"Not at all." This meant I would be glued to the script and ready to give a prompt if an actor called for a line.

"Okay. Let's get this baby rolling," Michael said to me with a grin, then announced: "Stand by everyone!" He called out, "And we're going to black in three, two, one," as a substitute for the real lighting cues, which wouldn't be there until Margot got her work done. Two actors came out and stood at opposite corners of the square space as he noted the start time in his book.

"And lights up!"

The two actors began, imagining themselves on the dark, windy ramparts of Elsinore, knowing that the ghost of Old Hamlet could rise up before them at any second.

> *Who's there?*
> *Nay, answer me. Stand and unfold yourself.*
> *Long live the king!*
> *Bernardo?*
> *He.*

The opening dialogue was off to a good start, but then almost immediately the actor playing Francisco stumbled and called for a line.

"*For this relief much thanks. Tis bitter cold and I am sick at heart,*" I said clearly, feeding it to him. Not a good sign, but to my surprise they got right back in stride. Over the last few nights the overall pace had improved and the sense of haste and urgency was finding its way into the scenes. The first half of our production galloped by.

We had placed the intermission at the end of Act 3, scene 1. The devastated Ophelia is left on stage as Claudius begins to grasp the real threat that Hamlet represents.

"*Madness in great ones must not unwatched go.*"

"And lights down. End of part one everybody. Good work. Fifteen minutes."

Michael sounded pleased and everyone rushed into the dressing room to prepare for part two.

The first part had taken an hour and twenty-five minutes. The goal was to tighten it up and get it down to an hour fifteen.

Margot was making little drawings and writing notes like a fiend.

"What did you think?" I asked her.

"Awesome," she said, not looking up from her writing. She seemed just a tad overwhelmed. Well, good luck to her, I thought. She has a mountain to climb in the next few days. I stood and stretched my back and walked over to where Harvie was sitting.

"I love it Roz! Everyone is so good. Sophie is heartbreaking."

"Isn't she fabulous?"

"I thoroughly enjoyed it. The text is really clear and well focused. Good for you."

"Thanks Harvie." I smiled, feeling energized by his enthusiasm.

"I'm so sorry I have to miss the second part but I have a meeting set up for 8:30, so I'd better dash."

"That's okay. Hey, they all die at the end, anyway."

"Oh man, I thought it was a comedy. Okay, I'm off." He was putting his coat on.

"Well, I hope you're planning to join us for the opening, so you get to see it with lights, music and full costume—not to mention the party."

"Definitely. I want to be there on opening night."

"Next Friday, one week from now," I said. "I'll book your ticket."

"Can I be your date?"

"We're on."

"In the meantime we've got a lot of work to do," he said running up the little stone stairwell to the door.

"I'm on for that, too," I called after him.

Chapter Twenty-six

MONDAY WAS MY FIRST DAY AS A RESEARCHER at the Crown Prosecutor's Office. Arbuckle had begun to work the previous week on preparing the charges. He was coming in at two o'clock to meet with Harvie, and I asked if I could join them.

When Arbuckle arrived we sat down in a well-appointed meeting room, and an assistant named Melanie brought in coffee and biscuits. This is a far cry from McBride's kitchen, I thought to myself, looking at my reflection in the polished mahogany table.

"I'm assuming they both have lawyers by now," Harvie said to Arbuckle.

"Spiegle's finally hired one. He's maintained his right to counsel so I wasn't able to question him last week."

"Who did he end up with?"

"Ralph McFadden."

"The Pugilist," Harvie said.

"What?"

"Yeah, that's our nickname for him. Well known for delivering the knockout punch too."

"Greta does not have a lawyer," Arbuckle said. "She seems to think she can handle this on her own and she has one strategy: denial with a capital 'D.' She won't even discuss her background, her family history, where she's from, how she met her husband. She's made herself into a fortress of secrets."

"Let's get Daniel in here," Harvie said to me. "We can ask him how their meeting went and suggest that he look after securing counsel for her."

I called the King house and left a message for Daniel, then noticed that I had an Ontario cell number for him. I dialed it and he answered. He was downtown at the bank, still sorting out some details of Peter's estate. I asked him how he was doing and he said he was making progress with the estate, but still feeling stunned by the extent of his mother's apparent involvement. I asked him if he would mind coming in to see us, and he agreed to join us within the hour.

Harvie cut to the chase. "So, what's the best approach, Donald? Do we try them together for the murder?"

"Greta King will be charged separately for her actions against Aziz, and in my opinion, it would be best to try that case later—by then all the groundwork regarding the poison will have been done."

I nodded in agreement.

"With regard to Spiegle," he continued, "I'm having my first interview with him as soon as possible. In the meantime, I've been working on all the evidence we've got in terms of sequence of events and on what I've been able to get out of those two clowns that worked for Spiegle. We also have the background information from Aziz's file."

"That's a good starting point for your research, Roz," Harvie said. "Find out the scope of those overseas projects, what Spiegle had to gain and what he had already lost and was going to lose because of Peter's actions. Spiegle didn't want Aziz's file to come to light and likely that's because it provides motive. All of Peter's files were packed in boxes and are still at his firm. Let's have them picked up and get as much information as we can out of them."

"I'll get them delivered first thing," I said, savouring the feeling of swinging into action as a Crown researcher. "There's also an email Daniel received from Peter the week prior to his death, saying that the situation he was involved in was heating up. I believe Spiegle may have been involved in that deal as well—I'll get a copy of that email."

"As for Greta," Arbuckle continued, "she's still denying even knowing Spiegle for heaven's sake."

"If she didn't know Spiegle, why would she steal the file? Why would she pay that deadly visit to Aziz? We have McBride witnessing them together at the house, which, by the way, I'd prefer we keep to ourselves for the time being. I hope none of us has let her know that she was seen there." Harvie said this looking at us to make it clear. It was interesting to observe him in his professional role. He was methodically getting control of this large, potentially unwieldy case.

"No. I agree that this is a revelation that could be useful later," Arbuckle said.

I jumped in. "And let's not forget the detail that alerted me to their connection in the first place—Daniel's telephone message to me saying that she had gone to Paris and that the contact name was Spiegle."

"Back to the question," Harvie said. "We can't charge them both with Peter's murder unless we can demonstrate there's a conspiracy."

"But if we can gather enough evidence to establish motive on Spiegle's part we can certainly charge him with the murder," Arbuckle said. "There's a record of him being on the premises when the ambulance came for Peter."

"It's the poison that complicates things," I said. "The yew tree that produced the taxine grows on the King property, and we have every reason to believe Greta had it in her possession the morning she visited Aziz."

"If Greta prepared the taxine for the purpose of poisoning her husband, that certainly makes her at the very least an accessory before the fact if not an accomplice to the murder. In fact, if she administered it to her husband, that could make her the murderer and Spiegle the accomplice," Harvie said.

"Or maybe Carl Spiegle really was an innocent bystander," Arbuckle said.

Melanie came into the room to let us know that Daniel had arrived.

"Good, oh good. Okay—show him in," Harvie said. "Why don't you initiate discussion with him, Roz."

Greetings were exchanged all round and Daniel sat down with us.

"Daniel, how have your meetings with your mother been going?" I asked.

"Meet*ing*. I've only seen her the once. She's not forthcoming, if that's what you mean."

"We're concerned that she does not have counsel. She's potentially facing very serious charges and she needs to have a lawyer to advise her and to help her through the process," I said.

"She says she lived with a lawyer for so many years, she knows how they think."

"But she herself is not thinking clearly, so for her to try to provide her own defence…it's ludicrous." Arbuckle stopped there. He didn't want to offend Daniel or come right out and say Greta wasn't in her right mind, but that's what was in the air.

"Is there someone you know that she would trust?" Harvie asked.

"Well, at one time, that would have been you," Daniel said.

"That's right, I crossed the floor. No more defence law for me," Harvie said. "And I was celebrating the fact that I would be in a position to help prosecute your father's perpetrator. But I certainly didn't anticipate that your mother would end up being a suspect. Life is never simple."

"Can you give me an indication of what the charges may be?" Daniel asked.

I looked at Harvie. He nodded. "Well…we now know your father was poisoned, and it's looking very much like your mother may somehow have been a party to it. She may have been an accomplice, so she will need an experienced criminal lawyer."

"An accomplice to this man Carl Spiegle?"

"That's right, Daniel."

Daniel suddenly looked at me and said "Roz…could I speak to you privately?"

"Of course," I said without hesitating. I could feel something troublesome brewing under the surface. I looked at Harvie.

"Go ahead."

"I'll come out with you now. Let's go somewhere."

Daniel and I left the Maritime Centre and walked along Barrington Street in silence. It was chilly, so we turned in at the Mediterraneo diner. There were a number of regulars in for their afternoon coffees, perusing *The Coast* or *The Daily News*. Some were just having breakfast. There were several art college students, including a group energetically discussing their film projects. Compared to the intensity I could feel coming from Daniel, the clientele seemed carefree. We found an out-of-the-way booth and sat down."What's up?" I said, stirring a little milk into my coffee.

"It's—there's a memory that's come back to me. It's the kind of memory that feels like a dream, because I was so young—but it's very clear." He paused.

"Please," I said. "I'd like to hear it."

"I'm seven, maybe. I'm in Zurich with my mother. We're visiting because my grandmother is dying of lung cancer. I'm sitting at my grandmother's antique dressing table—you know, the kind with a large central mirror and two side panels. I have a picture book my mother has given me to look at, Hans Christian Andersen, I think. But when I look up into the mirror, I can see my grandmother in the big bed and my mother beside the bed on a straight back chair.

"I remember my grandmother's breathing being very laboured. This must have been just before she died. Then, as I watch them, she says, 'I know how much you hate coming here.' And my mother says, 'That's not true. Just be quiet and rest.' My grandmother says, 'You hate coming here because you blame yourself. But it was my fault—I never should have let your father move the boy in here to begin with. It was a mistake and I knew it right from the start.' Then my mother says, 'Please don't talk about it.' And my grandmother says, 'It killed him in the end. That's why he killed himself—because of you and Carl.'"

Daniel looked at me. "That's it. I can't remember anything more. But I think it's key to whatever is going on here."

I nodded and silently reviewed what he had just said. He seemed relieved to have told me. He let out a long breath, picked up his coffee for the first time and took a drink.

"When you say it's key, do you mean you think the Carl in the memory is Carl Spiegle?"

"I think that's why the memory's come back to me. Because suddenly there's this person Carl, with whom my mother is apparently involved but whom she's never ever mentioned, as far as I know."

"Well, according to the CV that Harvic saw during his days at City Council, Carl Spiegle is from Zurich."

"There you go, it really could be him."

"And Daniel, is it true that your grandfather killed himself?"

"I knew he had died in the sixties and it was something no one ever talked about. My mother's relationship with her mother was not warm. I think my grandmother was right when she said my mother hated going there—and we only went that time because my grandmother was on her deathbed."

"So that summer years later when you went to take the architecture course…You said you stayed with cousins. Who were they?"

"They were actually second cousins, the family of my grandmother's sister. One of her daughters, who would actually be my mother's cousin, was a childhood pal of my mother, and so she invited me to stay with them."

"When you were there, did your mother's cousin talk about your mother, about growing up?"

"Only to say how much she missed my mother after she left at sixteen. My mother went to study in France then had gone on to England, where she eventually met my father, and they pretty much lost contact after that. But now that you ask, I do recall her saying that my mother's departure had been unexpected, that she left abruptly when her father died, so his death must have been what triggered it."

"And if it was suicide, and if your mother did blame herself, that would be a lot for her to handle."

"Yes."

"And your mother's cousin—what's her name?"

"Helga."

"You don't recall Helga ever referring to someone in your mother's household named Carl?"

"No, I don't. But when I was there, I was always busy at class or doing the assignments. And I knew that my mother's relationship with her own family had been rancorous. It just wasn't something we naturally spoke about."

"Is Helga still there? Is she alive and well?"

"I can try to find out. I must still have the telephone number for them."

"Daniel, if you could call and ask her if she recalls anything about this boy your grandmother referred to, that would be helpful to us. I realize it may be a bit awkward."

"I can figure out a way to ask her," he said, "and keep the explanations minimal for the time being." We got the bill; Daniel picked it up off the table and walked over to the cash. The art college students, both boys and girls, were checking him out with interest. He's definitely got the good looks going for him, I thought as I watched him. How would he manage over the next while, I wondered. I stood and put my coat on.

"I appreciate your telling me about this. It's extremely helpful." I wanted to encourage him.

"Thanks for listening," he said.

We walked out the door and onto Barrington Street.

"So you'll let me know if you find out anything more from your mother's cousin? And also you'll work on engaging a lawyer for your mother. Would anyone in your father's firm be able to send you in the right direction?"

"That's a good idea, Roz—I'll start there. I know my father would want her to have the best possible defence."

We parted ways and I walked back to the office. His story had been so vivid—I couldn't help picturing the two women in the mirror through the eyes of the seven-year-old boy.

When I got back, Melanie informed me that Arbuckle had gone and that Harvie had to attend a meeting out of the office. I called over to Peter's firm and arranged to have the boxes of his files delivered the following morning. I was at a loss. I needed to get perspective on what was happening with the case. I dialed McBride.

"You just caught me," he said. "I'm about to take Molly out onto the Commons for a run."

"Can I join you? I want to ask you about something."

"Do you miss me, Roz?"

"Every minute, McBride. Go on ahead—I'll find you there."

I walked up Spring Garden Road, past the School of Architecture, on past the beautifully dressed windows of Mills Brothers, the oldest family-run department store in Canada, and turned right on to South Park. I walked along beside the Public Gardens, closed for the winter. I looked in through the iron fence. The gardens were still in the midst of restoration from the damage done by the hurricane. I turned up Bell Road towards the open green space of the Commons. I had read that in the early days of Halifax, the Commons had been established so the whole community could pasture their livestock—hence the name. That made me think of Peter King and his philosophical position on water as part of the Commons. He was the heart of this case for me. Who would do his work now that he was gone, I wondered.

I looked across the snow-dusted grounds and my spirits lightened to see Molly bounding after an orange ball that McBride was throwing for her. It wasn't quite four o'clock, but would soon be dark—still heading for the nadir.

Molly ran towards me with an enthusiastic greeting and dropped the ball at my feet. I tossed it into mid-field and watched her race for it. We walked around on the grounds and I caught McBride up on what little was happening so far, and Greta's continuing silence, then told him the story of Daniel's childhood memory.

"So, there's a reason for Greta's behaviour after all. She's not just a run-of-the-mill nutbar. If this relationship goes all the way back to when she was fifteen or sixteen, it might explain why she stole the file and tried to eliminate Aziz. She's torn between protecting Carl and running away from him."

"So what's the next step here do you think? How can we get her to open up and tell us what's going on?"

"Wait and see if Daniel comes up with some information from the cousin. It might shed more light. My instinct would be to somehow provoke a reaction from her. Perhaps tell her that Carl is being charged with Peter's murder, even if they're not ready to really lay the charges. That might crack her open."

"That sounds scary…should we let Daniel be present?"

"I think so. That's why he told you about the memory, Roz. He needs to know what's going on with his mother. He can't be protected from that—and he shouldn't be."

We turned and started walking back towards North Park. Molly trotted along with the ball in her mouth.

"I better get back," I said.

"Punching a clock eh, Roz."

"You're jealous, McBride. You wish you had a job."

He laughed.

"Where are you off to now?" I asked.

"Molly and I are going to take a walk over to Sophie's. She hasn't been able to put her bed back together since they turned her place upside down. I'm going to help her out with that."

"Regular handyman."

"That's me. And then we're going to watch a movie."

"*Strangers on a Train*?"

"That's the one! Keep me posted."

I headed back the way I had come and was standing at the light at South Park and Spring Garden when a woman's voice from behind me said, "Hey, Rosalind. What happened to that lunch we were going to have?"

I turned. It was Eloise Radner from Ecology Counts.

"Hey! How are you? Good to see you."

"Likewise," she said.

"How about right now?" I said on impulse. "Have you got time for a drink?"

"I'd love a drink—it's been one crazy day. Honestly, those Tories are going to put me in the loony bin."

"Let's go in right here, to the pub in the Lord Nelson."

"Perfect," she said. "I can feel a martini coming towards me."

We got comfortable. I ordered a Keith's and Eloise ordered a vodka martini straight up with extra olives. The pub was quite dark with little lamps and cozy booths.

The after-work crowd was starting to fill the place up.

"They're two for one," the waiter said. "Happy Hour."

"Two would definitely be better than one," Eloise said. "So...

what's the news? The last time I saw you, you were getting Peter King's report on the Europa deal."

"That's right. A lot has happened, Eloise, a lot of 'blood under the bridge' as Albee says."

"You've lost me."

"Playwright. *Who's Afraid of Virginia Woolf?* Anyway, some happy developments as well. I'm working as a contract researcher for your old friend Harvie Greenblatt at the Public Prosecution office at the moment. Remember you gave me his card?"

"Good for you, Roz. It's so fantastic that Harvie took that new job. He'll be a welcome asset to the ever-fraught Prosecutor's Office."

"We've become really good friends through this Peter King case. Anyway, as I say, we're working on it and you'll be interested to know there's a murder charge pending."

She had picked up a few peanuts and was about to put them in her mouth, but she stopped short and looked at me, startled.

"Are you serious? Who killed him—his crazy wife?"

"Wow, Eloise. That didn't come out of nowhere. Do you know Greta?"

The waiter set down our drinks. Eloise knocked back a good portion of one martini and dug for an olive.

"Look, Roz, Peter's gone now, and I might as well come clean…I was involved with him for years. He loved his wife very much. He would never have left her, but she was…I don't know…a cold fish. And she was basically miserable most of the time. He and I worked together often and we enjoyed each other. We laughed a lot, you know? So, this one time—Greta was away in Europe and we were working long hours developing some policy initiatives, and the next thing you know, we were sleeping together. The truth is I was crazy about him."

I was kind of in shock. This was an aspect of Peter I hadn't even considered. Could this have played into Greta's actions somehow?

"When are you referring to, that she was in Europe?"

"Oh, seven years ago. Something like that. It was just after Peter had come back from his first trip to Bolivia in '98."

So, I thought, before Spiegle came to Halifax. "What was she doing in Europe, do you know?"

"I had the impression it was a mental health vacation, went to visit friends or something."

"Did she know about you?"

"I always think women know, don't you? But if she did, Peter never mentioned it. I mean, he was clear about things right from the beginning. And I'm a grown-up. I valued his company too much to throw a scene. I knew he'd stay with her if push came to shove."

She drained her first martini. "As I said to you that day you came to the office, I miss him terribly. If someone killed him, I hope they rot in jail for the rest of their lives. Good men like him are too few and far between. You're not actually looking at Greta for it are you?"

"He was poisoned. She's one of a couple of suspects. I would get into details Eloise, but it's early days and anything is possible at this point. I shouldn't be speculating out loud, but I know you'll keep this to yourself."

"My life is one long confidentiality clause. Not to worry. In fact, you're the first person I've ever told about my relationship with Peter, and I don't want that to get around either, so we're even." She held up her glass and we had a silent toast and drank. But she stopped as the glass got to her lips, looked at me and said, "Greta wouldn't have poisoned him because she found out about me, I hope."

"Crime of passion. Stranger things have happened. But I think she would have killed you, not him. Or at least killed you first," I said, teasing her.

"Is she behind bars?"

"For the moment. But she'll probably be out and about on bail soon, so lock your doors."

"That's not funny, Roz."

"But listen," I said, "during those last couple of weeks that Peter was alive, he was working on some international projects. Do you know anything about that? Were there any details about throwing roadblocks in the way of certain corporations or anything?"

"I can remember a couple of things he told me about. One was that he was able to force the same company that was originally contracted here—"

"Europa?" I said.

"That's right. Through some obscure WTO regulation he managed to force them out of this big water privatization scheme in West Africa. They were just one part of a multinational conglomerate, and that was only the beginning for Peter. He was determined to get all those companies out of there. He was working on behalf of a people's united action front. He was actually getting ready to go over there in the next few weeks, and was pulling in major support from water activists around the world."

"Impressive work."

"Oh yeah. And he had also gotten a temporary injunction to stop this German bottled water company from obtaining rights to Canadian bulk water. That was one of Peter's big concerns. He said he felt like the boy with his thumb in the dyke. Once one international corporation gained access to Canadian bulk water, it would change the picture forever. Commodification. It's a very frightening prospect, and Peter was on the front line like a ferocious guard dog."

"Now that he's gone, I guess it's only a matter of time, eh? Bye, bye water."

"There are other wonderful fighters, but he was hard to beat because he was such a brilliant lawyer."

"To Peter," I said, holding up my beer glass.

"And to all those brave people around the world trying to keep water off the market."

We finished our drinks and parted with promises to stay in touch. I watched her walk down South Park towards Morris Street. I remembered she lived on the little tiny street behind Morris that backed onto a large cemetery. She had kept our conversation fairly light, and I knew she was tough, but I had felt the depth of her pain when she spoke about missing Peter. Seven years is a long time to be involved—and to think she never told a soul. So she would have gone through the funeral and the grieving entirely alone. I recalled seeing her name in the guest book. I thought about Peter King in this new light and realized I didn't hold it against him. It kind of humanized him for me.

But the important things I had learned from Eloise were about Peter's recent actions in West Africa and Germany. In both cases, preventing these companies from proceeding would have had a major impact on Carl Spiegle. He would have been set to see big profits from their endeavours, and may have lost initial investment money to boot. I would spend the next morning diving into those files that were being delivered from Peter's office.

Chapter Twenty-seven

When I got home, I started making a little dinner for myself with some of the food I had bought with Harvie. That Saturday morning at the market now seemed like years ago. I had put some lamb chops into the freezer and managed to pull one out to defrost before I left for work that morning.

"What are you going to have?" I asked the cat. "Unfortunately I only thawed one chop."

I picked her up. She wasn't a lap cat by nature, but she must have missed me because she seemed willing to go for a little affectionate scratching and purring this evening. She put her head back and closed her eyes as I rubbed her chin. The phone rang and she leaped to the floor.

"So much for that," I said, going to the phone.

It was Daniel King. I asked how he was.

"I spoke to my mother's cousin Helga this afternoon."

"Fast work, Daniel. How did you approach it?"

"I didn't get into our circumstances here. I just said that I'd been having this memory about my grandmother and that my mother wouldn't talk about it. I asked her if she knew who the boy was, and if it was true about my grandfather."

"And?"

"She seemed hesitant at first, but I coaxed her along. She said she did remember the boy and confirmed that his name was Carl. Apparently, he was German. He'd been orphaned, and my grandfather—Heinrich Brunner—had known about him and wanted to help. He was fourteen or fifteen when he was brought into the house—around the same age as my mother."

"How long was he there? Did she say?"

"She thought it was at least a year, maybe a year and a half, before everything went awry. She said he and my mother became really close—inseparable."

"Did she confirm that your grandfather killed himself?"

"Yes. She said it was horrible for the family and that no one understood it. My mother was very upset and left almost immediately to go to school in France, and Carl left as well. She said my grandmother told him he couldn't stay on. He went to some kind of state boarding school or something. Helga didn't really know what happened to him after that."

"What do you make of it, Daniel?"

"I don't know what to think. I keep going back to the memory, to my grandmother saying that she knew my mother blamed herself. So my mother must have done something that she believed caused my grandfather to kill himself. What could that be? Say it was a pregnancy. It would have been shameful at the time perhaps, but surely it wouldn't have led to suicide. My grandfather had gone through the war; he must have had a thick skin."

"And his suicide would have taken place in the mid sixties?"

"That's right—my mother was born in 1950."

"Thank you for making that call. I need to sleep on all this. Let me know if you have any other thoughts or memories."

Daniel surprised me then by saying he wanted to talk to his mother about the memory and see what she had to say. I was impressed with his desire to get to the bottom of the story, and I thought this might be the beginning of him finding the strength to really face her. I told him I thought that was an excellent idea and that I would pass it on to Arbuckle, and let him know when we could set up the session. We rang off.

I went back to my dinner preparations and realized I didn't quite know what to do with a lamb chop. I called Harvie the chef to get his advice.

"No rehearsal tonight?"

"It's Monday."

"Dark."

"That's right."

"So a lamb chop, eh? Aren't you lucky. They don't need much cooking. You could wrap it up with a lot of garlic and pop it in the oven. Have it with a green salad and mushrooms."

"What are you eating?"

"Leftovers. Why don't you bring your lamb chop over here and have me do a demonstration for you?"

"But aren't you—"

"What?"

"I don't know…sick of me?"

"Oh boy, have you got the wrong end of the stick, Roz. There's nothing I'd rather do. Besides, you have to catch me up on what happened with Daniel, right?"

"Right. See you in a minute." I hung up. Harvie had once again succeeded in making me feel pretty good about myself. I was enjoying his company so much. But now that we were actually working together, I wanted to be careful about getting too close personally. Even though my work with him was likely temporary, I'd always been stringent about drawing the line between work and play. Or maybe I was using that as an excuse not to get intimately involved. I had no idea what I'd actually do if Harvie came on strong. His shyness kind of suited me, and I loved feeling such a warm regard for him.

I looked at the cat. "You can't come with me but it's your lucky night—I'll open a can of your favourite." She went and stood by her dish. She always had her priorities straight.

"Wine?" Harvie asked as I plunked the wrapped lamb chop on his counter.

"Not yet. I've already had a beer today. With Eloise. I bumped into her on the street and we had a drink. She had some very intriguing information about Peter's intervention in a couple of those international water deals that Spiegle was involved with. Apparently, Peter had succeeded in getting an injunction to stop the bottled water company from proceeding."

"Really. That's exactly the kind of information we need."

"I know, it was perfect timing to run into her. She's thrilled about you having this new job, by the way."

"She's a smart cookie, that one."

"She must be—she's the one who gave me your number in the first place."

"Yes, because otherwise you would have starved to death by now," Harvie said, unwrapping the meat I had brought over. "I just happen to have my own chop in the fridge, so we'll each have one. Much more interesting than my original plan."

He had already peeled and sliced several cloves of garlic. He rubbed the chops with oil and laid the garlic on some foil and put the lamb on top of it. Then he sprinkled a little lemon juice over the chops and put more garlic on top. Lastly, he added some ground pepper and a few small sprigs of rosemary, which he cut from a plant on his windowsill. He folded the foil around them and set the package in a dish—ready for the oven. I watched all this with a mixture of joy and fascination. He was doing this for me. Well, for himself too of course, but in my experience, food had never been so much fun.

"Yum," I said.

"Well, those won't take long. Let's have a drink while they're cooking. I've already made the salad. We just have to fry the mushrooms up. Would you like a beer? I've got Stella and Corona."

"Corona with lime would be great," I said.

"Done. Shall we be radical and go sit in the living room?"

Harvie sat in his well-worn leather easy chair and put his feet up, and I curled up on the end of the couch. As we relaxed, I recounted Daniel's story of his early memory and told Harvie about his follow-up call with Helga, his mother's cousin. I also told Harvie that Daniel had suggested to me that he would like to talk to Greta about it. "What do you think?"

"I think it could be productive. Any information is better that what we have now."

Then I caught him up on my conversation with McBride and his idea that telling Greta we were charging Carl with murder might provoke her to speak.

"We could try it. Now, would we do that in the same meeting, I wonder. Let's run this by Arbuckle tomorrow and see what he thinks."

"Great," I said.

"Now we're cooking," Harvie said.

"Cooking with gas," I said as we went back to the kitchen and got on with dinner.

The next day, I tackled the boxes of files that arrived just as I got to work. As Harvie was rushing off to court, he suggested I call Arbuckle and talk to him myself about setting up the interview with Greta. At around 10:30 I took a break from making an inventory of what was in the boxes and gave him a call, filling him in on Daniel's recollection and Helga's affirmation about the boy and the suicide.

"Very intriguing indeed," he said. "A possible connection with Spiegle that goes that far back. If Daniel's willing to try and talk to her about this, I think we should definitely go for it. I'd like to do it soon. How about tomorrow? Say, after lunch, around two o'clock."

"I'll contact Daniel and let him know the time."

"We should meet before the interview," he added.

I called and left a message for Daniel and then went back to work. I stood in the doorway and surveyed the boxes. There were a couple labelled "Bolivia." I opened one of them out of curiosity. Daniel had told me that Bolivia was where Peter's decision to become dedicated to the Water Wars had begun. I pulled out a couple of thick files. A book fell out of one of the folders. Not large—four by six, black with a flexible cover. I opened it and discovered it was a journal containing personal entries, handwritten by Peter.

It appeared to be a record of his trip in 1998, likely the trip that Eloise had referred to, just at the beginning of the Cochabamba conflict. I flipped through quickly, looking for his return to Canada. I saw notes on a flight itinerary, and turned the page. Then:

> Finally home. Lots of legal research to do re this Bolivia situation. Also overwhelmed with other work. Greta not well. Seems to be in emotional turmoil. Not dissimilar to some previous bouts of anxiety. She has asked to go to Europe for a few weeks. I can't object. It may sort her out. Life is about patience.

A couple of pages farther along I found:

> Took Greta to the airport today. She is flying to London and then going on to Germany to see other friends. She seems already less stressed and more affectionate. She let me kiss her goodbye. Perhaps she's right, this is what she needs.

I flipped through the book looking for other personal notes about Greta, or about their marriage, but could find nothing.

I went back to taking inventory from the boxes that contained the most recent files. I found a whole file on Aqua Laben—the

German bottled water corporation—and detailed notes that Peter had compiled to bring about the injunction, along with lists of Canadian federal and provincial officials whom he had notified. There was also a list of the individuals on the Board of Directors of Aqua Laben. My eye was caught by one name that was underlined by hand—the name was H. Brunner. Next to it in handwritten letters were the initials C. S. and beside them an exclamation mark. A little bell was ringing in my head…what was it? How much had Peter figured out? I looked at the array of boxes. I had my work cut out for me. Slowly, I could feel the puzzle pieces coming together, but the whole picture still eluded me.

At noon, Daniel returned my call and confirmed that he would be available to do the interview with his mother at two o'clock the following day. I mentioned that Arbuckle would like to meet with us beforehand.

"I'll be there," he said.

"Oh, and Daniel…Your mother's maiden name, it was Brunner?"

"That's right."

I needed to think. I decided to clear my head and go for a walk. I'll go home and feed the cat, I thought. On my way past Cogswell Street, I decided to run up to the police station and set a time for the next day's advance meeting with Arbuckle. I found him just on his way into an interview with McFadden and Spiegle.

"He's got his lawyer here at last, so I can finally get started," he said.

"Look, I've just been reading Peter's files about some of the deals Spiegle was involved with and I'm trying to unravel it all. Can I observe the interview?"

"Why not?" he replied. "Sergeant, can you show my friend Roz into the observation room?"

The observation room was classic—a long narrow room with a

door at the end, and uninterrupted glass all along one side that allowed for a view of the interview room. The opposite side of the glass had a mirrored surface that prevented those in the interview room from being able to see those who were observing.

There were high stools with backs on them and speakers on either side and above the window. The sergeant showed me how to adjust the volume on the speakers so I could clearly hear what was being said.

I got out my notebook and made myself comfortable on one of the stools while Arbuckle cued up the recorder.

Ralph McFadden, whom Harvie had referred to as "The Pugilist," was a stocky red-headed Celt with close-set blue eyes. He did look as though he would prefer punching people out to talking. Spiegle seemed to have a penchant for surrounding himself with thugs.

"Okay, let's get things cleared up. It's high time you told us exactly what you are charging my client with," McFadden said, as though he had just heard the bell to signal round one. "Otherwise, spring him until you can get your act together."

"Your client's been a busy boy." Arbuckle said, as though to rankle McFadden a little.

"Busy or not— what are the charges? I like to get it straight from the horse's mouth."

"So far, he's charged with accomplice to kidnapping, unlawfully holding a person against their will, refusing to comply with instructions from a police officer—that officer being me, by the way—possession of an unregistered firearm, illegally discharging said firearm, and two counts of attempted murder, the first, against the young woman when the firearm was discharged, and the second, against the student when your client ordered his employee to pursue, abduct, beat up and leave the young man Aziz Mouwad for dead in the railway cut."

McFadden grunted loudly and said, "Most of those charges don't hold water. He didn't do any of those things himself except shoot the gun and he wasn't attempting murder—the gun went off by accident. Was she hit? No, she wasn't."

"He was out of control, McFadden. I was there, I witnessed it myself."

"Okay, so you were there, you witnessed it yourself—so what? You think you can make these charges stick? You're going to be the one with egg all over your face. What else is on your list?"

"Premeditated murder."

"What are you talking about?"

"As if you didn't know. I'm talking about Peter King. That's what all this thuggery and kidnapping and harassment has been all about—trying to duck that murder. That's where this whole thing started."

"You're talking too much! Did you say you're charging him here and now with that murder?"

"Not today. I've still got a lot of evidence to go through."

"I did not do that murder." Spiegle spoke for the first time. He had a very slight German accent.

"There. See. My client didn't do that murder."

"There was no murder," Spiegle continued calmly. "He died. He died of heart failure. I was there. I witnessed it myself," he added, with a little edge, echoing Arbuckle.

"Let's go back. One Sunday afternoon in October you were visiting Peter King and during your visit, he collapsed."

"That's correct."

"How long had you been there when that happened?"

"I don't know, not even an hour. Maybe forty-five minutes. He was puttering around in the garden while we talked."

"Then he collapsed and you called an ambulance."

"His wife called the ambulance."

"And he was taken to the hospital and pronounced dead on arrival."

"Yes, from heart failure. It was official."

"Did you hear that, Arbuckle?" McFadden interjected. "What more do you need?"

"Whose idea was it to have this meeting at the house?"

"It was my idea. I thought if I could talk to him at home, in a casual meeting, he might be more open to understanding my business situation. I wanted to get him to stop targeting me."

"He was targeting you?"

"He had threatened to do so and he was doing it. It was costing me money, and I wanted him to stop."

"Well a good way to stop him would be to kill him, wouldn't it?"

"But I didn't kill him."

"So luckily for you he died."

"He collapsed. It was a terrible shock."

"He was poisoned, Spiegle. We've had him dug up; we've done the autopsy."

"I'm telling you—I didn't touch him."

"So you got your girlfriend to do it. Is that what you're saying?"

"What girlfriend?"

"Your old girlfriend from Zurich, Greta King."

"Well the only Greta King I know is Peter King's wife."

"But you knew her in Zurich, did you not?"

"That doesn't make her my girlfriend."

"But you did know her in Zurich."

"Is it a crime? We were kids—sixteen years old."

Spiegle looked at McFadden.

"That's enough, detective. Are you accusing my client of something here?"

"Look, there were two people present that afternoon with Peter

King. Your client and Peter King's wife, Greta. Somebody poisoned Peter King. Your client says he didn't do it. He also admits to having known Greta King since they were sixteen years old. If your client and Greta King know each other, it's possible they were working together on this murder. It's just logic, McFadden."

"My client is innocent. He had nothing to do with it."

"Was Peter King aware that you knew Greta many years ago?"

"I don't know what he was aware of."

"You never told him?"

"It was irrelevant."

"Perhaps he was targeting you precisely because of your relationship with his wife and not because of the business affairs."

"What relationship?"

"After the funeral, you found out that Daniel King had hired a private investigator to look into the circumstances of his father's death. How did you find that out?"

"You hear things. I just heard it around."

"Did you hear it from Greta King?"

"Greta King was gone. She went to England."

"How do you know that?"

"I saw her at the funeral. She told me she was going."

"You had heard that one of your employees had been spying on you and had gathered some compromising details about your affairs, details he then wanted to share with the private investigator that Daniel King hired. And so you set out to scare the boy off, and you also had the investigator assaulted."

"Not true."

"What then?"

"This kid had been observed spying on me by one of the secretaries. He was apparently eavesdropping on a discussion that I was having with Peter King, and using his camera. She told me about it. I'm a reasonable person and I didn't want to fire him without cause, so I asked a couple of the fellows who work in security to keep an eye on him. That's all. I was going on vacation. I had nothing to do with any assault. They got carried away."

"You're telling me they were proceeding entirely on their own, threatening and injuring people, kidnapping people, endangering people's lives, and just not bothering to check in with you."

"I told you—I just asked them to keep an eye on the kid for me. One thing led to another."

"Well what it led to was trouble. Big trouble for you," Arbuckle said.

"Are you done, detective?" McFadden said. "This is just bluster. I'm not hearing any new questions."

"Done for now."

"So, when's the arraignment on these so-called charges that have already been laid? What's the big delay? Let's get him in front of a judge and get him out of here."

"Don't get your boxer shorts in a knot, McFadden. All in good time. The sooner we get to the bottom of this, the sooner we'll have him out of here."

"You're barking up the wrong tree. My client is a reputable City administrator, and you can bet he won't stop short of suing you for damages."

Arbuckle just laughed at this. "You're really scaring me, McFadden. Trying to drum up business?"

A sergeant came in to escort Spiegle back to his cell. McFadden packed up and left. Arbuckle came into the observation room. "It's a beginning," he said.

"A good beginning," I replied. "You got him to admit to knowing Greta in Zurich—that's a major step."

Arbuckle and I talked about the following day and confirmed that Daniel would be asking Greta about the details from his childhood memory. Arbuckle suggested I take the opportunity to question her as well.

"Really?" I said, flattered that he would consider inviting me to interrogate a prime suspect.

"I'm sure you have a few ideas and we need to come at her from as many directions as possible."

"I'll prepare something," I said.

I left the station invigorated, feeling like this was a chance to prove I was more than someone else's perpetual assistant. I determined to figure out a way to make some real discoveries in my interview with Greta.

Chapter Twenty-eight

The following day, Daniel, Harvie and I met with Arbuckle, who felt we needed more than one interview to get through to Greta and suggested we be prepared to come back the next day if necessary. Harvie, who wanted to observe the entire interview, said he had to be in court the following day but that we could schedule a second interview with her for Friday. We decided that the beginning of the interview should be between Greta and her son only, to allow the conversation to be as personal as possible.

"Were you able to work on getting her a lawyer?" Arbuckle asked Daniel.

"I've had a good conversation with someone highly recommended, but she's not available to come on board until next week. I'm hoping my mother will be receptive to hiring her."

"Well, it simplifies things for us, and since Greta is refusing a lawyer at this point, we're not denying her the right," Arbuckle said. "However, she could stop this process at any time and demand a lawyer, so we need to be aware of that possibility when we're putting pressure on her."

Harvie and I were directed into the observation area. A policewoman brought Greta into the interview room. Though she couldn't see us, she stared straight ahead, directly towards us. Her face looked thinner and there was a weariness in her eyes, but her posture was strong and upright and she was surprisingly well groomed and ready for her close-up. A beautiful woman.

Suddenly the door of our observation room opened and we turned to see Daniel enter abruptly, followed by Arbuckle. "I don't think

I can go first," Daniel said. Clearly, his earlier composure had dissolved. "I'm sorry to change the plan at the last minute."

I looked at Arbuckle. "I don't mind starting," I said.

"What will you talk about?" Harvie asked, surprised by this development.

"Gardening." They looked somewhat perplexed, but Arbuckle gestured for me to go ahead.

A sergeant showed me in to the interview room. I stopped just inside the doorway and looked at Greta. I felt like I was stepping into a cage with an exotic bird.

"Hi Greta. It's Rosalind."

She glanced at me, but remained in the same still position, staring forward. Was she steeling herself? Or in some kind of trance? I couldn't tell. She asked me what I was doing there.

"I wanted to ask you about your roses."

"My roses? Whatever for?"

"I was at your house one morning a few weeks ago speaking with Daniel, and I saw the roses. Daniel said it was your rose garden. I noticed that they had been wrapped in burlap. Is that your customary winter practice?"

"Peter did it—he always wrapped them for me. As a matter of fact, that's what we were doing that day—the last day."

"It's something the two of you did together?"

"First I would go out and pick the hips, then he would wrap them."

"Rosehips?"

There was an edge of disdain in her voice as she explained that there were several bushes that yielded good, large rosehips, and that when she was growing up her mother always made a winter tonic from them full of vitamin C and other good things.

"Peter swore by it," she added. "He said that's why he so rarely got sick. Anyway, yes, that was our annual routine."

"So that Sunday in October you were making a winter tonic from the rosehips and Peter was wrapping the bushes. And what about pruning—some people prune in the fall, others leave it until the spring."

She looked directly at me for the first time and her impatience was showing.

"You know, you can get this information from any common gardener's guide, but if you must know, I take the dead canes out in the fall, but I don't prune the bushes back until spring. Peter would always do a lot of tidying up all over the garden, trimming dead wood but not pruning per se."

"Daniel mentioned to me that Peter would cut the red arils off the yew tree in the fall. Why would he do that?"

"It was just a precaution, that's all." I sensed that her annoyance was growing. Was it because I was getting close to something she didn't want to discuss?

"A precaution against what?" I pressed.

"Those berries are very toxic. Occasionally, squirrels and birds would eat them and get sick, sometimes die. Most birds are not affected; the seeds go right through them undigested. And they're a very bright red, very eye-catching. We certainly didn't want over-curious children in the neighbourhood to eat them."

"So, obviously you were well aware of their danger. Was Peter trimming the arils from the tree that day?" I was watching her closely. I wondered if the others in the observation room could detect her increasing pulse rate. To me, it was palpable, a quiver under the surface, though she appeared to be completely still.

"It's quite possible."

"How would he normally dispose of these dangerous arils?"

"He would put them in a large canvas bucket as he trimmed them off and then burn them in an incinerating barrel he kept in the garden. That way the seeds would not contaminate the compost."

"Was he burning things that day?"

"No. He probably intended to do that later."

"But his chores were interrupted by a visitor?" I asked, carefully introducing the presence of Carl into the events of that day.

She paused and shifted slightly in her chair. She crossed her legs. "That's right."

"Was it unexpected?"

"Peter received a call on his cellphone just prior to the visit."

"Did he tell you who was coming over?"

"He said it was someone from the City who apparently had some urgent business. Peter was always making himself available to people when he should have been relaxing!" She was exhibiting a caring, wifely sort of exasperation here. On purpose, or was it genuine?

"Did he tell you the person's name?"

"He said it was Carl somebody."

"Did you know this person, had you met him before?"

"Do you suppose they'd let me have a cigarette in here?" She uncrossed her legs and shifted again, restlessly.

"I doubt it. It seems to be a big no-no everywhere. Would you like some water?"

"Not really." She put her right hand on the interview table and restlessly drummed her fingers. I sensed my time with her was coming to an end.

"So this person, Carl, arrived and was talking to Peter. Did Peter stay out in the garden, or did they come inside the house?"

"They came inside for a moment. Peter washed his hands and I offered them some coffee."

"Did Peter wash his hands in the kitchen or in the bathroom off the front hall?"

She darted a look at me that showed genuine irritation, perhaps because I was so familiar with her house.

"In the bathroom," she clipped.

"Did you speak to this Carl person when he was in the kitchen with you?"

"I was polite, of course."

"Did he ask you what you were making?"

"He was interested. Some of the tonic was already cooling. I mixed it with apple juice to sweeten it and offered him a glass."

"Did he try it?"

"I think so. I had to leave the room—someone came to the front door."

"Who?"

"Mormons." The answer surprised me. It seemed too convenient. Handy, anonymous callers suddenly arrive and remove her from the action. Was she lying? I decided to investigate her trip to the door, and asked her if she'd met up with Peter in the front hall.

"Yes, I did as a matter of fact. He had just come out of the washroom. He was on his way upstairs to get a heavier sweater. I told him I'd get the door. He even said to me, 'It's probably the Mormons,' and he was right. We seemed to be on their route." She smiled as though she knew it was a good, thorough answer. Was this a game to her?

I asked her what happened after the Mormons were dealt with.

"When I returned to the kitchen, the men had gone back out into the garden."

"Was the glass empty? The one you had offered to Carl."

"Yes, it was sitting by the sink."

"Did you wash it?"

"Of course. I had a few things to wash up." She let out an exasperated sigh, as though talking about washing dishes was a barely tolerable line of questioning that revealed my stupidity. She looked towards the door as though hoping someone would rescue her from the interview.

"Then what happened?" I was pushing her steadily towards the moment of Peter's death, and trying hard not to let her attitude affect the tone of my questions.

She paused, and crossed her arms. "After a while, Carl came in to say something was seriously wrong with Peter and I called the ambulance. You know, I'm finding it very difficult to think about Peter's death. Could I have a break?"

"Perfectly understandable. How's fifteen minutes?"

She nodded.

I looked at the policewoman and she opened the door for me. The sergeant entered as I went out.

I went into the observation room.

"You've got her talking," Arbuckle said.

"Do you think it's true about the Mormons?"

"Coming to the door? We can find out," Arbuckle said.

"It's certainly true that they have come frequently in the past," Daniel said.

"And the rosehip tonic. That was a bit of good information I hadn't expected."

"I know," Harvie said. "And the tonic is something Peter liked and would drink, so it could well be the method of introducing the poison."

I nodded in agreement. "Exactly," I chimed in. "I was just asking her about the roses in order to work my way around to the arils, but we got something very valuable there."

"How will we proceed after her break? Did you want to continue, Roz?" Harvie said.

"I think I've hit a wall with her. What about you, Daniel?"

"I can speak with her now," Daniel said. He had recovered from his panic.

Greta returned to the room and appeared to be much more relaxed. She must have gotten someone to take her out for a smoke.

The sergeant brought Daniel in. He didn't hesitate, but went right to her, bent over and kissed her on both cheeks.

"What a surprise!" she said. She took his hands and held them for a moment.

"How are you?" he asked her.

"I miss your father."

"Me too. I'm working on getting you a lawyer. Someone Dad would have recommended."

She let his hands go. "I told them I don't want a lawyer. But I do need someone to help get me out of here."

"You do, and I'll have someone here first thing next week."

"Thank you, Daniel. You're your father's son." I could see the relief on Daniel's face. He had presented the idea of the lawyer and she had accepted it. He smiled, then sat down and leaned into the table so he could see her face.

"Mom, I want to ask you about something. It's a memory I've had from when I was little."

"Oh yes?" Daniel's question seemed to catch her interest. She looked at him curiously, her elbow on the table and her chin on her hand.

"When grandmother was dying from cancer, you took me with you to Zurich—"

"You were just seven or eight." There was a fleeting moment of tenderness as she pictured him as a young boy.

"That's right." He pushed on bravely. "We were in the big bedroom with her and she was in the bed, and she had a hold of your hand. I remember she was gripping it. She told you that you shouldn't blame yourself for Grandpa's death. She said that he killed himself. Is it true that Grandpa killed himself?"

She paused and looked down at the table. Finally, she said, "He did, yes. I was sixteen years old. I left home after that. I couldn't stay there."

"You've never talked to me about that."

She shook her head. "It was just too painful. You didn't need to hear about it."

"Was it too painful because you blamed yourself? Was Grandma right about that?"

"I think when someone commits suicide, people always wonder if it's their fault. It's such a hard thing to grasp, to understand."

"You're right, because I remember Grandma saying that really it was her fault. And this is the part I'm really wondering about. She told you she never should have allowed Grandpa to move the boy into the house. What did she mean by that?"

Greta looked momentarily startled by this question. But she quickly looked away and assumed a casual air.

"I'm…not sure."

"Well, was there a boy that Grandpa moved into the house?"

"Yes, a German boy. He was an orphan."

"Do you remember him?"

"Barely."

"What was his name?"

She shrugged and opened her hands, as though to indicate she had no idea.

"Well, in my memory of what Grandma was saying to you that day, she said his name was Carl."

"Did she? Then it must have been. I can't recall."

"How old was the boy? Was he your age?"

"Look. It was a long time ago. I really don't remember." Her tone was icy and she had pulled back from the table. She was on edge now, and I knew that he was very vulnerable to her anger. Hang in, Daniel. You can do it.

"Alright. So when you went away, you went to school?"

"Yes, in France, to an international school in Paris. Eventually I went to college in England. That's where I met your father." I saw her tension ease as though she were on safer ground.

"Did you know right away that you would marry him?"

"We knew it was something special." She leaned forward and put her hands on the table. "Please, Daniel. I can't talk about him." She was appealing to him now. He reached out and took one of her hands.

"There are so many things you don't want to talk about. It's hard to...know you."

"I've always been a very private person. That's just the way I am. Take it or leave it."

"But are you upset with me?"

"No. It's just...it isn't easy talking about your father."

"Do you remember when I wanted to hire a private investigator after he died?"

"Yes." She pulled away and put her hands in her lap.

"You didn't want me to do that."

"Of course I didn't. I don't like our personal lives being dragged into the spotlight. It's nobody's business," she said.

"Was there a spotlight on you and your family when Grandpa committed suicide?" asked Daniel.

"Yes, it was terrible. And look what you've stirred up here. Look at the mess we're in now because of that investigation you started." Her tone was accusing.

He tensed. "But don't you think my father deserves justice—if he *was* murdered."

"He wasn't murdered. It was heart failure."

At that moment, the door opened and Arbuckle entered the interview room and stopped the interview. "Sorry to interrupt, but that's all for today. Thank you for coming in, Daniel. I hope you had a good meeting. You can rest now Mrs. King. Take her back please."

Greta stood up and looked down at her son. "I'm sorry," she said.

"For what?"

"The way it's all turned out. I'm sorry." She left quickly.

"Shall we meet for a few minutes?" Arbuckle suggested.

"How are you, Daniel?" I said.

"I do feel so guilty about what's happened to her. Was it okay?"

"More than okay," Arbuckle said. "Let's go to my office."

We all found places to sit in his small office. There was an old credenza along the side that Harvie perched on while Daniel and I took the two unmatched chairs. Arbuckle stood for a moment behind his desk.

"Thoughts?" he said.

"Was there a reason you interrupted us when you did?" Daniel said.

"Harvie and I would like her to open up about the relationship with Carl before we get to the poison. It's the same reason I asked you not to reveal the poisoning evidence to her when I took you to see her the first time. And just now, when she maintained it was heart failure, you had no choice but to tell her how he died."

"That makes sense to me," I said. "You did such a great job of getting her to talk about the past. I mean, she did acknowledge that her father killed himself and that there was a boy in the house. Slowly, we're getting closer." I was trying to keep his spirits up.

"So. The day after tomorrow we'll talk to her again. Friday morning?" Arbuckle said. "In the meantime, I'm going to have another go at Spiegle."

As everyone was making their way out of the station, I turned to the detective, "May I observe your next interview with Spiegle?"

"I was hoping you would."

It was Wednesday, the night of the first *Hamlet* preview. I was obsessing over the interviews and the evidence, but I wanted Sophie to know I was thinking about her. I called her before I left work to see if she felt ready.

"Oh, definitely. Time for an audience. I'm up for it."

"I'll be there," I said. "I don't know how much use I'll be at this point. Everyone has so much to think about and remember."

"Well, if you've got any acting or text notes for me, I'll be happy to get them afterwards, and I'm sure that goes for the others as well, Roz. I'm thrilled that you're coming tonight."

"How are the lights?"

"Margot's still working like a demon, but it's coming."

We talked about Margot's determination to do a good job, and Sophie told me she'd had to put in a couple of all-nighters, but I realized this aspect of the production was not something Sophie needed to be worrying about at this point.

"Well, I can't wait. I'll see you soon," I said.

I left the office and walked along Barrington, towards home, reviewing in my mind the interviews with Greta. It was so difficult to tell whether she was completely in control or in genuine denial about Carl's presence in her life. We didn't know with absolute certainty it had been Spiegle that her father had brought home. But the coincidence of him being from Zurich and the apparent involvement between them that McBride had witnessed at the King house pointed to this. And the previous day Carl had acknowledged that he knew her when they were kids. I was standing at Barrington and Duke ruminating, waiting for the light, when I heard a familiar beep.

It was McBride, coming up Duke Street in Ruby Sube. He turned the corner and stopped in front of the Delta Barrington to wait for me as I crossed the street. I bent down and looked in the passenger window.

"Hop in, I'll take you up the hill." He took several items off the passenger seat and put them on the floor in the back.

"Good," I said, getting into the car. "I'm exhausted. I think I'm getting a sore throat and I have to get to the preview soon." I looked in the back seat. McBride's characteristic debris was everywhere, but there was no dog. "Where's Molly?"

"Probably sitting at the door waiting for me to come home and take her for a walk. How's work?"

"The interviews have begun. It's slow going. No revelations yet, except for the rosehip tonic. Greta revealed that she made some the day Peter died and I think it's relevant, somehow. She's still not talking about Carl, but don't worry, I'll let you know when there's a breakthrough. Where were you?" I said, digging in my bag for a throat lozenge.

"Crikey, I just spent two hours in the passport office." The light changed and he turned up Cogswell towards Brunswick.

"Why...what are you, a masochist?"

"Well, my passport's expired. I have to get it renewed."

"What for? Are you planning on going somewhere?"

"Well, yes."

"Where?"

"Well...can you keep this to yourself?"

"Duh. You know me."

"Sophie and I are getting hitched."

I stopped digging in my purse and looked at him with my mouth open. I was having trouble breathing. "What?"

"Yeah."

"No, you're not."

"Yeah, we are. On the Solstice. The night *Hamlet* closes."

"What? No, you're not. That's ridiculous! It's crazy!"

"No, it's not ridiculous. It's great. It's a great, wonderful thing.

We're getting married at midnight and the next morning we're blowing this popstand and going to Cuba for two weeks."

"McBride! For heaven's sake!"

"Roz. Why are you crying?"

"I'm not—I'm—why are you telling me this! What am I supposed to do with this information! God, McBride, you're so…distracting! I've got a lot on my mind right now, you know. Stop laughing at me. It's not funny."

"Sorry. It's just not quite the response I expected. Here's your house."

"Thanks for the ride." I opened the door, still blubbering.

"See you at the opening. Wait! Don't forget your bag."

He drove away and I stood on the doorstep blowing my nose. I was completely overcome with emotion. What an idiot I am!

It took me forever to find my keys but when I finally let myself into the house, I put down my bag and went immediately to the hall phone and dialed McBride's number, hoping he wouldn't be in his door yet. I left a message.

"It's me. God! Sorry about all that. I must be really messed up. I was just so overcome with…anyway…enough about me. Congratulations McBride!"

I hung up, went into the kitchen and reached up into the cupboard for the last of the Scotch. I poured the shot into a little glass. "Here's looking at you, kid," I said to the cat as I knocked the drink back.

The preview ended at 10:40. Not a bad length for *Hamlet*, I thought. The show had grown enormously. There were a few line confusions, but for the most part the text was solid and clear. The entrances and exits still needed more alacrity—both actors and technical cues. But that would come with practice. The preview audience had responded warmly, and I was sure that was what the cast had really needed—the opportunity to have someone there to tell the story to.

I walked over to Michael's little tucked-away, stage-management table from which he called all the sound and light cues.

"Everything's good, Michael," I said. "The lights are going to be fine. The music's fantastic and the costumes are beautiful."

"Was I quiet enough calling the cues? Could you hear me?"

"No, I didn't hear a thing. You were really quiet and your timing on the cues is good too. I can't believe how much you've all done since I saw it on Friday."

"Oh, I know. They've worked hard. So this must be strange for you Roz—your work on *Hamlet* is done. Do you feel good about it?"

"I feel great, but you're right—I'm really going to miss the rehearsals."

"Well, I wanted to talk to you about something." He explained to me that they were forming another independent co-op in the new year to produce Sam Shepard's *Fool for Love*. "Sophie's going to be in it...so we want you to come on board to help us out with that."

"Are you serious? I'm definitely interested. I'll take a look at it."

"I have a copy right here. Why don't you borrow it?" As he rcached into his knapsack to get the play, I could tell that he was pleased and excited.

"Thanks, Michael. I'll get it back to you as soon as I read it."

"You'll love it. And it's a lot shorter than *Hamlet*," he said laughing. "Oops, I'd better get backstage and give them tomorrow's call before they all disappear."

"I'll come backstage with you."

"You're off and running!" I said to everyone. "It's powerful—and beautiful. Shakespeare would be proud." I gave Tom a much-deserved hug. "I even cried."

"You always cry, Roz. I've seen you cry in rehearsal," George said, putting his arms around the two of us.

"I do? I always think of myself as being tough and cynical."

"Are you kidding?" George said. "We know you're a total softie."

"Even you got to me, George, with your perfectly delivered 'flights of angels' line."

"Really?" He looked chuffed.

Sophie came out of the little curtained area they had improvised into a separate dressing room for the two women in the cast.

"Oh my god," she said. "It was just so good to have an audience. It's like you start hearing the play in a completely new way. You can feel it landing on people."

"And that will get even stronger," I said. "It's amazing how much the audience teaches you about the play, isn't it?"

Sophie looked at me. "Are you okay?"

"Why?"

"I don't know. You look...like something's on your mind. Is it an acting note?"

"No no, not at all. It's all there, Sophie. It's great work."

"Well, what then?"

"What are you doing—are you going out?"

"God no. No going out until after it's open. But tea, maybe. Do you want to come back for a chai?"

"Perfect."

We got into Old Solid and talked about the performance all the way across town to the North End. As we were walking upstairs to Sophie's apartment, I realized I hadn't been there since the day she was abducted.

"How's your place?" I said.

"You'll see. It's pretty much back in order."

"Yeah, McBride mentioned he was coming over the other night to help you put the bed together."

"I know. The bed frame was actually in pieces. It was crazy." She opened the door.

The apartment had been restored to its familiar Bohemian charm.

"I'll put the kettle on."

"So, how are you, Sophie? Are you going through feelings of violation or side effects from everything that happened to you?" I said, watching her and leaning on her kitchen door.

"I've been so distracted by *Hamlet*, I haven't had time to dwell on it. I mean, you hear about trauma and things coming back on people for years. I hope that doesn't happen. Once was enough." She poured the water over the tea and the familiar spicy aroma filled the kitchen.

"So," I said.

"So?"

"Do you have some news for me?" I observed her closely as she took her attention away from the tea things and looked up at me with a little grin. She raised her eyebrows.

"He told you."

"Yup—earlier today."

Now she was beaming. "So what do you think?"

"I seem to recall warning you about this very thing not so long ago."

"Listen Roz, I took that warning seriously. And I'm not going into this lightly. But with everything that just happened—me thinking I was going to die down there in that freezing excavation site, and then really seeing what a good guy McBride is, discovering how much we cared about each other...We're bonded. It's really happening. Suddenly life is short, my eyes are open—and this feels right."

"When McBride told me today, I was really taken by surprise—shocked actually. I thought maybe it was a little impulsive. I care about you Sophie and I don't want you to get hurt, or disillusioned. But you know what? Everything you've just said makes sense. So,

I'm there, I'm with you, and you're right—life is short. So congrats!" I hugged her and actually managed to refrain from crying.

As we clinked our teacups in a toast she said, "Keep it under wraps. We're going to announce it at the opening night party and completely surprise everyone!" She got that familiar mischievous look on her face and rubbed her hands together in anticipation of telling everyone. I told myself I would get used to the idea, and resolved to keep any reservations to myself. Who was I to spoil their happiness? Besides, they were grown-ups. I changed the subject.

"So Michael told me about this *Fool for Love* idea. What's that all about?"

"Oh it's such a cool play, Roz. It's about these two completely obsessed lovers, May and Eddie, who are actually half-brother and sister. I would play May, who is determined to start a new life on her own. But Eddie always tracks her down. And their father, the Old Man, is ever-present, but he's really a ghost."

"Not another ghost!" I said.

"—and then May's date, Martin, arrives and it all gets pretty crazy and pretty funny too. The whole thing takes place in a motel room in the Mojave Desert and we're thinking about doing it in this little storefront on Agricola Street, so the audience is kind of compressed into the motel room with them. And you'll love the language—gorgeous writing. It's very mythic too—brother and sister—like Isis and Osiris. Symbols. Magic realism. Passion, fire, horses—lots to think about. So there you go! Will you do it? Maybe you could actually direct it, rather than just working on the text."

"You think?"

"I think you'd be a wonderful director, and we'll really need one."

"I'll think about it Sophie—that would be amazing."

I didn't stay any longer. I was exhausted and I knew that Sophie always tried to get to bed early when she was performing. I was exhilarated by this notion of working on *Fool for Love*, possibly as a director, and was thinking about Sophie's description of the play as I drove home. I could feel the idea of the play drawing me in and I felt compelled to read it immediately. So when I got home, I fed the cat and changed into my coziest pyjamas. I put the old chenille robe on over them and pulled on my sheepskin slippers. On the book cover was a compelling, sexy photo of a man and woman touching tongues. Sitting in the kitchen next to the radiator, I devoured the whole play in less than an hour. When I finished reading it, my brain was on fire. All my worlds were colliding.

Chapter Twenty-nine

THE SPIEGLE INTERVIEW HAD BEEN SET for eleven o'clock. I spent the earlier part of the morning pouring over some of the notes Peter King had been compiling on the Aqua Laben deal that Spiegle was connected with.

At 10:45 I walked over to the police station. I took my place in the observation room and watched as they brought Spiegle in. McFadden was next—slowly hauling his sizable girth into the small room. He sat at the end of the table and heaved a sigh as though he were extremely hard done by. His dramatic entrance made me smile.

Arbuckle entered last. "Okay," he said, "let's get rolling." He set up the recorder and identified the date and the participants.

McFadden pronounced that he was expecting something new and exciting to take place in the interview, and Arbuckle ignored him and jumped in.

"So, on that day in October when you visited Peter King, did you go to the front door or did you just go straight into the garden?"

McFadden bleated. "Did you hear what I just said? This is not new!"

"You're welcome to leave if I'm keeping you from something more important." Arbuckle turned back to Spiegle and asked if he should repeat the question.

Unlike his lawyer, Spiegle seemed unperturbed and confident, as though he had nothing to hide. "King had told me on the phone he would likely be in the garden, so I just went through the gate at the side of the house."

"And at any point during the visit did you go into the house?"

"King and I went in not long after I arrived."

"And when you went into the house, you saw Mrs. King for the first time that day?"

"No. When I first got there, she was in the garden too."

Arbuckle, clearly surprised by this new information, asked what she was doing there.

"Cleaning up the yard, I suppose." Spiegle continued in his unruffled manner. "She was carrying around a bucket of clippings or something. But just after I arrived she went into the house."

"What kind of a bucket was she carrying around?"

"A bucket is a bucket!" This was McFadden.

"It was one of those collapsible canvas buckets from garden stores."

"What did she do with this bucket of clippings?"

"I don't remember."

"So then a few minutes later you went into the house with Peter King."

"Wait." Spiegle sat up straighter and leaned forward. "Now I do remember what she did with it because when we went in to the house, the bucket was sitting on the walk just by the side door. In fact, King asked her what it was doing there, and she said something about taking it to the compost, and then he instructed her not to do that because he was planning to incinerate it."

"I see. And then you entered the house?" As the questioning continued, I found my mind going back to the bucket of arils sitting just outside the kitchen door.

"We went up into the kitchen. He said he was going to wash his hands, and he went into the hall, to the water closet out there."

"So you must have had a conversation with Mrs. King at that point?"

"She wanted me to try this winter tonic she had cooked up with rosehips. She had it in the blender."

"In the blender?" Greta had not said anything about a blender. Arbuckle was intrigued with this new development. I leaned forward on my stool. Things were getting interesting.

"Yes. She said she had added apple juice to sweeten it. She poured me a glass and handed it to me. She told me to drink it all—that it would be good for me. Then the doorbell rang. She went out into the hall to answer the door." Arbuckle nodded. This corroborated what Greta had said about the Mormons. He then asked, "Did you drink the tonic?"

"I'd had rosehip tonic before—when I was kid. I never really liked it. I just set it down on the counter."

"And she returned to the kitchen?"

"No, Peter King came back then and he asked me if I'd gotten coffee. I said no, that she'd offered me the tonic but I told him I would prefer coffee. So he poured me a cup of coffee and then picked up the glass and drank the tonic himself, right down. Then we went back outside, and while he worked, I helped him with this and that and tried to talk with him about the project in Germany."

"Did the conversation become heated? Were you arguing?"

"I was frustrated. But I had come over to try to make him see reason and so I just kept trying. And then he suddenly stopped talking and sat down on a bench and said he wasn't feeling well. He seemed a bit shaky. Then he grabbed his chest and looked like he was in terrible pain. That's when I rushed to the house and told his wife to call the ambulance."

"And did she do that?"

"She became very distraught when I told her. But yes, of course, she called."

"Did she say anything?"

"She just kept saying, 'No, oh no, oh no.'"

Arbuckle stopped the interview at that point and suggested a short break.

McFadden leaned back in his chair and stretched. He loosened his tie. "Well Arbuckle, I hate to disappoint you but what I heard during that interview was the testimony of an innocent bystander."

Arbuckle came into the observation room and said, "Let's go to my office."

When we got there, we sat down and looked at each other.

"So Spiegle didn't do it?" I said. "What are you thinking?"

"It looks like a real fluke—she was trying to get Spiegle but Peter ended up drinking the poisoned tonic. She inadvertently killed her husband."

"So, she would have taken the arils from the bucket outside the kitchen door and put them in the blender with the tonic and apple juice. That would have been an efficient way to grind the seeds and release a maximum amount of taxine."

We continued hashing it over and tried to figure out why, if Greta had intended to kill Spiegle, she would help him later by retrieving the file and trying to get Aziz out of the way. Arbuckle also wondered why, if Spiegle hadn't killed King, he would go to such risky extremes to try and get Aziz's evidence.

"Time to get back in there. Why don't you join me this time?" Arbuckle said.

"You're on," I said. "I do have a few queries."

"I thought you might," Arbuckle said.

Just as we were leaving Arbuckle's office, Harvie appeared.

"What's happening? They let me out of court early and I thought I'd plug in."

"Good timing. The observation room is all yours," Arbuckle said. "We're both going in to interview Spiegle."

As I entered the interview room with Arbuckle, he said to them, "This is Roz. She's going to join us for this session."

"Who's this exactly?" McFadden asked.

"I'm working with the Prosecutor's Office," I said. "Nice to meet you too, Mr. McFadden. You're a legend." I held out my hand to McFadden. He looked wary, but shook my hand. His hand felt kind of damp and meaty.

Arbuckle set up the recorder again, entering the time and adding my name to the list of people in the room. He looked at me and gestured for me to begin.

I said, "Mr. Spiegle, do you have an official business connection with Aqua Laben, the bottled water company in Germany, that you were trying to talk with Peter King about that day?"

"No. I have a moderate financial investment in that company."

"Really? So you're not on the Board of Directors or anything."

"No."

"That company is attempting to secure the rights to Canadian bulk water, aren't they?"

"They were, until Peter King got a temporary injunction."

"As an administrator working for our fair city, would you think it inappropriate to also be a member of such a board?"

"What do you mean?"

"Where's all this going? My client has just told you he's not on the Board of Directors of that company. Are you deaf or stupid?"

I levelled an unflinching look at "the Pugilist" and started firing my imaginary rockets in his direction, one by one.

"Well, I think there's a reason why your client hired those so-called security boys to prevent Mr. Aziz Mouwad from passing his file of information to the private investigator and a reason why the information in that file could be dangerous to your client if it got into the wrong hands."

"Okay. Cut the drama. What's the reason?"

"That file contained many pertinent facts about your client which Mr. Mouwad got from Peter King's office back in August, and there's one tiny detail in that file that could almost go unnoticed."

"I'm all ears."

"It's the suggestion that your client Carl Spiegle conducts some if not all of his business affairs in Europe under another name. And under that name he is—are you ready?—a prominent member of the Board of Directors for Aqua Laben." There was a moment's pause while the bomb dropped.

"That's the most—What do you think you're talking about?" McFadden sputtered, hitting the table with his meaty hand. "A suggestion, you say? A suggestion is not proof. Where's the proof?"

"I have proof, Ralph. I have Peter King's recent detailed research on this. Research that is far more thorough and up-to-date than what Aziz had in that file. Research that indicates that the bulk water that Aqua Laben was after was to be obtained through a very sweet deal being arranged by your client right here in Canada's Ocean Playground!" I turned to face Spiegle. "Because of your position here, you were able to facilitate access to Nova Scotia water for this German corporation at a cost of next to nothing, and you intended to personally profit by it when it was sold on the world market in the form of Aqua Laben bottled water. Would that be considered, let me see, a conflict of interest? Or maybe just plain illegal? In fact, isn't that an indictable offence?"

I glanced quickly around the room. McFadden was narrowing his eyes at me. His cheek was twitching. Arbuckle was clearly enjoying the show. I knew I couldn't drop the ball now—I kept going.

"And Mr. Spiegle, the real reason that you went to see Peter King that Sunday in October was because the jig was up. He had already obtained a temporary injunction, and his next step would be to call you up on the carpet and expose your second identity and your position with Aqua Laben. A conflict of interest that could cause you to lose your job, and probably land you in jail for quite some time. Isn't that right, Carl—or should I say Heinrich?"

"I need to speak to my client." McFadden shouted. "What is this Heinrich stuff? What's she talking about?"

"Oh good question," I said. "It's a question with a very long answer. But the short answer is Heinrich Brunner, isn't it Carl? A name that you come by somewhat honestly because it's the name of the man that took you in when you were orphaned. And that man was Greta King's father."

I stopped short and looked at Arbuckle. "Oh, my god."

"What is it?" Arbuckle asked.

I got up and paced around the room for a moment to try and think clearly. I was nodding my head every few seconds as the picture began to come into focus. I knew they were all looking at me like I'd just lost my mind, but I needed to put it all together and I really didn't want them to take a break.

I looked at Arbuckle again. "Bear with me. I just want to go over the story of that afternoon in October one more time."

"Oh for Christ's sake! This is beyond reason!" McFadden threw up his hands.

"Sorry to tax your patience, but we have your client's version and we have Greta King's version, but neither of those is the truth. When you arrived in the garden, Mr. Spiegle, you did help Peter out with some tasks, just as you said. One of which was trimming the arils from the yew tree. Peter likely even explained to you why he was doing it: to prevent small animals and birds or neighbourhood children from poisoning themselves.

"At the same time, you were trying to talk to Peter about the Aqua Laben deal and he adamantly refused to back down and give you a break. That upset you—understandably. King had already been instrumental in the collapse of the Europa deal with the City. Then he had turned around and forced Europa out of the privatization scheme you were involved with in West Africa. And now, this very lucrative secret arrangement was going down the toilet, and you were about to get nailed. So, when Peter suggested that you come inside for some coffee, or for a taste of Greta's rosehip tonic, you agreed. As he headed in, you followed, taking a pocketful of those freshly trimmed arils with you.

"When you got inside, Peter went to wash his hands and Greta offered you some tonic sweetened with apple juice. She was just ready to turn on the blender when someone came to the front door. So she turned it on, and left it with you. Then she left the kitchen. And that was the perfect opportunity—you added the arils to the tonic in the blender, and blended them in. Then you poured it all into the glass, set it on the counter and waited.

"When Peter came downstairs and re-entered the kitchen, you told him that Greta had prepared you the tonic, but you'd rather have coffee. He poured you some coffee and you invited him to drink the tonic instead, and, without hesitating, he picked up the glass and drank the tonic down, then set the glass by the sink. And that's how you engineered the death of Peter King."

Spiegle was shaking with rage by the time I finished my version of the story.

"He was a self-righteous bastard!" he seethed. "He deserved it—he took everything from me."

"Everything? You mean, money, power and Greta?" I asked.

"Don't say another word Spiegle!" McFadden said. "What's going on here Arbuckle? I've heard enough of these outrageous fantasies."

I ignored McFadden and pressed on. "You do mean Greta, don't you? She was yours once, wasn't she Carl? When you moved into that house, you two became deeply involved with one another. And then her father committed suicide and everything fell apart." He looked at me. I could see him struggling hard to cope with the force of the truth as it began to come forward. He had his fist pushed up against mouth, as if to stop the words from coming out. But they came out anyway.

"At first, she blamed herself. Then she blamed me. But I…I didn't know How could I know? He had never told me."

I decided it was time to take the leap. "Heinrich Brunner hadn't told you that he was your real father. Isn't that what you mean?"

There was a pause as we all looked at Carl Spiegle.

"Yes. I was his son." He was gripping the table. "I was his son," he said again.

Arbuckle suddenly rose from his chair. "Carry on," he said and left the room.

McFadden leaned back in his chair and crossed his arms over his belly. There was no choice now but to listen.

"So Heinrich Brunner had a secret liaison with your mother?"

"He'd met my mother years before," Spiegle continued. "He worked on the trains during the war, keeping the rail line going between Germany and Italy. It was one of the reasons that Hitler never invaded Switzerland—the Germans needed that line. He met my mother on the train. Like so many others, she was escaping from Germany into Switzerland and he helped her, found her a place to live in a small village. After the war, she stayed on. I was born in 1950. He often came to visit us, right up to the mid sixties when she died. But I never knew that he was my father."

The door to the meeting room had opened and Greta was standing there with Arbuckle.

Spiegle turned his focus to her and continued talking. "When my mother died, I was fifteen years old and I had no one, so he brought me home to his family, to the big farmhouse on the outskirts of Zurich. He told everyone I was an orphan from one of the villages, and as far as I knew, that was the truth."

Arbuckle moved further into the room and got one of chairs. He set it over by the wall across from Spiegle and Greta sat down in it. She pulled herself up straight and looked directly at him. Her jaw was tight.

"You promised me you would never talk about this to anyone—ever," she said.

"It's too late, Greta. This can't stay hidden forever. Besides, we were innocent when it began! All we knew was that we needed to be together from the moment he brought me there. We were completely connected, weren't we? Admit it!"

There was a pause. I looked over at her. She began to speak to him. She was dredging it up after years of denial and it wasn't easy, but she had begun to talk. Her voice sounded completely different, perhaps because she was finally speaking the truth.

"A year after you moved in, my father caught us sleeping together," Greta said. "It put him into a panic. He tried to stop us, but we didn't understand what the problem was. It seemed so simple to us. It was August and we just flew out of that house every day into the sunshine and went everywhere together.

"And then one night we stayed out all night. By that time my mother had figured out who you were; she could see the resemblance between you and my father. And when we came home early that morning, she sat us down at the kitchen table and she confronted my father with the truth. And my father broke down and confessed. He told her all about your mother and he told us that we were half-brother and sister. And then he went out of the house and across the road into the forest and shot himself with the old World War II revolver he had always carried on the trains.

"It was horrible. We didn't know what to do. I was ashamed. I felt so very guilty. I didn't know what to say to my mother. I couldn't look at Carl anymore. I couldn't even look into a mirror." Greta's shell was cracking. She began to weep silently.

"What happened then?" I said to Carl.

"Greta went away to school almost immediately. She wouldn't let me come and see her in France and then later she went to England and met Peter. She married him. I tried to reach her, but she was determined to cut me out of her life."

"Until you came here?" I said.

"No!" He paused and looked at Greta. "Long before that she found me—in Europe." Greta was staring down at her knees. Her hands were on her temples as she listened. "It was maybe fifteen years ago. I was working in Germany and she tracked me down. I was using the Brunner name. I have a right to that name; it was my father's name after all," he said directly to me. "Suddenly, there she was again. I couldn't believe it. It was like my life had been on hold waiting for her."

"But why?" I said to Greta. "Wasn't it long over?"

She shook her head. "I thought it was. But it came back on me like a curse. I was compelled to find him. When we saw each other, it started up all over again."

"Every couple of years she would come to Europe and see me for two or three weeks and then she would leave me and go back to her life. Then there was a job posting for the City Planning department here and she pleaded with me to apply. She said she needed me to be near her. So I went after it and I got it. But when I got here, suddenly it was a different story. She was terrified that her husband would find out about me. And the irony was that I ended up in direct opposition to her husband anyway, for reasons that were entirely unrelated to her and me. Peter King became my true nemesis." He stopped and there was silence in the room.

There was nothing more to say.

Arbuckle solemnly wrapped up the day at that point. He suggested we meet with Greta in the morning to address some remaining questions.

"Well, that was…the real thing," I said. We stepped into the observation room to see Harvie. Daniel was there as well.

"I called Daniel in," Harvie said. "I thought it was important for him to be here."

"When did you arrive? Did you hear everything?"

"I heard part of the story about how my grandfather met Carl's mother," he said. "I'd like to go and see my mother now." Arbuckle called the sergeant to take Daniel to see Greta.

"You knew, Roz. How did you figure it out?" Harvie asked.

"Synchronicity," I said. "Life imitates art yet again."

"What do you mean?"

"Well, people always say that art imitates life, but the truth always comes to me the other way around. Like, this play I read last night helped me today to see into the enigma of Greta and Carl, to have insight into the complexity of their relationship. It all came together in a kind of flash. I knew that Carl must have done the murder and that his impulse to kill Peter went much deeper than thwarted water contracts."

"How about we grab a drink?"

"Excellent idea. I'm still dizzy from the force of this long-buried truth pushing its way into the light."

Chapter Thirty

THE FOLLOWING MORNING, Arbuckle, Harvie and I met early. We needed to get answers out of Greta about the theft of the file and the assault on Aziz. Arbuckle and Harvie would work out what the murder charge against Carl would be, as well as taking a careful look into the information that had surfaced about his second identity. It was obvious there needed to be a major probe into all his water resource schemes—and that could take some time.

"Looks like we'll need you to stick around the Prosecutor's Office to help with this research, Roz," Harvie said.

Nothing could have made me happier. It was the change I'd been looking for, and, under Peter King's influence, I felt like I was becoming a warrior in the Water Wars.

Arbuckle and I went in with Greta at ten o'clock, while Harvie observed.

"Thank you for co-operating yesterday, Mrs. King," Arbuckle said. "There are just a few details to clear up."

She nodded and looked down at the table.

"After your husband's funeral, did you meet up with Carl Spiegle in Europe?"

"Yes, in Paris. He initiated the meeting. I was in London. He wanted me to come and talk with him about our situation. He believed that everything would be easy, that with Peter gone, we could just be together. That's what he'd always wanted."

"What was your response?"

"I couldn't comply. I was very distressed by Peter's death, and for me there was something so much deeper standing in the way; yet I had always been so vulnerable to anything Carl wanted. Part of me is still that fifteen-year-old girl who fell down a well. Anyway, because I was resisting, Carl got enraged and told me how Peter had set out to destroy his career. Then he revealed how he had impulsively made the poisoned tonic for Peter, and how shockingly quickly Peter had died.

"I was horrified. I accused him of destroying the only person I had ever truly loved—the person who had saved my life when I was a young woman in despair. Carl retaliated saying that if I hadn't begged him to come to Halifax he would never be in such a dreadful situation now.

"I had to admit he was right. It was my fault. I had ruined everything for him. He also blamed me for allowing Daniel to start the private investigation, saying it led to terrible complications for him.

"I felt trapped. I called Daniel and he said there were papers to sign, so I immediately booked a flight out of there. Then Carl got word from those two miscreants he had hired. When he found out they had taken the actress, he knew they were completely out of control. He suddenly appeared at the airport. He was coming back with me. I couldn't stop him."

"So, when you arrived back here, you went directly to your house."

"Yes. It was quite late. I was shocked to discover that Carl had allowed one of his gang to set himself up in the house—he had been interrogating the boy, Aziz, about what he knew, what he had done with the information. Later that night the boy somehow managed to escape. Carl wanted him caught and brought back."

"But we know now that he was pursued, beaten and left for dead in the railway cut," I said.

"Yes, and then the culprit went after you, I believe," she said.

"That's exactly when I had my little encounter with Scarface," I replied.

"Then the next morning, early, the other one showed up with the girl, and they couldn't get anything out of her so they wanted me to talk to her. I couldn't go along with it. I made a decision to walk away from everything."

Arbuckle and I looked at each other. This tallied with what McBride had witnessed.

"So how did you get drawn back in? Why did you steal the file?" I asked.

"It's the story of my life, isn't it? Carl couldn't leave me out of it. After he was arrested that afternoon at the house, he called me on my cellphone. He begged me to help him. He told me he had heard from this…Scarface, who had called him from the hospital. He told Carl where he thought the file was—in your bedroom closet under the floorboards—and he also said he had found out that Aziz was still alive and in the hospital, but apparently in a coma.

"Carl asked me to try and get the file and told me if Aziz came out of the coma to do something to shut him up. I asked him how on earth he expected me to do that. He said that he had made more of the poison with the arils that night at the house, intending to use it on the boy when they caught him. He said it was in a small jar in the freezer.

"He said I had put him in this terrible position and now I could save him. I felt as though I had no choice. I decided to do this last thing for him then leave, and let the chips fall."

"So I know how you got the file—but tell us about the poisoning of Aziz," I said.

"After I left you that night, I took a cab to my house. I was amazed that I had succeeded in getting the file—it had been easy. So I called the hospital and found out that Aziz had in fact come out of his coma and that he was doing quite well and could take visitors the following day.

"I found the concoction in the freezer—just as Carl had said—and put it out to thaw. In the morning I took the little jar with me to the hospital. I introduced myself to Aziz as Peter King's wife and he was happy to meet me. He chatted to me a bit about Peter. Then he went into the bathroom with the assistance of an orderly. That's when his breakfast arrived. I quickly stirred the poison into what looked like tapioca. When he came back to the bed, I made my excuses and left. I'm very glad that he lived—and not just for my sake."

"Thank you Mrs. King," Arbuckle said. "That's all we need for now."

"What's going to happen to me?"

"Mr. Greenblatt and I will be preparing the charges against you. Daniel said he has found you a lawyer who can start on Monday—and that's a very good thing. Your involvement in all this is certainly not as serious as that of Mr. Spiegle, but it will be grave enough. Your co-operation here will work in your favour."

That was it. They took Greta back to her cell. We watched her go. "She seems lighter now, doesn't she?" I said.

"Relieved," he said.

Harvie came into the meeting room. "That was a good week's work. You saved the taxpayers a lot of money and the Prosecution Service a lot of time. And you were instrumental in that, Roz."

"It's uncanny," Arbuckle said to me. "You seem to have the mind of a criminal."

I realized he was teasing me. Getting to know Arbuckle was turning out to be a treat.

Harvie told me I'd exceeded my research quota for the week and gave me the rest of the day off, and I reminded him that we had an important date that night. "It's the *Hamlet* opening!"

"I haven't forgotten," he said. "I'll pick you up early so we can get good seats."

That afternoon, I ran around to the shops and picked up some cards and champagne for the cast and crew and then went home and had a leisurely, uninterrupted bath. Uninterrupted apart from the cat, who promised me loudly that she wouldn't fall in. I let her join me, and she kept her word.

I decided to wear something kind of chic and looked hopefully through my closet. I took out a little black dress that I could still manage to get into. I was surprised when I looked at myself in the mirror. I hadn't worn a dress in forever. Somehow they didn't suit the criminologist's lifestyle. I turned sideways. Maybe a better bra. I curled my hair with the curling iron, noticing a few grey strands creeping into my brunette tresses. Then I put on some lipstick, eyeliner and shadow, and assessed the result. "Pretty racy, Roz," I said to myself.

I got a dark red pashmina out of the drawer to keep the chill of the Crypt off me and poked through the footwear on my closet floor for some high-heeled black boots. "You'd think it was all about me," I said to the cat, who actually looked confused when she saw me.

Harvie was early as promised, looking pretty sharp himself wearing a striking Hugo Boss suit. Each of us was dumbstruck by the transformation of the other.

"Hey, you clean up good," I managed.

All he said was, "Wow."

I put the long stem red rose he brought me in a vase on the hall table and instructed the cat not to knock it over. He brought one for Sophie too, which we took with us to the theatre.

As planned, we arrived at the cathedral early, hoping to get seats together. There were, after all, only sixty seats in total.

"There should be comps for us here," I said.

"No way," Harvie said. "I'm buying our tickets. Can't think of a better way to spend my money than on a production of *Hamlet*."

"You're crazy," I smiled at him. "You must like *Hamlet* as much as I do."

"I do," he said.

I opened the greenroom door and passed in the opening night greeting cards I had prepared that afternoon, along with Harvie's rose for Sophie and the bottle of champagne for after the show.

"Thanks Roz!" George said. "Enjoy yourself out there."

"Break a leg everybody. Merde!" I closed the door and went and found Harvie again.

There was already a crowd milling around—friends and family of the company.

Walking towards the archway into the Crypt, I was amazed at who was just ahead of me.

"Aziz! Look at you! It's Roz." I reached out my hand. "McBride and I visited you that day in the hospital."

"Of course I remember you—you saved my life. Sophie called and invited me. And look, I brought my camera. Don't worry," he said, noticing the alarm on my face. "I won't be taking pictures during the show, but I'm hoping to interview people afterwards. All part of the doc I'm making about…well, everything."

"You can interview me, if you want. Aziz, this is Harvie Greenblatt, a lawyer with the Proscćution. He's been working with the police on the case."

"Good to meet you," Harvie said. "How are you feeling?"

"Every day I'm stronger. I'm happy to be alive."

"I'm happy that you're alive too." It was a voice behind me. I turned to see Daniel King standing there.

"Oh, good," I said. "Aziz, this is Peter's son, Daniel King. He's the one that got the investigation rolling in the first place. This is Aziz."

They shook hands. "This is my partner, John, everyone," Daniel said, putting his hand on the arm of the man beside him. "He just flew in this afternoon. Moral support and all that."

After exchanging greetings, we all crowded our way into the Crypt proper. Harvie and I managed to get two seats together, but the place was filling up fast. There was a seat on the aisle just in front of me and I put my coat on it.

"McBride will show up just as the lights are going down," I said.

"He cuts it close, does he?"

"Too close," I said. "He almost missed the train that day."

"You can have a relaxing weekend now, Roz. It's all over but the crying."

"I think I've done enough of that already," I said.

Just as Michael was finishing his "no cellphones, no candy wrappers" speech to the audience, McBride slipped in. I reached out and tapped him on the shoulder. "There's a seat for you right there." I pulled my coat off the chair.

"Great. Thanks kiddo." The house lights started going to black. The deep foreboding cello notes of the score began to sound. I grabbed Harvie's hand and squeezed it. He looked kind of startled.

"I'm nervous," I said.

"It's going to be great, Roz," he said returning the squeeze.

And he was right. It was.